CW01262675

I Give You My Heart

Book I

By: Kelly A. Cole

I Give You My Heart © Copyright 2023 Kelly A Cole

Hardback: 9798833432112

Paperback: 9798833386767

eBook: B0C3WZS1RJ

All rights reserved. No part of this book may be reproduced in any manner without prior written permission of the copyright owner, except for brief quotations in a book review.

All images present were paid for, and designed by the author.

To all the friends, and family who supported me on this journey; I could not have done it without you!

NOCFEYNIR

EROCAELI

ERADUUN

PYRAMORIR

HELIOAGUAS

Table of Contents

Prologue..9
Kat...20
Daniel..37
The Spear and Thistle...........................54
After the River.....................................76
Revelations and Ramifications............95
The Thistle and the Wolf....................113
Seasons Change................................. 138
The Festival..158
The Tournament.................................179
How to Say Goodbye..........................197
Legacies.. 219
The Pendant....................................... 242
The Story... 261
Birthday Surprise............................... 273
Sweet Dreams.................................... 291
Unanswered Questions...................... 301
The Suitors Feast................................314
Confrontation in the Garden..............334
Reap What You Sow.......................... 347
Emerlyn Mae Scott.............................357

Prologue

"Once upon a time, our now magnificent land lay fractured into four very different regions," the mother began.

"Erocaeli, Helioaguas, Pyramorir, and Nocfeynir!" Her young son interrupted proudly. "Hey! I wanted to say that part!" her daughter protested. The young boy stuck his tongue out at his sister, taunting her. Before her daughter could retaliate, the mother stifled a smile and calmed the situation with a single question. "Do you want to hear the story or not?"

The children gasped at the implied threat, then quieted and swiftly cuddled into each side of their mother. She smiled and gave a small squeeze as she wrapped her arms around them.

"Where was I? Ah yes! Each region provided something important to its neighboring nation. Lumber, furs, and game from the north; precious gems, coal, and mined stone from the east; fish, fruit, and spices from the south; and wheat, grain, and produce from the west.

The people of Erocaeli were generous; the earth around them was rich with minerals to grow anything the mind could imagine, and they had no qualms about sharing their abundance. In Helioaguas, to the south, the people lived and died by sun and sea; they were carefree and thrived in the waters that surrounded them. The people of Pyramorir were wild and hard; their Stony and unforgiving landscapes made it possible to hide the jewels and riches they found just below the surface. The people of Nocfeynir were proud and righteous; their days were warm and full of work, their nights long– giving a certain power to the moon. At the crossroads of these four great regions sat a small village.`

"Eraduun!" the young girl exclaimed. The mother chuckled as her daughter sent a sly glance towards her son, but then quickly continued.

"Yes, my darling, the village of Eraduun. For centuries, the four regions lived in peace, using Eraduun as a trading post between them. Small groups of people from each region had settled there, living and working as one. Together, they built the thriving post that soon became a large, bustling village.

Through the years, each region had *tried* and *failed* to lay claim to the village; Until, the rulers finally realized what had made Eraduun so special to begin with. Eraduun did not belong to just one of them, but *all of them*. The lords of the four nations held a summit to discuss the prospect of unifying their lands once and for all. Each ruler agreed the union would be advantageous, but-"

"What's advin... adavin-tigious mean?" the small girl whispered to her brother. He let out a small huff and rolled his eyes. His sister had not only interrupted the story, she had also mispronounced the word. Their mother said nothing and waited to see how her son would respond. "Advantageous means it was to everyone's advantage," the boy stated proudly.

His sister cocked her head to the side, still not understanding. He sighed once more. "It means it would help everyone."

"Oh!" The girl grinned, then looked back up at her mother, ready for her to go on. Their mother twisted her mouth into an amused smile, then continued on as if nothing had happened.

"Though it was *advantageous,* each region had its own customs and traditions. Because of this, choosing just one leader was rather difficult. After a lengthy debate, the rulers agreed that in order for the nations to combine peacefully, it must be done through marriage."

The young boy groaned as his sister giggled with delight, knowing her favorite part was coming.

"Three of the great lords, not wanting to relinquish their power completely, offered their children, or equivalents, as prospective matches. The Lord of Erocaeli was an older man. He had no children of his own, so he offered his great nephews as worthy husbands. The Lord of Helioaguas was a fair-minded man, who had only one son and so offered him. The Lord of Pyramorir was a hard man who had reared several sons and daughters but offered only his sons as potential matches. The Lord of Nocfeynir, however, was a proud man, blessed with three beautiful daughters that he loved with his whole heart and would not offer against their will.

The other lords demanded that the Lord of Nocfeynir match each of his daughters to one of their boys. They decided that whoever the northern lord matched with the eldest of his daughters, the most intelligent and beautiful of the three; would become king over all. But, even knowing that his daughter would be queen, the Lord of Nocfeynir would not force her to match. Instead, he let his daughters decide.

The three daughters of Nocfeynir formed an agreement. They would host a grand feast to celebrate the beginning of the harvest season, allowing *any* young man who sought their hand to attend. There, the sisters would choose their husbands. Though reluctant at first, the lords agreed.

The day the festival began was a monumental occasion, and after an evening of food and frivolity, all the would-be suitors were called forward. The sisters stood poised and graceful before the crowd of eager young men, as the northern lord announced that whomever each of his daughters chose as her first dance partner would become their husband. Then, slowly, the three sisters made their way through the sea of suitors; who, upon inspection, stood a little straighter.

The youngest sister offered her hand to one of the great nephews of the western lord. The next sister, much to the dismay of her father and the other lords, offered her hand to a young northern warrior. As the eldest sister stepped forward, a hush came over the crowd. She walked the line of suitors carefully. She passed by the great nephews of the west, the sons of the east, then every other young man in attendance. Until finally, she stopped in front of the young southern prince.

He was handsome to be sure, but the time she spent with him earlier in the evening also told her he was intelligent, kind, loyal, and brave. The eldest sister presented her hand to the southern lord, but to everyone's shock, he did not accept it. 'I am honored to be your dance partner Princess. However, I do not wish to be chosen as your husband this night. For if you are to be at my side the rest of our days, let me win your affection. If, in one year's time, I am still your choice, my lady, choose me then.'"

The young girl sighed wistfully, and her brother made a retching noise. Their mother smiled and continued on.

"The boy's response outraged the lords, but the eldest daughter smiled and agreed. The young southern prince spent the next year courting his fair lady. He had loved her from the moment they met, but he knew it wasn't fair to assume she felt the same.

The harvest season arrived once again, and once again, it was time for the princess to choose a worthy husband. They held yet another grand feast and would-be suitors flocked to the north in droves, hoping she may have changed her mind.

Just as before, when it came time for her to choose her partner, she paused in front of the southern prince. To everyone's surprise, though, he repeated his original message. 'I am honored to be your dance partner Princess. However, I do not wish to be chosen as your husband this night. For if you are to be at my side the rest of our days, let me win your affection. If, in one year's time, I am still your choice, my lady, choose me then.'

The princess smiled sadly, but nodded in agreement. The lords of the land cried out in protest. Though none more so than the lords of Helioaguas and Pyramorir.

The southern ruler couldn't understand why his foolish son was letting the chance to be king slip through his fingers. The eastern lord, however, felt slighted and annoyed that she had rejected his sons once more. All four great rulers were growing more restless and irritated with the situation, but reluctantly agreed to wait *one more year*.

The lords of the east and west sent their suitors to spend the year in the north; hoping in that time, they would win the princess over once and for all. Seeing all the attention she was receiving, the young southern lord took a step back, but hoped she would not forget him.

Another year passed, and the day came for the eldest daughter of Nocfeynir to host what all hoped would be her last feast. It was the grandest of them all, and each lord and suitor waited anxiously for it to pass.

Just as before, when the eager young men lined up, she walked the line carefully and thoughtfully, knowing she could not possibly make them all wait another year. Nor did she desire to. The princess had made her choice long ago, and she prayed they would soon be spending the rest of their lives together.

She walked through the crowd, hoping her prince would finally accept her hand, but when she did not see him, her heart dropped. Frantically, she scanned the crowd once more, but it was to no avail. *Had he left? Did he not love her as she loved him?*

Feeling panicked and overwhelmed, she turned to her father and pleaded with him. 'Please Lord Father, the man I choose is not here.' He frowned and glanced at the other lords. They would not prolong this decision another year, let alone another moment.

A low murmur moved through the crowd. The young men all called out. 'She must make another choice.' 'He who is not here forfeits the right to her hand.' The young girl's father looked at her, sorrow filling his eyes. 'You must choose someone else then, my darling.'

His daughter's eyes filled with tears. She glanced at the line of young men, and just as she had given up all hope, the crowd parted. To her delight, the young southern prince presented himself before her, offering instead *his* hand to *her*.

'My lord, you have been my choice these past three years, and you will continue to be my choice for all the years to come.' she said to him with a tearful smile.

'Forgive me for making you wait, my love. I did not want you to settle for any less than your heart's desire.'

They made the match at last, and a wedding date was set. The young lovers were finally married and crowned the King and Queen. To bind their union and the nation for years to come, the king created a new sigil for himself and his bride: a golden sun intertwined with a crescent moon.

He declared that the ruling family would keep this sigil to remind them where they came from. To show them there must always be a balance, and that one is not complete without the other. From that point forward, Erocaeli, Helioaguas, Pyramorir, and Nocfeynir became one nation. A nation that would always remember to look to its heart to lead and guide them."

With the story finally completed, the mother stood, then tucked her children into their bed.

"But what about the king and queen?" The young girl yawned.

"Yeah, and what about the other lords? Weren't they mad?" her brother asked.

"The king and queen lived happily ever after, sharing a love so deep, none could ever compare," the mother said with a smile.

Content with the story's end, the young girl nuzzled into her pillow, shut her eyes, and fell instantly asleep. The mother chuckled to herself, as she leaned down to kiss her daughter's forehead. "And as for the other lords..." she said, turning to her son. "Because they had all agreed to the terms of the arrangement, none could contest its outcome."

The mother lovingly swept a bit of hair from her son's forehead and kissed it. "Good night, my darlings," she whispered, then turned to walk away.

"I think you're wrong," a small voice said, halting her exit. The mother stopped and turned back to face her son. "About what, my love?"

The young boy rose sleepily in his bed as his mother sat in front of him. "About the *'love so deep, none could ever compare.'*"

The mother smiled sweetly at her boy. "Oh?" she said, waiting for him to elaborate. He looked past his mother to the nursery door, where his father had just appeared. Then looked back at his mother and smiled. "I think I know of an even greater love than that."

Kat

It was a gorgeous spring morning in Eraduun. The air was crisp and cool as a slight mist rose from the river; and a thin layer of dew covered the village and dripped as though the buildings themselves were melting. It had rained night and day for two weeks, making the ground soft and soggy, but the sunrise brought with it a swirl of color and bright blue, clear skies that seemed to lift the spirits of all who witnessed it.

The village was just waking. The windows of homes everywhere swung out welcoming the soft spring breeze and missed rays of light, while businesses and shops opened their doors to greet the new day. It wasn't long before the streets of the village and courtyard of the castle were bustling with tradesmen, shopkeepers, scullery maids, knights, nobles of the court, and everyone else in between. Amidst this lovely, bright, though slightly sodden spring morning, there was one particular bedroom that remained silent.

Between drawn curtains, small beams of light shone into a darkened room. One of which landed on the still sleeping face of a rather pretty girl. She stirred some as a muffled voice spoke, and the room grew suddenly brighter. Not quite ready to greet the new day, she held her breath until the sound of the door closing told her the visiting voice had left, and she was alone once more.

Slowly the young girl opened one eye, just enough for the bright light of day to pierce it. She groaned at the inconvenience, and pulled the covers over her head. Beneath the shade her blankets provided, she screwed her eyes shut, and silently willed the sun to go back down, hoping she could return to the rather pleasant dream she had been having.

Before long, her body and mind seemed to relax and the tantalizing notion of returning to her deep, peaceful slumber was within her grasp. That is until a sudden loud banging at her door caused her to sit up in alarm, erasing any expectations she had of falling back to sleep.

"GOOD MORNING SISTER DEAREST!" an annoying voice rang out. The girl groaned, then collapsed back into her mattress as the door opened just enough for the enormous head of her older brother to fit through.

"Go away!" she protested.

"Still in bed?! I am SHOCKED!" he said sarcastically.

"I said, *GO AWAY!*" she answered, growing more annoyed.

"Oh, come now, Kitty Kat, don't be that way."

Instinctively, his sister reached for the hairbrush on her side table, and without hesitation, hurled it at the door, just missing his head. "Well, at least your aim is improving," he teased.

The girl kicked the blanket off of her, rather petulantly, then lazily swung her legs off the side of her bed. She sat hunched on the edge of her mattress, contemplating all the possible ways she *could have* begun her morning. The thought that her day should begin *like this,* aggravated her, and she did her best not to let her brother sabotage it further. She stretched her still sleeping muscles, then let out a satisfactory yawn, and sighed.

"We *are* lively this morning, aren't we?" her brother prodded further.

"Don't you have anything better to do than irritate me?"

"My *dear* sister, whatever could you mean? All I want is to spend some quality time with you," he said, giving her an exaggerated wink. His sister rose from her bed, and swaggered over to the door. "My *dear* brother, you are so *completely* full of it."

She batted her eyelashes innocently at him. He snorted, then raised one eyebrow as he looked her up and down. "That may be so. But at least I look better than... *it!*"

"*Goodbye Jerren.*" she said, narrowing her eyes. "Farewell for... *meow.*"

He laughed as his sister huffed and shut the door hard in his face, knowing he had won the game. Jerren was hardly older than she, and they had been the best of friends when they were younger. Now though, things were a bit... different. Because they were close in age, they competed at nearly everything: who was taller, who was stronger, who was better at games; the list was endless. They taunted each other constantly, trying to see who might break first, and unfortunately, the young girl found herself on the losing end of that battle almost constantly.

She used to be just as tall and strong as he was. Now, she seemed short, wimpy, and though she hated to admit it, almost homely next to her "mature" looking brother, who had finally hit a growth spurt. And though it was impossible to make herself grow physically, she rose far above her brother in other ways.

She tried her hardest to be as responsible, dependable, and mature as she could. As hard as she tried though, she found she was not always so successful. She had been known to throw the occasional temper-tantrum, *or two*. But, she figured it all balanced out, because it seemed as though Jerren had never taken a moment in his life seriously; and surely that meant she was allowed a slip up now and again.

The young girl walked back over to her bed, contemplating whether she should even attempt climbing back in, when a knock at the door gave her answer. "Princess Katiana, the day grows late!"

"I'll be down in a moment Mara!" she replied as sweetly as she could through clenched teeth. '*Princess Katiana,*' she mimicked rudely in her head. She walked over to the small balcony that overlooked the main courtyard, leaned against the door frame, and watched the bustling crowd below. She groaned internally, wishing she could be another face in that crowd, instead of the princess. The door cracked open behind her, and she had been so fixated on her own thoughts, she paid it no attention.

"Princess…" a kind middle-aged woman urged as she entered the room. The woman had hardly taken a step, when she felt a mass under her foot. She glanced down at the brush the princess had thrown at her brother, then gave her a knowing look, and retrieved it from the ground. "I thought he looked a little too pleased with himself."

The princess giggled, knowing the woman understood exactly what had transpired between the two siblings. "Come now. I'll help you with your hair." the woman said, crossing to the ornate vanity near the window.

"Oh Mara, can I just... *not* today?"

Mara stood stoically, giving nothing away. She smiled and waited patiently for the girl to come to the most obvious decision.

"Okay... I'll do it... *If* you'll finally agree to call me Kat."

Mara's kind smile turned almost stern and disapproving. "I have addressed you as Princess Katiana from the moment you were born, and I will continue to do so until I am no longer able."

"Can't blame me for trying," Kat shrugged as she plopped herself on the small bench that faced the vanity.

She was born *Princess Katiana Renea Scarborough*, and as a small child, she thought being the princess was an answered prayer. Always having loads of pretty dresses, going to all kinds of fancy parties, people waiting on her hand and foot; her life was nothing short of a fantasy. As she got older, though, she realized being a princess wasn't at all what she assumed it would be.

Between the grueling public appearances, where perfection was not just expected but demanded; and the constant chaperones that did not allow her a moment's peace; She had no desire to be a princess, and she wished everyone would just call her *Kat.*

Kat just seemed to fit her better: it was fun; it was simple. 'Kat' didn't carry any weight or expectations. It was the perfect reflection of the life she saw for herself; but the furthest thing from the life she actually lived. Despite several attempts to make the nickname stick, only one other person outside her direct family used it; and since that person was more like family than anything else, she didn't think they actually counted.

Kat watched in the mirror as Mara swiftly and effortlessly made a neat braid down her back; twisted it up into a bun, then slid an elegant comb into place, securing it. "There now."

Mara smiled at Kat's reflection, then sighed. "Every day, you look more like her."

Kat smiled back to be polite, but it was far from genuine. The *'her'* Mara had referred to was Kat's mother; *Queen Roslin*, who died several years before. The death of her mother had been hard for her to process; she was young, and didn't fully understand how or why her mother was no longer there. Everyone told her to be strong, and even suggested that the pain of losing her would dull with time; it was a comforting notion, though she found no such relief. It had been years since that fateful day, but her blossoming adolescence made it feel as though no time had passed at all. She missed her constantly and craved her presence like she never had before, making the reminder of losing her cut a little deeper each time.

"Shall I help you dress, Princess?" Mara asked.

Kat shook her head. After the mention of her mother, she just wanted to be left alone. "No, thank you Mara. I promise to be down soon."

The nanny gave Kat a curious look, knowing full well that *'soon'* was never soon enough. Kat put her grievances to the side for a moment to give Mara a convincing smile, winning the nanny over. Mara let out a light chuckle, then left her in peace.

Once the door closed, Kat turned her attention back to her reflection, and stared at it long and hard, searching for *something*. Some small glimpse of her mother, or even the slightest clue to who *she* was supposed to be.

Since her mother's passing, many people had claimed to have seen the queen in her, but Kat was not one of them. The older she became, the more she dreaded the comparison altogether.

Queen Roslin had been beautiful in every sense of the word. Kat thought she was fair enough, but nothing compared to the beauty she found in the memories, stories, and portraits of her mother. And though she admitted to possessing several of her mother's traits, she refused to believe that hers were in any way comparable.

Her chestnut hair didn't seem to shine and flow the way her mother's hair had. Her green eyes didn't sparkle or gleam. The bridge of her nose had a light dusting of freckles, where her mother's skin had been flawless. Her mother was elegant and regal; Kat was a little gawky and awkward.

The more everyone compared her to Queen Roslin, the more she wanted to be herself. The more she wanted to just be 'Kat'. It was frightening to think people could see her mother in her. *What if she did something wrong? Or made a mistake? What if she was foolish?* How could she let any memory of her mother become tarnished that way? She felt like it was an impossible standard she could never live up to, and it devastated her to think how disappointed her mother would be if she couldn't.

Unwilling to go the rest of the day with Mara's words haunting her, she tried her best to obscure the image of her mother by pulling the delicate comb from her hair. The neat braid fell down her back with a flop, but it still wasn't enough. She loosened a few strands from the top and sides of her head to shape her face and break up her perfectly smoothed crown. It wasn't much, but the finished result was cute and unpolished. It was simply... *Kat*.

She walked to her window once more and let the warm beams of morning shine on her face hoping to lift her spirits. Glimpsing what was sure to be an undeniably lovely day, she couldn't imagine being stuck inside after enduring so much rain. Attending various lessons; listening to the idle gossip of the ladies of the court; going to court in general; it all just seemed so... *dreadful*. The thought annoyed her so much she had to scrunch her nose up at it. She sighed, resigned as always, to do the expected, and walked over to her closet to dress.

She was choosing between changing into a lovely maroon and gold trimmed gown, or staying in her cotton nightdress just to see the shock on everyone's faces, when Mara called from the other side of the door. "Don't forget about your lesson with Mistress Hilda this morning, Princess. She expects you... *presently.*"

Kat groaned.

"Are you alright, Princess?"

"Yes, thank you Mara. I'm just finishing," she replied. As the footsteps of the nanny faded, Kat fell back onto her bed in frustration. "Of all days! Of course I'd have a lesson with the *Kitchen Witch*!" she said aloud, feeling defeated.

A sudden clamor from the courtyard distracted her from her woes, and she scurried to her balcony to investigate. As she scanned the area below, she found her uncle scolding his ward and her brother. And though she hadn't seen the mischief, she suspected a knocked over fruit cart had been involved.

Kat waited till her uncle disappeared from the scene, and chuckled to herself as the two boys began to begrudgingly clean up the mess they made. "Trouble again boys?" she called down to them.

The two boys glanced toward her balcony at the sound of her voice, and while her brother rolled his eyes at her obvious amusement, her uncle's ward smirked. "Had *His Royal Highness* caught the ball like he was supposed to, there wouldn't have been!"

Kat laughed more still as her brother threw an apple at the boy standing not ten feet from him, and missed. "A lousy catch and a lousy shot, as well."

The boy laughed.

"Laugh it up, Kitty Kat! Uncle's on his way to see you and you've not even made it out of bed yet!"

Kat scoffed, unbothered by her brother's warning. But as she looked to the horizon and the village that lay before her, an idea struck her. Her eyes glowed and her smile oozed excitement. Racing to her closet, she grabbed a plain navy gown, and her simplest pair of boots, then dressed as quickly as she could.

Kat loved her uncle and typically would welcome his presence, but she had slept in almost every day since the rain began and knew he was growing impatient with her laziness. In that moment, she couldn't help but wish her father would finally return from his trip to the western lands; for it was much easier to get things past him. But, while he was away, he left Kat in her uncle's charge, and she knew her spark of an idea would fail if he caught her just barely out of bed.

She opened her bedroom door just enough to peer down the hall, making sure the coast was clear. As quietly as she could, she headed towards the northern staircase, only to turn around at the sound of her uncle's voice drawing closer. She was about halfway down the hall heading the opposite direction when he called out to her. She let out a small, silent huff, straightened her face into a smile, then turned to greet him. "Good morning uncle!"

"I missed you at breakfast Princess… *again*." her uncle said. Kat bit her lip slightly, and shrugged, hoping to charm her uncle enough to get out of a lecture. He smiled, and she knew it had worked, and before he could change his mind, or worse, uncover her true motive for the day, she was already saying goodbye.

"Sorry uncle, I can't stay and talk just now. I'm on my way to a lesson with Madame Hilda, and I simply cannot be late!"

She jumped up and left a sweet kiss on his cheek, hoping the gesture would distract him enough to not investigate further. Her uncle smiled, and as he did, Kat turned and raced down the hall.

"Princesses shouldn't run in the halls!" he called after her.

"My apologies, Sir William, it won't happen again!" she quipped back as she rushed down the stairs, leaving her uncle chuckling to himself.

As Kat reached the last step, an enormous, mean-looking woman, who was obviously on a warpath, emerged from the kitchens.

"You were supposed to escort the princess back, Gerald!"

"I'm sorry mistress, she was absent from the hall," the meek young man that followed behind the woman stuttered.

Kat slipped into a cubby behind a suit of armor. She felt a little guilty, seeing how the woman blamed the boy, and questioned if she should make herself known, but as Kat listened to the groaning complaints of the woman, she knew she had made the right choice. "If we wait much longer, my custard will burn!" she screeched.

Kat rolled her eyes and waited for the pair to clear the hall. She glanced towards the kitchens, and her stomach rumbled; the detour was not part of her original plan, but she couldn't resist the thought. Not only could she sneak away unseen, but she'd be free to grab a bit of breakfast on her way out.

She smiled to herself, snuck towards the kitchen and carefully peered inward. *It was empty.* She swung the door open, then pranced across the threshold, finding the welcoming aroma of the room as divine as she imagined. As much disdain as she held for the kitchen witch, Kat couldn't deny that she was a wonderful cook.

She scanned the room thoughtfully, and her eyes landed on a tray full of still steaming meat hand pies. Her stomach growled, and she licked her lips. Grabbing a nearby cloth, she fanned the tray, knowing from experience, how hot they could be. Then, carefully, she picked up a pie and wrapped it in the cloth. A noise from the hall startled her, and she sprinted toward the back door, hoping she still had time to escape.

She chanced a look over her shoulder to be sure nobody was behind her, but as she did, she slammed into a very tall, very strong, *very handsome*, young man. The boy was her uncle's ward, *Daniel*.

The abrupt stop sent Kat to the ground along with her meat pie. "*DANIEL!*" she whined, though she knew it was her fault more than his.

He discarded the basket of fruit he was carrying and quickly bent to help her up. "Are you alright, Princess?"

Kat dusted herself off and looked pathetically at the mangled cloth, now filled with crushed pastry and oozing gravy. "Yes..." she said sadly.

The sound of the kitchen door opening behind them made the pair jump. Kat darted beneath the windowsill, and pulled Daniel down with her as she did.

"Hey! What are yo-"
"SH!"

Mistress Hilda growled. "I just can't imagine where she could be. Are you sure you reminded Miss Mara of the lesson today, Gerald?"

Daniel glanced at Kat through the corner of his eye and gave her a broad grin, suddenly understanding why they hid. Kat shook her head.

"Oh, shut up." she whispered, biting the insides of her cheeks to keep from grinning back. Daniel tapped his nose, obviously feeling mischievous. Then, and despite Kat's attempts to keep him down, he stood up. Her heart began to race. Kat had never even tried to skip a lesson before, and she fully expected Daniel to rat her out. Feeling defeated, she pulled her knees to her chest, then buried her face in her hands and waited for the repercussion that would surely follow.

"*Good morning Madame!*" Daniel shouted, startling the Kitchen Witch. He waltzed into the kitchen with his basket of fruit, and Mistress Hilda scoffed. "I don't have time for you this morning boy, I'm expecting the princess at any moment."

"But, Madam Hilda... I've just come from the princess, who sends her *sincerest* apologies that she is unable to attend her lesson this morning. She's sent me to deliver her message, along with this basket of fresh fruit, hoping it may beg your forgiveness."

Kat clapped her hands over her mouth to suppress the giggle that threatened to escape her throat at Daniel's explanation, and her eyes sparkled with glee. *He wasn't ratting her out at all!*

The Kitchen Witch eyed Daniel suspiciously for a moment. "What have you done to this fruit?" she said as she ripped the basket from his hands.

Daniel gasped and feigned offense. "Why Madame! It wounds me to know you think so little of me!"

"You've delivered your message, and your fruit... Now, leave my kitchen!" she barked.

Daniel bowed low, hiding his wicked smile. "Have a *pleasant* day, Madame!"

He took a couple of steps backward to cover the doorway, then leaned back to see if Kat was still there. She smiled up at him, and he rewarded her with a playful wink, then signaled for her to cross behind him. She nodded, took his direction, and had just made it to the other side when the Kitchen Witch turned back.

"I thought I said leave!"

Smiling at the Kitchen Witch, Daniel bowed once more, and sauntered away. He meandered casually down the back wall towards Kat, all the while keeping a close eye out for any trouble. Then, taking one last survey of the area, he reached down and helped the princess to her feet. But, before she could even mutter a 'thank you', he walked away.

Kat cast her gaze to the ground, as she awkwardly shuffled her feet. She hadn't expected to make it this far, and wasn't sure what to do next. She glanced anxiously at her surroundings, and waited for inspiration to strike. Suddenly her eyes fell on Daniel. He and her brother, she knew, were well-versed in the art of playing hooky. She thought if anyone could help her prolong her campaign, it was him.

Daniel paused momentarily, feeling Kat's stare resting on the back of his head. He chuckled to himself, then glanced over his shoulder at her with a smirk. "You coming, or what?"

Daniel

"You didn't have to do that, Daniel... Thank you." Kat said as she caught up to him.

Daniel's lips rose into a crooked smile. "I couldn't very well leave the princess to the wrath of *the Kitchen Witch* on this lovely spring morning, now could I?"

He winked, and the lightest blush colored Kat's cheeks. She giggled and shook her head.

"I can't believe you still call her that..."

Daniel chuckled. "What else should I call her?"

"Do you remember the day we gave her that nickname?"

Daniel half snorted, as though she had asked a rather ridiculous question. "I remember *you* ruining her dessert trays, and *me* coming to the rescue, only to end up scrubbing pots and pans after every meal for three weeks." He said a little snidely, though Kat could see the humor in his eyes.

"Hey! No one asked you to take the blame for me," she replied matter-of-factly. Daniel answered with an offhanded shrug and a slight smirk.

"Just be glad I did, princess... It has been years, but I still twitch a little every time I see a wooden spoon in that woman's hand."

Daniel visibly shook, and Kat giggled once more. The pair walked on a little ways in silence until Daniel let out a light chuckle.

"What?" Kat asked.

"Nothing... Just thinking about how some things will never change."

Kat's brow furrowed, making Daniel chuckle again.

"You sneak into the kitchens for a snack, only for it to end up on the ground, and then I have to come bail you out. It could practically be a tradition."

Kat half scoffed, though she wore a grin. "If I remember correctly, the only reason *anything* ended up on the ground was because you have a habit of popping out of nowhere at the most inconvenient times."

"And you are very welcome for that, princess." Daniel chided.

Kat couldn't help but laugh to herself; he was right, of course. She seemed to have a losing streak with sneaking in and out of the kitchens, but somehow, he always kept her out of trouble. She didn't understand *why* he had done it, but she also never thought to question it... until now. Suddenly, she realized her close encounters with the Kitchen Witch were not the only memories she had of Daniel coming to her rescue. Thinking back to the very beginning of their friendship, she realized Daniel had *always* been there to help her.

He picked her up whenever she fell and dried her tears whenever she cried. He was always first in line to dance with her at important gatherings, and even stood up to Jerren when he thought he had taken a joke on her too far. The more she thought about everything he had done, the more questions she had. Kat followed Daniel through the orchard, deep in thought, silently replaying every distressing moment Daniel had saved her from.

"What is it now?" he asked, seeing the thoughtful expression on her face.

"Can I ask you something?"

Kat stopped to face him, and he shrugged in response. "You always look out for me."

"That's not a question…"

Kat rolled her eyes. "My question is… *why*?"

Daniel cocked his head to the side and rubbed the back of his neck. Kat smiled, knowing he had learned this mannerism from her uncle, who did something similar when he wasn't entirely sure what to say. "I can stop if you like."

"No, I didn't mean it was a bad thing. I just mean you always do. You have since… well, since you first got here. I was just curious to know why?"

"Well isn't that kind of what Sir William's training me for? To look after and protect the royal family...?"

Kat made no reply and cast her eyes down. It somehow disappointed her that his explanation was so ordinary. She was obviously reading too much into the situation, and she felt foolish for thinking it had been for any other reason.

Daniel saw the reaction on her face and gave her a curious look. "Were you hoping for a different answer, Kitty Kat?"

Kat knew he had used the name on purpose, and it soured her mood. "I told you, don't call me that!"

She pushed him hard, but he only laughed, then put his hands up in surrender. "I'm sorry, I couldn't resist."

Kat rolled her eyes and put her back to him. *Why did he always have to do that?*

"You've turned into a real jerk since you came home last year. Gods only know how stupid you'll get when you leave again this summer..."

"Hey, where are you going?" Daniel called as Kat marched away.

"None of your business," she sneered.

"Oh, don't be such a snob."

Kat gasped, and Daniel tried to stifle a laugh at her shocked expression. She narrowed her eyes at him and again marched away, but Daniel cut in front of her. "I'm sorry, Okay? I didn't mean it."

He gave her his most charming smile, and Kat's heart fluttered a little at his expression. Something in the way he looked at her made her feel... *special*.

"Now.." He said, stepping closer. "Catch me if you can, Kitty Kat."

Daniel leaned in slightly and Kat's heart raced. Before she knew what was happening, he left a quick kiss on her cheek, then sprinted off towards the stables. Kat turned a dark shade of pink, and it took her longer than she liked to regain her composure. Once she had, she screeched, and chased after him.

Had it been a real kiss, she may not have minded, but she knew he was only trying to get a rise out of her, and it had worked. Kat hated being teased. One of the greatest perks of being a princess was, no one dared to tease her. Well, no one except her brother and Daniel, who did it frequently. For her brother to do it was one thing, but Daniel... She and Daniel used to be just as close and she and Jerren were, but now he teased her any chance he got, and the whole situation gave Kat mixed feelings.

If she was being honest with herself, receiving *any* sort of attention from Daniel flustered her. When he smiled, she couldn't help but smile back. When he was upset about something, Kat wanted to do anything in her power to fix it; and when he teased her, it made her as sad as it did angry.

It was like he had some secret power over her. In mere seconds he could make her heart swell, make her blood boil, and then send her into a fit of laughter. She had no way to explain it, or her true feelings for him.

He was her best friend, except when he wasn't. Or maybe he was like a brother, but not like Jerren. All she knew for certain was that Daniel was one of the most important people in her life, and no matter how much he teased her, she never wanted that to change.

Kat was breathless as she reached the back side of the stables, but Daniel was nowhere to be found. She peered around the corner of the building, hoping she could surprise him, but she was so focused on not giving herself away that she didn't hear him sneaking up behind her.

Knowing he wouldn't be able to go unseen for long, he reached out and squeezed her sides, sending a jolt up her spine. She yelped at the sensation, and had she been an actual cat, she would have jumped ten feet in the air. Daniel broke into a fit of laughter, watching her reaction. Kat, though, was thoroughly *unamused*. She glared hard at him, but her expression only seemed to fuel his amusement.

"You scared me half to death!" she scolded.

"I'm sorry." Daniel said, attempting to quell his laughter.

Kat huffed and sat herself against the side of the stables. The whole situation irritated her and she could think of no other way to show it than to cross her arms and pout. Daniel, however, snorted at her tantrum, then slid down the wall to sit beside her, but Kat refused to look at him. He let out a long sigh, then nudged her with his shoulder, hoping it would soothe her mood, but it didn't work. Kat scooted away just enough, until they were no longer touching. Daniel, unwilling to let it go, followed closely beside, and repeated the action.

Kat swung her head over to glare at him, but when their eyes met, her stomach filled with butterflies. His bright eyes sparkled with joy, and the grin on his face was as genuine as it was charming. Kat tried her hardest to maintain her less than cheerful attitude, but the longer she looked into those stupid blue eyes, the lighter and happier she felt.

Seeing the slight struggle in Kat's expression, Daniel quickly contorted his face in the most ridiculous manner, effectively ending Kat's sour mood. She let a small laugh escape her throat, and Daniel beamed with pride.

"Oh, don't laugh. I was just practicing my impression of the prince."

Kat burst into laughter and shoved him slightly for his wicked remark. Daniel smiled, then chuckled along with her. As their laughter subsided, Kat leaned her head casually against his shoulder, and to her surprise, Daniel reciprocated in kind.

The sweet gesture had been just what Kat needed, and she thought that maybe this could be her happy place. Right here; sitting in a meadow next to Daniel on a cool, sunny, spring day.

A comfortable silence formed between them as they both took in the moment; until Daniel broke the silence with a confession. "You reminded me of Em."

Em? Kat didn't know who he meant, or why he had even made the comment. She looked up at him slightly confused, and he couldn't help but chuckle.

"Before... You asked why I always covered for you and looked out for you... You reminded me of my sister... Emerlyn."

The admission made Kat feel strangely relieved and dismayed all at the same time. "Oh..."

"We were really young... When it all happened, and I guess I felt like if I couldn't do it for *her,* at least I could do it for you..."

The way Daniel looked at her as he spoke, made Kat's heart beat a little faster. She could see the mixture of sadness, and hope in his eyes, and knew exactly how he must be feeling. She knew little about Emerlyn, just that she had been very important to him, and died much too young. Being a little nosy, she wanted to ask more, but knew it wasn't the right time. Instead, she smiled and said, "Well, I guess that's okay then."

They exchanged a small understanding look, then resumed their previous positions. Only this time, she noticed Daniel had leaned in a little closer.

"Can I ask you something else?" Kat asked hesitantly, unable to stop herself.

Daniel chuckled, recognizing her curious tone. "By all means."

"You said I *reminded* you of her... Do I *still*?"

"Do you still, what?"

"Remind you of her...?"

Kat bit her lip anxiously, not knowing what his response would be, or even what response she was hoping for. Daniel fumbled at finding the right words, and before he could attempt to clarify, an outside voice saved him.

"Awww, isn't this sweet?"

Kat sat up, feeling slightly embarrassed, and put just a little space between herself and Daniel. "What are you doing here?"

"Better question, sister dearest. What are *you* doing here?" Jerren said, raising a suspicious eyebrow, looking from Kat to Daniel and back again. Kat scoffed, stood, and dusted herself off.

"Not that it's any of *your* business, but we were in the middle of a conversation," she said, half glaring at him.

"Oh, I'll bet you were..." Jerren said with a wink.

Kat huffed, stomped her foot, then began to march away. Daniel rolled his eyes at the prince, giving him a playful shove.

"Hey!" Jerren called after his sister, who he noticed was not following her usual path. Within seconds, the boys caught up, flanking her on either side. "And where do you think you're going?"

"To the village."

The immediate answer along with the nonchalance in her voice momentarily halted her brother. Jerren looked around as though he had lost something, and Kat had the slightest suspicion, the *something* he had lost, was his mind.

"I'm sorry, I must have missed something.... Where are you going?"

"*I. Am. Go-ing. To. The. Vill-age.*" Kat said, articulating each syllable so that her dimwit brother could try to comprehend what she was saying.

Jerren laughed loudly and obnoxiously, until Kat groaned, and hastily marched forward.

"You're joking!" Jerren said in disbelief, as the boys caught up once more. "Daniel, this has to be a joke!"

Daniel looked from Kat back to Jerren. "No, I'm fairly certain she's serious."

Kat scoffed. "Of course I'm serious!"

"But there's no escort with you! There's no guide! And I know for a fact that you have already skipped out on a lesson with Madame Hilda. So you *can't* be serious."

Kat stopped cold in her tracks. It had only been a few minutes... *How could he possibly know already?*

"I overheard Gerald and Mara talking." Jerren shrugged, obviously proud of his eavesdropping skills. Kat huffed and rolled her eyes.

"Of course you did..." Daniel and Kat said in unison.

"Wait so, hang on!" He paused, cutting in front of his sister. "Let me get this straight... YOU, Katiana Scarborough, *Princess Perfect,* are planning on not only skipping out on *one* lesson, but the *whole* of your responsibilities today?!"

"Well, when you say it like that..."

"Oh, thank the Gods!"

Jerren grabbed her by the shoulders and left a loud kiss on her cheek.

"Ugh, what's wrong with you?" Kat whined, pushing him away.

"Do you know how long I've waited for this day?! Welcome to the land of the living sister! Let's go have some fun!"

Jerren draped his arm around her shoulder, then turned his attention to Daniel and asked a rather obvious sounding question. "The Inn?"

Daniel laughed and put his own arm around Kat's other shoulder. "Where else?"

Kat looked at them both in utter confusion. *Why were they so willing to include her now?* It had been so long since they had tried to drag her along anywhere. She was shocked and admittedly a little concerned. *What, in the last few moments, had changed?* She ducked beneath their arms and walked backwards, breaking free of their embrace.

"Hang on! What is going on? Why are you being so... *weird*? What's the Inn? And who said either of you were going anywhere with me?"

Jerren rolled his eyes and groaned. "Oh, please don't be so... *you* about it! I just started liking you again!"

"We're taking you to the village," Daniel said, interrupting before Kat could make a rebuttal to her brother's remark. "To my aunt's inn, to be more specific. We *are* going with you. Because, number one, there's no way we can leave you to go on your own; your uncle would kill us if he ever found out."

"Most definitely, *and* number two, because we're professionals." Jerren added.

Kat hesitated for a moment, questioning whether she was going to follow through with her plan. She knew she ought to turn back now and beg forgiveness from her uncle, Mara, and probably Mistress Hilda. If she did, maybe they wouldn't be too hard on her.

But then again...

She looked from Jerren to Daniel. The expectant and excited looks on each of their faces only encouraged her, and the tiniest hint of thrill spread through her at the very notion of her miniature rebellion. "It's just *one* day... Right?"

"YES!" Jerren exclaimed, clapping his hands together. He turned swiftly on his heels, then marched on, leading the way.

"After you, Princess." Daniel bowed, presenting the path to Kat. She giggled at the gesture, curtsied back to him, then skipped happily behind her brother.

The village wasn't far from the main gate, but taking that route meant there was a higher risk of attracting unwanted attention. Instead, they opted for the western gate. It was further out and surrounded by a meadow on both sides. It took a little more time to travel, but was much better for sneaking. The path had overgrown from lack of use, and because of all the rain it was almost marsh-like.

Kat had managed well enough for a short distance, but the mud grew thicker and harder to walk through with her boots, and dress. She hesitated at one point and wondered how the boys didn't seem to mind. Jerren rolled his eyes at her priss.

"It's just a little mud, Kat, it won't bite you…"

"Shut up, Jerren!"

Daniel rolled his eyes at the siblings' bickering, then offered a solution to stop it. "Here Kat, hop on my back."

"Really?!"

"Sure, why not?"

Kat skipped to Daniel and put her hands on his shoulders, but paused just before hoisting herself up. "I'm a little heavier than the last time we did this…"

Daniel couldn't help but chuckle at the ridiculous comment and her lack of faith in his abilities; he shook his head, then squatted a little lower, urging her on and up. "Don't worry, Princess… I've got you."

Daniel winked back at her, and it was all the encouragement she needed. Kat smiled excitedly, then jumped on to his back and was glad to find he walked on with ease. She playfully nuzzled the back of his head, and he laughed.

When Daniel had first arrived with Sir William, he had been a little shy and sad. Then again, so had Kat. Only a year had passed since losing her mother, and she was still struggling. When she and Jerren realized the loss Daniel had experienced, they rallied around him, and the resulting understanding that emerged between them formed an unshakable bond. One that said they had felt the same heartache, and they didn't have to suffer alone. Without even realizing it, they grew to rely on one another, and helped each other move forward.

Jerren and Daniel had always been inseparable, and it made Kat jealous that more often than not, they excluded her; especially in recent years. Today, though, it felt like it had when they were younger and spent every moment all together.

The entire way into the village, the three laughed, joked and played games. They didn't argue or bicker or tease each other. Everything was just as it used to be, almost as if nothing at all had changed. Even Jerren didn't seem as annoying and irksome as he typically did.

When they finally reached the bridge just before the village, Kat peered down the river and could see how much the rain had affected it. Anxiety grew in the pits of her stomach as she watched the rapid water rush unyielding beneath them. She looked from bank to bank, but could not see a definitive shore; the river had overflown so much it was as if one never existed.

"Wanna go for a swim, Kat?" Jerren teased.

"After you, big brother." Kat said as she stuck her tongue out at him.

Jerren rolled his eyes. "You can set her down now, Daniel... the path is stone from here."

Daniel looked up over his shoulder at Kat with a questioning grin. "Would you like me to set you down, Princess?"

Kat tapped her chin thoughtfully, as though the question were a difficult one. "I'm not sure. A girl could get used to this whole not walking thing."

"Get down, Kat. Stop being so lazy!"

"Uh, uh, uh, the Princess has spoken and so it shall be!" Daniel replied, holding up his hand. Kat giggled and squeezed Daniel a little tighter.

"Oh, come on Dan, I want to race!"

Daniel scoffed, "It's not like you'd beat me!"

"I one hundred percent would!"

"I'm sorry to be the one to tell you this, your Highness, but I'd still beat you, even with Kitty Kat here on my back."

"You are so on!" Jerren shot back, welcoming the challenge.

"First one to the inn wins?"

"Call it, sis!" Jerren ordered as the boys took their stances. Kat hesitated. She thought she'd slow Daniel down for sure; it didn't seem like a fair race at all.

"Come on, Kat..." her brother groaned. Daniel looked up at her with a confident smile, then winked.

"Alright..." she sighed. "On your marks... Get set..."

"Hang on tight, Princess."

Kat tightened her grip around Daniel. "GO!"

The boys took off down the lane and into the village. They dodged cart vendors left and right. They jumped down full sets of stairs and weaved seamlessly through the crowds in front of them. Kat squealed with delight and cheered Daniel on, very surprised that even with her extra weight, the boys were neck and neck. At one point, Jerren bolted ahead, but not far enough to worry Daniel.

Thinking quickly, he took a sharp turn down an alley. The path was narrow with twists and turns, but nothing seemed to slow him down. Daniel popped back onto the main street just ahead of Jerren, and Kat and Daniel laughed as they sped on to victory.

"We've arrived at our destination, Princess," Daniel half choked out as he finally came to a stop. He lowered himself slightly, and Kat quickly jumped down. The moment she did, Daniel fell back to rest on the bench beside them. Seeing him so out of breath and worn made her feel guilty, and so she awarded him with a gentle pat on his shoulder.

"You... cheated!" Jerren gasped, finally joining them at the finish line. Daniel scoffed. "Don't be a sore loser. You're just mad because I was right."

Jerren waved off Daniel's comments, too preoccupied by his own lack of oxygen. As the boys recovered their lung capacity, Kat looked around excitedly. She had been to the village many times before, but always for a specific purpose, with a specific destination and always with an escort. Seeing it all for herself made it feel brand new, and she couldn't decide where to go, or what to do first.

It was mid-day now and the world around her was alive, and filled with unique sights, sounds, smells, and all kinds of people. Her eyes lit up with excitement, and Jerren must have noticed just how much, because as she was about to walk towards a shop, he grabbed her arm, and pulled her back.

"Hey! What are you-"

Jerren sighed at his sister's argument, but made no verbal reply. He pointed to the sign directly above his head, and his semi-perturbed expression quickly shifted into an impish smirk.

The Spear and Thistle

"The Spear and Thistle Inn?"

Jerren gave a proud nod, as Daniel stood to join them. "The best spot in town!" he boasted.

"We're really just coming here?" Kat half whined. Jerren and Daniel rolled their eyes. "Have a little faith, would ya."

They had almost made it to the entrance when a blur of dark hair ran past Kat and straight at Daniel. The blur had nearly knocked him to the ground, but Daniel opened his arms just in time to catch a little boy leaping at him. He pulled the boy close and hugged him tight. "Hiya, squirt!"

Kat watched the interaction curiously. She couldn't remember a time she had seen Daniel look happier. She turned to Jerren with a questioning look, but he didn't notice. He was too focused on Daniel and the boy; he smiled, and something in his expression made Kat feel warm. She turned back to Daniel and realized the boy looked oddly familiar.

"Mommy will be so happy to see you!" he exclaimed. Kat saw Daniel's eyes light up at the boy's words, and she suddenly realized the boy looked so familiar because he looked just like Daniel. *It had to be one of his brothers.*

The younger Enid was in the middle of telling Daniel a story, but interrupted himself when he caught sight of Jerren. He squirmed from Daniel's hold and ran over to Jerren, then began a faux sparring match with him.

"Declan!" a woman's voice called out. The little boy looked over his shoulder and shouted. "Aunt Ada! Guess what!"

"What is it, darling?"

Daniel caught his brother just before he ran inside and whispered something to him. Declan laughed and nodded in agreement. Daniel released him, then tousled his hair.

"Nevermind!" Declan smiled back at his brother, then disappeared through the door.

"We'll meet you inside," Jerren said, clapping Daniel on the back. Kat looked at each of them not understanding what was going on. Jerren chuckled and put his arm around her shoulders, then ushered her into the Inn while Daniel disappeared around to the back alley.

"Sit anywhere you'd like, dears, I'll be with you in a moment," a very kind, jolly looking woman called out. Jerren lowered his head a bit and waved in acknowledgment. He directed Kat to a table along the back wall, pulled out a chair, then sat opposite her, somewhat concealing himself, while Kat scanned the space with mild scrutiny.

"What do you think?" Jerren asked.

The main floor of the inn was large. It was clean, cozy, and inviting. There was a small stage set up for musicians, and even space for dancing. The kitchen door swung open and a delicious symphony of smells wafted into Kat's nose. Her stomach growled, and it was just then she remembered she hadn't eaten breakfast. The sound her stomach made was so loud it made Jerren chuckle. "Just you wait!"

"I like it here… It feels…" She couldn't think of the word to describe it, but Jerren must have understood, because he nodded in agreement. "I know."

Kat had a million questions. *Why hadn't she been here before? How had she never met Daniel's family? How often had her brother come here?*

She was about to launch a full scale inquisition when the sight of Daniel climbing through an open window distracted her.

"What's he doing?"

Jerren followed Kat's gaze, then chuckled and shook his head. At the same moment, a pretty girl, around Daniel's age, placed two cups and a pitcher of water on the table in front of them, blocking Kat's view. Jerren looked up and grinned flirtatiously at her. The girl blushed, and smiled, then spun her head around to scan the room. Kat rolled her eyes at her brother, then smirked to see the girl seemed uninterested in his attempts.

The woman who had greeted them walked towards their table, still oblivious to who they were. "What can I get you dears today?"

Before Jerren could respond, Daniel picked the woman up from behind and swung her around. "Hi Aunt Ada!"

The woman yelped in surprise, but laughed. "Oh Danny! Put me down!"

Danny? Kat had never heard Daniel called that before. It sounded a little strange, but seemed to suit him. When he set the woman down, she engulfed him in a loving embrace, then held him at arm's length for inspection.

"Daniel Trystane Enid! It has been two months since I've seen you!"

Daniel laughed and shrugged. "I've been busy."

"Tsk, busy!" She playfully swatted his shoulder, making Daniel smile.

"Yeah, those crazy royals have him doing all kinds of nonsense," Jerren smirked.

The woman turned to him in shock, then smiled when she saw who it was. "Oh, you boys!" The woman pulled Jerren up and hugged him almost as fervently as she had hugged Daniel, then looked at both of them lovingly. "You two are growing into such fine young men."

"We do our best," Jerren said, straightening his shirt. Daniel rolled his eyes and walked over to Kat, who he could tell felt a little out of place. He bent slightly and offered her his hand, then helped her to her feet. He smiled, then without taking his eyes off of her, introduced her. "Aunt Ada," he said, "I would like to introduce-"

"Oh my heavens," she gasped, and immediately curtsied. "Princess Katiana, please forgive my rudeness."

How did she know? Kat blushed at the woman's instant, obvious recognition and the formal greeting.

"Oh no, please don't do that, Madame," Kat said politely. The woman looked a little confused. "There's no need to apologize... I get just as excited after not seeing Daniel for a couple of months... And please, call me Kat."

Daniel blushed slightly at Kat's words, and the woman smiled. "As you wish, Miss Kat, but only on the condition that while you're here, you call me Aunt Ada... Everyone does."

Kat beamed and nodded in agreement. No one had ever agreed to her request, and with so brief a hesitation; and she didn't want to say anything that may hinder the agreement.

"But, can I just say, what a great honor it is to have you here? These boys have told us so much about you."

It was Kat's turn to blush. She glanced over at Jerren and Daniel, a little flattered they had spent any time at all talking about her.

"Just wait till Lena hears."

Aunt Ada gasped, then looked over at Daniel, who beamed. "Lena!" she called. "Come and see!" Aunt Ada excused herself, then rushed up the back staircase.

"So, that's Aunt Ada," Daniel said with a chuckle. Kat smiled and just as she was about to say something, the girl that had brought the water ran up and flung her arms around Daniel, giving him a tight squeeze.

"Oh Danny! It's so good to see you!"

Daniel chuckled and accepted the embrace. Kat couldn't help but notice how excited the girl had been and was a little annoyed by it, and that she had called him Danny... Or maybe it was him not seeming to mind that bothered her more than anything else.

"It's good to see you too, Seydi."

Daniel cleared his throat a little and took a step back towards Kat. Seydi looked from Daniel to Kat and back again. Something in his expression must have irritated her, because when she looked back at Kat, she gave her a rather unimpressed glare, as though she were a bug in dire need of being squashed. She held her expression until Daniel told her who Kat was.

"*Princess Katiana*!" Seydi's face turned a pale shade of green as she curtsied. "What an honor to meet you..." she said in an apologetic sort of way. Kat responded cordially, but made it a point not to introduce herself as 'Kat'.

"Can I just say how pretty you are?" Seydi continued.

Kat knew she was embarrassed and trying to save face, so she took pity on her; smiled, thanked her, then paid her an equal compliment that seemed to settle the silent dispute. Before excusing herself, Seydi took one last glance at Daniel.

The longing expression on her face made Kat squirm, but she did her best to ignore it.

Suddenly Declan came barreling out of the stairwell, pulling the group's attention. Aunt Ada followed quickly behind, with another small boy, and another woman followed behind her. The second woman was tall, slender, and beautiful. She had light sandy hair, but her deep blue eyes, Kat would recognize anywhere.

"Danny!"

"Hi mum," Daniel smiled and crossed over to her. He hugged her tight and leaned back slightly, lifting her off the ground. She laughed, but tears sprang to her eyes.

When his mother was satisfied with the length of the embrace with her son, she fussed over him the same way his aunt had. Kat saw the color in Daniel's cheeks deepen; it was obvious he wasn't used to this sort of attention, especially around other people, and Kat couldn't help but think how sweet it was. Then, she couldn't help but think of her own mother and how much she wished she could be there to fuss over her.

A surge of emotion washed over her, and before she knew what was happening, the smallest of tears ran down her cheek. She wiped it quickly away, hoping no one else had noticed. She couldn't understand why she suddenly felt this way, and tried hard to suppress it.

A soft hand slipped into hers and squeezed. She looked up to find her brother's half smile. "I miss her too," he whispered. Kat dashed away any remaining tears with her free hand, then leaned on to her brother's shoulder. She was glad that no matter how much they fought or teased, she could always count on Jerren to understand just how she was feeling.

Right after they had lost their mother, Jerren had been there for her in a way no one else had. She remembered how late at night, after everyone else had gone to sleep, Jerren would come into her room and sit with her. Sometimes he sang; sometimes they talked; mostly though, he just sat with her and held her hand, just so she knew he was there and she wasn't alone. Those were the times she loved her brother the most.

Kat gave him a small smile and squeezed his hand. He nudged her with his elbow and she let out a weak laugh. When she lifted her head once more towards the Enid's, her eyes met those of Daniel's mother.

His mother's eyes were a rich blue, full of warmth and kindness, just like Daniel's. Lady Leanna loosened her grip on her son, and Daniel stepped to the side to present his guests.

Not wanting to just be in the background, Kat stepped forward before Daniel could say anything. She smiled and gave a polite curtsy. "Lady Leanna, it's so nice to meet you."

Daniel's mother smiled, then returned the formal gesture. "It's nice to meet you as well, Princess Katiana."

"Please, call me Kat…"

A curious expression flitted across Lady Leanna's face, almost as if she had unlocked a memory, and she smiled. "Then *I'm* Lena."

It surprised Kat how relaxed Daniel's family seemed to be, and how willing they had been to call her 'Kat'. A sudden tugging on her skirt brought her out of her thoughts and back to the present. She looked down to investigate, only to find the little sandy-haired boy Ada had been holding.

"Hello there, aren't you cute!" Kat said, squatting down to talk to him. She extended her hand to him and introduced herself. "I'm Kat. It's so very nice to meet you."

"My name's Archer Enid, and I think you're the most beautiful girl I have ever seen!"

Archer smiled and kissed Kat's hand, and she tried hard to suppress a giggle at the boy's cute greeting. "Well, that's very sweet of you to say *Archer Enid*."

"Will you marry me?" he asked suddenly. The question caught Kat off guard, and the extremely serious look in his eyes halted her. A light blush filled her cheeks, and when she looked up at the surrounding audience, hoping to find any sort of guidance on the matter, Jerren and Daniel didn't even try to hide their amusement. She shot them a pointed look, then turned back to Archer. Kat gave his tiny fingers a soft squeeze, and smiled as sweetly as she could.

"I'll tell you what, *Archer Enid*... You come find me when you can reach the top of that door frame without help from *anything, or anyone*, then we'll talk."

She winked at the boy, and he giggled, agreeing to the terms she set. Daniel squatted down to be level with his brother. He hugged him and then in a low voice asked, "Do you know who that is, pipsqueak?"

Archer shrugged and shook his head. Daniel laughed, looked at Kat out of the corner of his eye, then whispered something inaudible into his brother's ear. Archer looked wide-eyed up at Kat, turned bright red, then ran to hide behind the main counter. Daniel chuckled at his brother then stood, and offered his hand to help Kat up. She took his hand, but narrowed her eyes at him, wondering what he could have possibly said to torture the poor boy, but he gave nothing away.

Just then a very tall, very handsome older gentleman entered through the back door. Aunt Ada called him over and introduced him as 'Tom the caretaker.' After the introduction, Kat caught sight of a sweet look he and Ada had exchanged. But then, a nearby customer called out for service, and Tom dismissed himself to attend to the patron, effectively ending the moment. Kat watched as he walked away, and noticed that though the inn had been relatively empty when she first entered, there were now only a few vacant tables.

"Could I offer my help, Aunt Ada?" Kat asked, feeling a little guilty that she had taken up so much of their time... Jerren, Daniel, Lady Leanna and Aunt Ada gave her an odd, unsure look; like she had just grown a second head.

"Oh no, Princess, I couldn't-" Aunt Ada began, but Kat wouldn't take 'no' for an answer. "Please Aunt Ada, I insist."

Ada smiled and bowed her head. "That would be lovely, Kat."

Daniel coughed, clearing his throat, "I'd be glad to help too," he muttered. His mother put her arm around him and kissed his temple. The sweet gesture brought a smile to Kat's face. Her eyes met Daniel's, and she watched as color filled his cheeks. Hoping to save him some embarrassment and move the subject along, she gave her brother a stealthy kick of encouragement. Jerren laughed. "I'd rather sit back and watch the show, but of course I'd be glad to lend a hand."

Kat let out a small huff at her brother's response, then followed Ada into the kitchen. She donned an apron, rolled up her sleeves and rejoined the group in the dining room.

It was exciting to her that no one outside the Enid clan seemed to recognize who she, or her brother, had been; or maybe they just didn't care. Either way, she spent the early afternoon serving food and talking with all kinds of people. She sang tavern songs, danced on the stage, and in spare moments played a few games. Once Archer had recovered from his shyness, he scarcely left Kat's side. Meanwhile, Declan seemed to follow Jerren and Daniel around like a shadow.

Kat had felt almost like a normal girl. For once, she didn't have to worry so much about being prim and proper.

She felt relaxed, at ease, and maybe even a little playful. It was the most fun she'd had in a very long time.

Then, to cap it all off, after the service in the inn had slowed down, Ada treated them all to a small feast. Kat had never eaten so much in her life; and though she wasn't sure she could eat another bite, she could not resist Ada's famous lemon pie. It was the most delicious thing Kat had ever eaten. It was creamy, and smooth, and just the right level of tart and sweet.

She ate her piece quicker than anyone else, and even though her stomach was so full she thought she might burst, she couldn't stop herself from looking over at Daniel's piece. He hadn't even touched it, and part of her had hoped she knew the reason.

At feasts, or dinner parties, or anytime dessert was involved, or Kat *really* liked something, Daniel always offered his serving to her, and today was no exception. Kat gave him a knowing smile; he snickered, smiled back, then slid his dessert plate over to her.

She hadn't noticed it then, but Ada and Lady Leanna had exchanged a small look at the gesture. What she *had* noticed was that since sitting down for lunch, the lovely Miss Seydi had made several more attempts to get Daniel's attention. Kat was glad to find that he was too immersed in his family's company to notice, or maybe he was ignoring her advances on purpose; she liked to think it was the latter of the two options.

She wasn't sure why it had bothered her so much that a girl was paying him so much attention. She had seen lots of girls at court act silly around him, and it hadn't bothered her then. This felt different, though. *She* was too close, too familiar, and Kat didn't quite understand why, but she wasn't a fan of the situation.

It was late-afternoon when Kat, Jerren and Daniel thought it was time to leave the inn. The three took turns saying their goodbyes to Ada, Tom, and the two little boys; then they turned to Lady Leanna.

She announced that she and the little boys would be in town for the month until Daniel was ready to join them for the summer, and that Kat and Jerren were welcome to come visit anytime.

Leanna hugged her son tightly and whispered something into his ear. Daniel smiled and nodded in response. Then Kat watched as she hugged Jerren and told him to behave himself. Finally, Leanna turned towards her.

"Is it alright if I give you a hug?"

"Of course!" Kat replied. Though the instant they formed the connection, Kat wished she wouldn't have. Something stirred within her, a well of emotions that she didn't realize existed.

"I know it's not my place and I know I've only just met you..."

Lady Leanna hesitated, then pulled back from the embrace. "I was very close to your mother once upon a time, and I know how hard it is for a young girl to grow up without one." A small tear appeared in Lady Leanna's eye, and she wiped it away. "I just wanted to let you know if you ever need anything," she paused, "anything at all... You could come to me if you'd like."

A lump formed in Kat's throat as Lady Leanna cupped her hands around Kat's face.

"I'm sure you hear this all the time, but you look so much like her and I know she would be so *very* proud of you."

Lady Leanna's words pierced into Kat like shards of glass; she suddenly felt as though the air had been sucked from her lungs, and filling them again would be impossible. She smiled the best she could, then hugged Lady Leanna as tightly as if she were her mother, letting small strands of tears stream down her cheeks.

"Thank you," she whispered. Kat pulled away abruptly, then headed for the door, not waiting to see if Jerren or Daniel were behind her.

As she burst into the street, she felt raw and exposed. She did not like the idea of being out in the open. She crouched between the inn and the neighboring building, buried her face in her hands, and wept. The tears came on so suddenly and unexpectedly; she was a bit frustrated by it. *"Why are you crying?!"*

She felt foolish. Here she was, having the best day she'd had in a long while, only for it to end in tears. *And for what?* It's not as if Lady Leanna was the first person to say those words to her, but for some unknowable reason, they hit her differently.

It was obvious Lady Leanna was a wonderful mother. She was kind and genuine. She was beautiful, inside and out. In fact, she reminded Kat so much of her own mother that it was almost sickening. Maybe that was the real reason her words were so hard for Kat to swallow, or maybe she had just momentarily gone insane. Whatever the reason, Kat was in a very vulnerable state and she didn't like it. Every emotion she had ever felt pummeled her until the strongest one overcame the rest.

Anger completely consumed her. She was angry at Lady Leanna for saying what she did to make her feel this way. She was angry at her mother for not being here with her; at her father for being so absent all the time; at her uncle for being so overprotective and sheltering her; and at her brother because he had such an obvious connection to the outside world, and to this family in particular. Though no one angered her more than Daniel.

He had brought her to the inn. *He* had introduced her to his wonderful family… to his wonderful mother; who loved him more than words could describe. Why did *he* have that when *she* didn't? *How was that fair?*

Her anger had no real validity. It didn't even make sense; but that didn't seem to matter much at all. It didn't change the fact that her mother was gone, or what Lady

Leanna had said... It didn't change the fact that Kat felt so unbearably alone.

The front door of the inn opened, and Kat could hear Daniel and Jerren call back to say one last goodbye. She wiped her face as well as she could, hoping to disguise how much she was hurting, dusted herself off, then emerged from the alley and walked up the path that led home.

She had only taken a few steps when she heard Jerren say, "There she is. Hey Kat, wait up!"

The two boys jogged to catch up with her, but her pace didn't slow. Jerren dusted his shoulder and straightened his cuffs, as if he were important. "You're welcome."

Kat rolled her eyes but didn't respond.

"I think you're the favorite Scarborough of the Enid clan," Daniel smiled, though the smile didn't last long.

"Yippie..."

"Oh, come on, Kitty Kat, no clever remark?" Jerren teased.

Kat stopped and pushed Jerren hard causing him to stumble, and nearly knock over a flower stand. Jerren apologized to the vendor, then moved to confront his sister. Kat scowled at him, and he gladly returned the glower. He opened his mouth to reprimand her, but she turned and walked away before he could get a single syllable out.

"Are you alright, Kat?" Daniel asked. He barely tapped her shoulder, and she jerked away. Jerren was growing more heated by the second witnessing her rude attitude. He stepped in front of her to slow her, but she sidestepped him, only for Daniel to catch her forearm. "Kat, come on, what's going on?"

"Let go Daniel..." she warned, trying to rip her arm from his grip, which tightened as she wriggled.

"Just look at me for a second... Please."

Kat reared back and slapped him hard across the face. He released her, only to console his aching cheek. "I said let me go!"

"What is your problem?!" Jerren growled, stepping between her and Daniel. It was clear he had more than enough of whatever was bothering his sister. Kat's expression hardened and flared her nostrils, daring him to push her further, but Daniel quickly intervened. "It's fine. Let's just get her back."

"I don't need your help!" she screeched. Daniel looked back at her with wide, confused eyes, and Jerren's mouth formed a hard line, but Kat ignored them both, then marched on in a huff.

"No! It's not alright!" Jerren burst, chasing after her. "This is so typical Kat... I don't know what your problem is but-"

"I don't have a problem! Leave me alone!"

Jerren stepped in front of her and lowered his voice. "Knock it off, Kat, or I swear."

Kat rolled her eyes. "You'll what?"

"Just leave her be Jer. Whatever's going on, she doesn't want to talk about it." Daniel said, putting himself between them.

Kat took a deep breath. The rage within her was building higher and higher. She knew she shouldn't feel this way, but there was nothing to do to stop it. "What is *YOUR* deal? No one asks for your opinion and no one needs or wants your help!"

Daniel's brow furrowed in frustration. "That's not what it looked like this morning."

"This morning was... different."

Daniel gave a half-hearted laugh. "How?"

Kat couldn't stand that he had laughed at her, even if she had deserved it. She looked over at Jerren, who was fuming, back to Daniel, who she could tell was losing his patience with her as well. Her head swirled with so many emotions; sadness, bitterness, heartache, confusion. *How? or Why?* She had no way of knowing; but if she was going to feel this way, she'd make sure someone else did, too... unfortunately for Daniel, her target was obvious.

"It was different because this morning I was stupid enough to think you cared about me at all!"

Daniel and Jerren exchanged a confused glance. Daniel wanted to say something, but Kat stopped him before he could.

"No! Just shut up! I don't want to hear anything you have to say to me. The only reason I'm even here right now is so *you*," she looked at Jerren. "had an excuse to blow off whatever you were supposed to do today. And because *you*," she looked back at Daniel. "Think that being nice to me and 'protecting' me is somehow going to make up for your dead sister!"

"Kat!" Jerren warned sharply.

"Well, I'm not her and you know what? I'm glad I'm not her! Gods! I'd feel so bad for her if she was here, though! Can't you just back off?!"

"Kat, that's enough!" Jerren said, harsher this time.

Kat knew she had crossed a line, but her mouth moved faster than her senses and she just couldn't stop herself.

"I mean, honestly! Doesn't it *ever* get old? Good Ol' Daniel coming to the rescue! Do you get some weird thrill from it? Can't you just focus on your own life? I mean, look at you! You've got it all! The best of both worlds! Got the perfect little family, and all the perks of living at the castle without actually earning it in any way! Must be so nice for you! Livin' the dream and swooping in to solve everyone's problems. That certainly didn't get your father very far, though, did it?"

Jerren pushed past Daniel, which wasn't hard to do at that point, grabbed Kat firmly by the arm, leaned in close and stared her hard in the eyes. "I said, *enough*."

The seriousness in his eyes and voice was just enough to blink Kat out of her blind rage and back to a bit of sanity. "Jer, I-"

She looked over at Daniel, who was staring at the ground with his fists and jaw clenched tight, and his eyes full of pain. Kat's heart sank. *What was her problem?*

"Daniel-" She half quivered. He looked up at her and his typically warm, bright blue eyes were a dull, cold and empty gray. She lowered her head. "I'm so- I didn't mean-" Tears glossed her eyes. "I'm so sorry," she said, shaking her head in disbelief at her own behavior.

She knew Daniel well enough to know that he would take everything she had said to heart. *Why had she said any of those things at all? Why had she attacked him like that?* Daniel had never done anything but help people the best he could, *her in particular.*

Jerren's grip on her arm loosened, and she took full advantage. Mortified, and unable to articulate any sort of excuse, she turned around, then merged into the crowded path. She meandered through the street, bumping into another person or a cart and muttering an involuntary apology. All the while, trying to wipe away the flood of tears that wouldn't stop. Jerren called after her, but she ignored him. He called again, and she could tell he was closer this time.

Kat couldn't bear to face him, to face anyone. She ran... As fast and as hard as she could. Her vision blurred with tears as she did her best to follow the path that had brought her to the inn. Off in the distance, she could see the muddled image of the bridge that led to the western gate. If it was at all possible, she ran faster.

As she neared the bridge, the ground softened and became slick. She slowed her pace slightly, struggling to keep her balance, but she knew her brother was close behind. Unwilling to be caught, she sped up once more, not realizing how close she had gotten to the steep edge of the embankment.

She slipped, and screamed as she slid down the muddy slope. She tried desperately to grab hold of anything she could to avoid falling into the rushing river. Just as her feet hit the water, she caught herself on a small root that protruded from the ground.

"Kat!" Jerren yelled from near the bridge. Daniel didn't hesitate for a second. He slid himself down the embankment and tried his best to get to her.

"Just hang on!" Jerren called.

Kat fought hard to find her footing, but the mud was too slick and the passing water was moving too fast. Daniel was within arm's length, but hesitated to go any lower for fear of becoming stuck in the thick mud, or falling into the river himself.

"Kat, grab my hand and walk up to me!"

Terror flooded her system, her sole focus was on the root she clung to, which was now threatening to remove itself from the soft earth.

"Come on, Kat! You can do it!" her brother called down to her.

"I can't!" she screamed. Her feet slipped out beneath her, and the jolt of the small drop was just enough to cause the tip of the root to spring outward. Kat's hands slipped from the root, and she fell back, disappearing beneath the rushing river.

"Kat!"

The cold, murky water was deep. Between the rapids and the tears that overwhelmed her eyes, Kat couldn't make sense of what was up or down. Her head bobbed in and out of the river, and she splashed and spluttered between deep breaths and mouthfuls of water. When she surfaced, she could hear the faint, gargled sounds of her brother and Daniel calling out to her as she drifted downstream.

Kat tried her best to swim to the bank, but always seemed to be cut off by something; A rapid, large limbs, or jagged rocks that seemed more likely to impale her than help her.

She had nearly made it to a large log when a sweeping undercurrent grabbed her and pulled her beneath the surface. The current slammed her against the log, and what little light glistened above her head, faded quickly to black.

After the River

When Kat opened her eyes, she was on solid ground with Jerren, and a dripping wet Daniel, hovering over her. She spluttered as water rose from her throat, and Jerren turned her to the side to release it. Kat began to drag large breaths of air back into her lungs, and Jerren and Daniel let out a collective sigh of relief.

"Oh, thank the Gods!" Jerren exclaimed.

He pulled her up into a sitting position, then engulfed her in a loving embrace. The grip he had on her was so firm that even if she had tried to move, she knew he would be unwilling to release her. Out of the corner of her eye, Kat saw Daniel fall back onto the soft earth, and cover his face with his hands; she briefly wondered if his actions were out of relief, or maybe something else.

"Are you alright?" Jerren asked, giving her a quick, but thorough once over. Kat gave a tearful nod as he kissed her forehead, and a small tear ran down his cheek.

"I'm sorry Jer... I didn't mean..." Kat's voice cracked as she struggled to make an apology. Every emotion she had before falling into the river came rushing back, and mingled with the ebbing adrenaline that coursed through her.

"I know it, Kat... I know."

Jerren stroked her back as she sobbed into his shoulder, hoping he could soothe away her sorrow. When her tears slowed just enough, and she felt as though she could speak again, she pulled away from him and turned toward Daniel. She kept her eyes on the ground beside him, too ashamed to truly meet his gaze.

"Daniel, I-" she choked out. The lump that formed in her throat didn't let her say anymore, and before she could stop it from happening, tears overwhelmed her.

"Hey..." Daniel cooed. He slid his hand into hers and brushed his thumb across her fingers, then brought her hand to his lips and lightly kissed it.

Fueled with hope by the sweet gesture, Kat lifted her head. Daniel's bright blue eyes sparkled as he gave her a reassuring smile. "I'm just glad you're okay," he said softly.

Kat's heart swelled at his words, and she flung herself into his arms.

"I'm sorry. I'm so, so sorry," she sputtered out between light sobs. "I didn't mean any of it... I was being stupid," she continued, unable to stop. "You are amazing, and I was jealous... I was so jealous!"

Daniel's brow furrowed with confusion. *Jealous?* he mouthed to Jerren, who only shrugged.

"I didn't mean any of it! I'm sorry, I'm so sorry! Please believe I didn't mean it."

Daniel wrapped both arms around her and squeezed firmly. Tears brimmed in his eyes as he cradled her head and tried hard to process everything that had happened. Kat's grip on Daniel tightened, and she held onto him as if her very life depended on it, which less than half an hour ago, it had.

A hard breeze blew through the trees, and the cool spring air sent a shiver through the still sopping wet princess. It was just then that she realized how much the ordeal had affected her.

"We need to get you back," Jerren said, rubbing her arms to warm her.

"I'm so tired…" Kat said with a slight tremble.

"Come on, Princess, let's get you home."

Daniel stood and simultaneously picked her up off the ground. Jerren raised a questioning eyebrow, wondering if Daniel had enough strength left to carry her the whole way back. "We'll manage," he said, answering the prince's supposed inquiry. "Won't we, *Kitty Kat?*"

Daniel winked, and she gave him a half-hearted smirk, having no strength left to object to the use of the name. As Daniel walked on with Kat securely in his arms, she looked up at him with grateful, undeserving eyes.

"Daniel…"

The look in her eyes told him all she wanted to say. He pulled her a little closer and gave her a warm smile. "You should rest, Princess," he said, silencing her attempted, and unnecessary, atonement.

Kat mustered all her strength, pulled herself up, and gently kissed his cheek. The late afternoon sun blocked her vision, but she swore she saw a blush spread across his cheeks as he tried to contain a smile. Satisfied with his reaction, she snuggled happily back into the crook of his neck, closed her eyes and drifted into a light sleep.

It wasn't long till Jerren, Daniel, and Kat arrived at the western gate. As they approached, the two boys noticed a certain carriage waiting for them. They exchanged a weary look, knowing they had failed its passenger in so many ways. "We're nearly there, Princess," Daniel whispered, waking her.

The carriage door opened, and a very concerned looking Sir William appeared. He paused in order to inspect the trio. Kat and Daniel were soaking wet and looked exhausted, and Jerren, although mostly dry, seemed rather anxious. Sir William also noticed a consensual look of relief, guilt and remorse across each of their faces.

"What happened? Are you all alright?" Sir William asked, his voice laced with panic. He cradled Kat's cheeks, then gave Daniel and Jerren a quick once over.

"I thought it would be fun to go for an afternoon swim?"

Kat gave him a small guilty shrug paired with as playful a smile as she could muster. Her uncle, though, seemed unamused. "Let's get you inside."

Sir William scooped Kat out of Daniel's arms and placed her into the carriage. Daniel and Jerren clamored in on either side of her, leaving Sir William to sit across from them.

Kat shivered once more and Daniel helped wrap a rather heavy blanket around her. Grateful for his help, and of course for saving her life, she leaned over and rested her head on his shoulder. Sir William was half glaring in their direction, but at that moment, neither Kat nor Daniel seemed to notice.

"What happened?" Sir William asked again, more sternly this time. Knowing they were safe and seemingly unharmed put him at ease, though not enough to erase the anger that had built in their absence. In the confines of the carriage, he knew he could unleash at least enough anger to shame them.

Kat, Daniel, and Jerren exchanged a questioning look. *Who was going to go first?* Jerren swallowed, then took his chance. "We went to the Inn."

"Without an escort? Without fulfilling your duties? Telling no one where you'd gone or when you'd return?"

Sir William's voice crescendoed with each question. He closed his eyes and took a calming breath, reining in his emotions, and when he opened his eyes again, he was ready for answers.

Jerren opened his mouth once more, but Daniel spoke quicker. "It was my fault, my Lord. My mother and brothers arrived earlier than expected, and I wanted to see them, but didn't want to make the trip alone. I asked the prince and princess to accompany me, but convinced them we had no need for an escort, or time enough to ask permission. We were being a little careless, and Ka- *the Princess* fell into the river as we were returning."

Sir William took a moment to contemplate what Daniel had said. The time the knight spent with the three troublemakers had taught him two very important things.

Number one: Jerren and Kat were not easily persuaded to do things they didn't want to.

Number two: If Daniel was readily taking the blame for anything, he had to take whatever he said with a grain of salt.

Kat looked up at Daniel in total surprise, and he answered with a slightly bashful shrug. She glanced over to her uncle, who she knew wasn't buying much of Daniel's story, then back to Daniel, who was more than ready to take the fall for her... *again.* She couldn't let Daniel take the blame, not this time, not after everything he had done for her, and everything she had done to him.

"I'm the one that started all this," Kat admitted, surprising not only Daniel, but her uncle and brother as well.

Sir William sat back, crossed his arms and legs, then waited patiently for her explanation. Kat sat up a little taller, took a deep breath, then began her story with renewed confidence.

"I didn't want to go to my lessons this morning, and I talked Daniel into helping me get out of them. We ran into Jerren, and I begged them to take me on an adventure. They didn't want me wandering off alone, so they followed me to the village and insisted we go to the Inn; I assume to keep me out of trouble. When we got there, Daniel realized his mother and brothers were there. I wanted to meet them, and after I did… it was hard to say goodbye, besides Daniel never gets to see his family because he's always working so hard and they live so far away and I thought it was only fair to give him some well-deserved time with them… and we ended up staying a little longer than we meant to."

Kat paused to take a breath and noticed Daniel had goosebumps on his arm; so she shifted some of her blanket over to him, then turned her attention back to her uncle.

"When we were leaving the inn, I got upset, and lost my temper… I was acting foolishly, and didn't want to be around anyone, so I pushed Jerren over and ran off on my own. When I made it to the western bridge, I wasn't paying attention to where I was stepping and slipped down the embankment and into the river. I would've drowned, had Jerren and Daniel not been there."

Kat eyed her uncle intently, trying to gauge what his reaction would be. Sir William said nothing, nor did he give anything away. He squinted his eyes and looked at each of them skeptically, trying to decide if he had gotten the whole truth. Kat was so anxious about his response, she hadn't even realized she was holding her breath until he started to speak.

"I am very relieved you are all alright," he began. "However... I'm very disappointed in each of you." The trio lowered their heads simultaneously.

"Jerren, Katiana, while your father is away, you are in my charge. Imagine him coming home to find his children missing. And not just his children, *the crown Prince and Princess.*"

Kat and Jerren understood the emphasis he had placed on their titles almost immediately, and they shrunk inwardly. "There are responsibilities you have to fulfill and priorities that need your attention. You are supposed to be setting the example, not gallivanting across the village, breaking all the rules. I know your lessons can seem tedious, and I know attending council meetings is boring."

The expression on the knight's face softened, and he took Kat and Jarren's hands in each of his. "But... I promise you this; One day, when you've grown a bit more and all the kingdom is at your fingertips, you'll be grateful for the lessons and time spent learning them."

Sir William kept hold of his niece and nephew's hand, but glanced over at Daniel, who lifted his gaze just enough to meet the knight's. "You *all* have very important roles to play in our future as a kingdom."

Sir William released Kat and Jerren's hands, then sat back to continue his sermon. "You two are extremely lucky to have a friend like Daniel."

"We know." Kat said with a smile, sliding her hand into his, and giving it a gentle squeeze. Daniel could feel his cheeks warm, but tried his best to hide it.

"And you two," Sir William said, pointing to each of the boys, "Stop corrupting the Princess."

Kat scoffed at the idea of anyone 'corrupting' her, making the two boys and even Sir William chuckle. When Kat met her uncle's gaze once more, he smirked, reminding her that just because she did something amusing didn't mean she was out of trouble. Her eyes softened and her lip pouted slightly, and Sir William snickered and shook his head.

"After all the trouble you three have caused me today, I have to say - it is nice to see you all together getting into mischief again. I'm glad you're looking out for one another."

At the admission, the trio quickly passed one another a consequential look of agreement, as if to say 'this was only the beginning.'

Soon after, the carriage arrived in front of the main entrance of the castle. Sir William emerged first, and immediately doled out instructions. "Jerren, go get yourself cleaned up. We have a council meeting before supper."

"Yes, uncle."

He stood to leave, but rethinking his exit, turned his head toward Daniel.

"He'll be joining us a little later," Sir William said, answering his nephew's unasked question. Jerren nodded in response, then turned his attention to his sister. "I'm glad you're alright."

He kissed her hair, then wrapped his arms tightly around her. Her brother's unexpected display made Kat's eyes water and reminded her that maybe he wasn't quite so irritating after all. Before breaking the embrace, Jerren lifted his eyes to meet Daniel's. "Thank you," he mouthed. Daniel answered with a sympathetic nod, then watched as Jerren made his way into the keep.

Sir William smiled to himself at the sweet moment, but before he could direct anyone further, Kat turned quickly to Daniel. "What he said."

"No thanks necessary, Princess."

Kat and Daniel had been so focused on one another that Sir William had to clear his throat to remind them he was still there. The slightest bit of color rose in each of their cheeks as they realized what had happened, and the fact they were still holding hands didn't help the situation. They quickly released hands, then began scanning the carriage as though they were looking for something. Sir William bit back his amused smile and became commanding once more.

"You two are coming with me to see the healers," he said with finality.

Daniel and Kat protested one after the other, both insisting they were fine and had no reason to see the healers, but their plights fell on deaf ears, and were immediately silenced by the raise of Sir William's hand.

Kat jumped to her feet, not thinking about how the quick shift in her movements might affect her. Her head spun, and her legs wobbled, causing her to stumble back slightly. Daniel rushed to steady her, and caught her just in time.

"I'm just a little tired..." she said sheepishly, to Sir WIlliam, who's concern for her well-being had grown exponentially. "Come on, Princess," he said, scooping her out of the carriage. "You too, Daniel."

Daniel stood to follow behind and felt a sudden and intense soreness radiating across his ribs, and to his back. He ignored it the best he could, then jumped down from the carriage behind Sir William, which was apparently the wrong thing to do. The second his feet hit solid ground, his knees buckled, and the soreness in his ribs became a sharp pain. He straightened himself quickly, hoping the knight hadn't seen the ordeal, and was relieved to see he hadn't. The concerned look on Kat's face though, told him *she* had.

He shrugged, dismissing the situation, then darted his eyes towards the keep, and back to Kat. He smirked at her as if to suggest there was a certain favor she could return. Kat frowned. She knew he was asking for help to get out going to the healers, but after seeing what she had, a part of her felt as though he needed to be seen. He made one last silent plea, and she sighed; after everything, it was the least she could do.

"Uncle Will?"

"Yes, princess?"

"Are you sure you want Jerren *alone* in the council meeting?"

Sir William paused, contemplating the idea for a moment, then shook his head, dismissing a rogue thought. "He'll be just fine."

Kat scrunched her nose up at the idea. Sir William paused and let out a heavy sigh. "Daniel? Are you positive you're alright?" he asked, turning back to him.

Daniel stood as tall and strong as he could. "Yes, my Lord."

Sir William quickly scanned him up and down, then sighed once more. "Go get cleaned up and meet the Prince *outside* the council room."

Daniel nodded, then waited for Sir William to turn back towards the healer's tower. Kat looked over her uncle's shoulder at Daniel, who smiled and gave her a playful wink. She returned his smile with a rather weak, concerned smile of her own, then watched as he disappeared in the same direction her brother had.

Kat rested her head on her uncle's shoulder and was suddenly glad to be back home and safe. She wished she could see her father, but she knew how disappointed he would be with her. Her uncle was much more observant, but he was also much more lenient, especially towards her. She hadn't thought about it before, but after the conversation she had with Daniel that morning, she suspected his leniency had something to do with the fact that she reminded him of his own little sister; her mother.

"Uncle Will?"

"Yes, Princess?"

"I said some awful things to Daniel today..."

The knight's eyebrows perked up with intrigue, but he made no reply, and waited for her to elaborate.

"He told me I reminded him of his sister, and then took me to meet his family and I had the best time, but then..."

"What is it, Kitty Kat?"

An involuntary look of annoyance passed across Kat's face, making Sir William frown. "I'm sorry, I forgot... You're too old for that now..."

'Kitty Kat' had been his pet name for her since before she could remember. It was only in the past couple years that Jerren and Daniel had overheard and completely ruined it for her. The disappointment on her uncle's face though, was harder to swallow, than hearing a couple of meows and hisses. She chewed her lip slightly, contemplating the situation at hand, until finally she decided on the matter.

"No, it's just my head," she said with a convincing smile. "I like when *you* call me Kitty Kat."

"Are you sure?" he asked skeptically.

"Positive!"

Her uncle smirked and gave her a tight squeeze, then waited for her to continue on with her story.

"Anyway, Lena- *Lady Leanna*, I mean, told me she knew mother, that I looked like her, and how proud she would be of me." Kat paused, thinking that maybe she wouldn't be so proud of her at that moment. "She told me I could come to her anytime I wished, about anything..."

Sir William gave Kat a warm, yet sad smile she didn't fully understand, then waited once more.

"Well... She had been so kind and seeing how she was with Daniel and his brothers, even Jerren and I... It made me miss mother. Then, I was jealous... Jealous that Daniel had a mother that was so beautiful, and wonderful, and loving."

Kat lowered her head, disappointed in herself for what she was about to say next. "Anger just took over, and I wanted to make him feel as bad as I did..."

Sir William could see the embarrassment on her face, and knew she had already condemned her own actions. He wanted to probe further, but knew it wasn't the time. As they reached the healer's tower, he put the conversation on hold, leaving Kat in the care of the healers and Mara, who escorted her back to her room when they had finished, then put her to bed.

When Kat opened her eyes again, she felt warm, almost uncomfortably so. The fire in her fireplace was larger than usual, and she had three extra blankets on top of her. To her right, she could see a tray of food, and to her left, near the window, stood the silhouettes of two men whispering. Kat cleared her throat to announce she had woken, and the men turned their attention to her.

"You're home!" Kat said happily.

Her father crossed the room, sat on the bed beside her, and gently caressed her cheek. "I hear you've had quite the day..."

His face was full of concern, and Kat lowered her head in shame as tears welled in her eyes.

"Oh, my Katiana..."

Her father engulfed her in a loving embrace that seemed to warm her soul. It touched her so much that the internal dam that held her emotions once again broke. She couldn't help but sob in his arms. "Hush now, darling, everything is alright," he cooed as he rocked her.

"I'm sorry, father..."

Kat sniffled and her father cupped her face in his hands, much like Lady Leanna had, then wiped her tears away.

"There's no need to apologize. I'm just glad you're safe."

Her father smiled at her, but she could see the slightest hint of tears brimming his eyes. A light knock at the door interrupted the tender moment, and one of her father's guards appeared, and bent down to whisper something into his ear. The king nodded, dismissing the guard, and Kat frowned; she knew it meant he was needed elsewhere. Her father saw the disappointment on her face and, as a way of apology, leaned down and kissed her hair. "I'll only be gone a few minutes, love."

"I'm glad you're home."

"Me too, darling... I'll be back soon."

The King closed the door behind him, then Sir William, who lingered behind, took her father's place on the bed in front of her.

"Feeling better Kitty Kat?"

"A bit."

"Hungry?" Her uncle asked, presenting the tray of food to her. She smiled and gave a small shrug. Not only was she still full from the feast Ada had given, but after everything that happened her appetite was lacking.

As she picked at the plate he had given her, her eyes wandered around the room, then landed on her side table, where she noticed a small vase filled with wildflowers. They were obviously hand picked, and it made her smile that someone had been kind enough to do that for her.

"Daniel snuck those in when he thought no one was looking," Sir William smiled.

Kat frowned. The thought of Daniel doing anything kind for her after the way she treated him made her lose what little appetite she had. She pushed the tray aside, then pulled her knees to her chest, hugging them.

"What is it, Princess?"

Kat looked up at her uncle with watery eyes. "Why is he so nice to me? I mean, after everything I did, everything I said..."

"Daniel cares about you... Quite a lot, if you ask me." he said, as he removed the tray of food from the bed.

"Because I remind him of his sister or because you're training him to watch over Jerren and I?"

Sir William smiled to himself, knowing neither reason was the full truth. "When I was about his age, I had a friend I really cared about. She was a little younger than myself and I teased her constantly," he half chuckled. "She and your mother would get so angry at me. But, no matter how mad she got at me, no matter what she said or did... I always did anything I could to make sure she was safe and happy."

"*But why*? Who was she?"

Kat had never heard her uncle talk about anyone so fondly, let alone some girl, well maybe besides her mother, but she didn't think his sister counted. Sir William smiled again.

"She was one of my best friends. I made sure she was safe and happy, simply because... I liked to see her smile."

Kat sighed, a little aggravated. "That look you have on your face says she wasn't *just* a friend. What happened to her?"

Sir William laughed and rubbed the back of his neck. "We grew up. She fell in love with a noble knight. They moved on, started a family, and lived - relatively, happily ever after."

Kat scrunched up her face. *"That's it?"* she asked, unsatisfied with his response.

"That's it."

Kat eyed her uncle carefully, but he gave nothing away. She thought about arguing, but knew better, and so dropped the subject. "Do you think Daniel will really forgive me?" she asked, unsure if her actions were at all forgivable. Sir William smiled and gave her foot a tender pat.

"Without a doubt... Now, get some rest. Hm?"

Kat gave him a half smile, then snuggled down into her bed. Sir William kissed the top of her head, then quietly left the room. But Kat's head was too full to sleep. She couldn't wrap her mind around everything that had happened. Her thoughts raced, but at the same time felt so empty... All she could do was stare at the flowers Daniel brought her and reflect on her day.

It had begun so ordinarily with Mara; *daisies.* Finding the courage to do something rebellious; *violets.* Laughing and joking with Jerren and Daniel; *corncockle.* Meeting Daniel's family; *buttercup.* Singing and dancing with strangers and new friends; *primrose.* The small conversation with Lady Leanna; *red clover.* Running off and falling into the river; *chicory.* Daniel and Jerren consoling her at the river's edge; *honeysuckle.* Her uncle taking care of her; *jasmine.* Waking to find her father home once more; *poppies.*

Kat pulled her eyes away from the flowers, and caught her reflection in the mirror above her vanity. It was just a quick glance, but the more she focused on it, the more she realized something in it had changed. It was no longer just *her* reflection, but her mother's. Her hair shone a little more, and her eyes had a slight sparkle in them. She smiled, and saw there was something else in her reflection she couldn't quite give a name to, but she knew it could have only come from *her*.

Maybe it wouldn't be so bad to be compared to her mother. *Would she be proud of her?* Kat wished with all her heart that she could know for sure. She took a deep breath and a warmth spread through her, yet tears welled in her eyes.

"I miss you," she whispered into the air.

Katiana Scarborough drifted to sleep that night full of hope that tomorrow would always be a new day; and the knowledge that love surrounded her.

The love of her mother, who she knew was always looking over her; and of her father, who would return any minute to be at her side. She knew her uncle loved her, and that she could always count on him, and she knew her brother loved her, and cared enough about her to tell her when she was wrong. She thought maybe even Daniel loved her... Or at least she hoped he did. *Thistle.*

Revelations and Ramifications

Kat woke the next morning to find her father fast asleep in a chair beside her bed. His facial hair left a shadow across his cheeks, and it was obvious he was weary from his travels, but even with the stubble and worry lines cascading across his face, her father seemed peaceful and even looked much younger. She smiled seeing how much Jerren took after him.

Kat carefully pulled back her covers, got out of bed, and laid a warm blanket over her father. She tiptoed across the room to her closet, and very quietly readied herself for the day, hoping she could exit the room without disturbing him. Then, hoping to make amends for her transgressions the previous day, she made her way down to the kitchens, where she apologized to Mistress Hilda for missing her lesson, and offered to help her with breakfast.

Kat couldn't ignore the look of shock on her father's, her uncle's, or her brother's face as she entered the small hall with a tray full of their favorite breakfast foods. She presented the tray proudly, and to her delight, they had all seemed rather impressed with her work; and even more so that it had all been done before mid-morning.

After breakfast, Kat's father pulled her aside. They sat and had a long talk about everything that had happened the day before and how she had been feeling; from her anguish of trying to live up to her mother's image, to her doubts about who she really was.

"I just don't think the Gods meant for me to live the life of a princess..."

"Oh, my darling girl."

Her father sighed, and Kat lowered her head, sensing his disappointment, but relaxed some when he reached out to lift her gaze, only to find love and maybe a little humor glistening in his eyes.

"*No one* is *meant* for this life," he said with a smile. "We pass it down from generation to generation in the hopes that one day our children may *earn it*."

Though she knew her father's words were meant to be comforting, they had hardly succeeded. "And what if I can't *earn it?*"

Her father smiled as he stroked her cheek. "You will," he insisted.

"How could you know that? I'm not like you... I'm not like *her*..."

Kat's eyes lifted past her father to the portrait of her mother, which seemed to loom over her. Her father chuckled, catching her off guard.

"Katiana, you are more like *her* than you know."

Kat shook her head, not truly believing her father's words. "I don't just mean how I look..."

"And neither do I."

The king lifted his daughter's disheartened gaze once more to him.

"You have your mother's spirit, my darling, and for too long, even I have tried to keep it tucked away." he paused and let out a soft chuckle that somewhat confused her. "Your mother was *not at all* suited for the life of a royal. She was clumsy, uncertain, short-tempered... She was not afraid to speak her mind to *anyone*, and she never cared to be the most fashionable lady in the court."

Kat listened in wonderment. She had never heard her mother described in a way that felt so similar to herself.

"The first time your grandfather introduced me to your mother, she was just about your age... she told me I was pompous and ridiculous, and when she turned away, thinking she had gotten the last word, she knocked over an entire row of armor."

Kat giggled at the thought, and a bit of hope bloomed in her chest. If her mother could go from making clumsy mistakes to commanding rooms full of people, perhaps she could too.

"You're young... You're still learning. Enjoy it while you can," her father said. "Don't worry about what *others* expect from you. Try to figure out what *you* expect of yourself."

The king pulled his daughter into a warm embrace, then kissed the top of her head. "I am so proud of the young woman you are becoming," he began, but Kat could hear a struggle in his voice. "And though the gods were cruel to take your mother away from me... I will sing their praises every day, for sending me *you*."

Kat walked down the hall to her lessons, deep in thought. Everything her father said left her with more questions, but also a weird sense of relief. She certainly was her mother's daughter, and it seemed she was the only one who was unsure of it until now.

As she passed a well-polished suit of armor, she stopped and carefully examined her reflection, then smiled. She swelled with pride at having even the smallest piece of Queen Roslin's reflection shown in her. From that point forward, Kat was determined to do whatever it took to prove her worth; to her father, her mother, the kingdom, but mostly... to herself.

After her world-altering self realization, the morning and early afternoon flew by with ease, and her lessons were over before she knew it. As she exited the small hall, she came across her brother sitting in a stairwell, eating an apple and reading a book. She smiled mischievously to herself, then snuck up behind him.

"Who are we hiding from?" she whispered in his ear, startling him.

"You really are part cat, aren't you? You scared me half to death!"

Kat laughed, sat down beside him and helped herself to a bite of his apple.

"By all means, help yourself…"

"I will, thank you!" she said, wiping a bit of juice from the corner of her mouth. Jerren chuckled at her rather unladylike behavior. "I'm glad you're doing better. Yesterday was… eventful."

It was Kat's turn to chuckle. "I am sorry for how I behaved… before… you know," she said, lowering her head in shame. This was far from the first time Kat had to apologize for her behavior, but it was nice to see that Jerren was still understanding enough to forgive her. He gave her an empathetic smile and nudged her shoulder. "I know it… and, apology accepted, Kitty Kat."

Kat rolled her eyes, and Jerren laughed. He put his arm around his sister's neck, hugged her and then made kissing noises near her face.

"Alright, alright! Enough weirdness. I liked you better when you meowed and hissed at me…"

"Well, then! Farewell for *meow*, madame *hiss!*" Jerren stood and bowed dramatically; Kat chortled and shook her head at him.

"Hey!" she called out as he climbed the steps. When Jerren looked back, she chewed her lip, unsure whether he would answer her next question. "Any idea where Daniel might be?"

Jerren threw his head back with a huff. "Alas, I do not. A Royal decree was announced and we have been 'hereby' separated for the remainder of the week."

Kat giggled. "I am sorry... I know how much your boyfriend means to you."

"HA! I'll remember *you* said that! But, if I had to guess, I'd bet he's doing his penance by working more than he ought to in the stables."

"Thanks Jer."

"No problem... Just try to leave him the way you found him... Or improved! I believe in you!" he called down to her.

Kat shook her head. "Shall I give him your love?" she called back.

"Please do!"

Kat made her way to the main doors and out towards the stables. She opened the door carefully, and peered inside. It was quiet, aside from the soft shuffle of hooves, and the random whinny. She called out to Daniel, but there was no response. She sighed, unsure of what to do next, but not wanting to waste a trip to the stables, began to meander down the line, petting each mare and stallion, giving extra attention to any pony she came across.

She sighed once more as she reached the last stall, but a noise from outside caught her attention. Hopeful it could be Daniel, she stepped through the back door, and peered down the side of the building that faced the meadow. Daniel was about half way down, and facing the opposite direction. For a moment Kat considered sneaking up on him, the way she had with Jerren, but something seemed off. She noticed his movements were stiff and strained, and he twisted his torso with care as he pitched hay into the wagon beside him. She wasn't sure why, but she suddenly felt nervous.

Everything felt different for her now. *She felt different. What if he did, too?* Not ready to face him, but hoping to get a better look, Kat snuck across the opening and crouched behind a large bale of hay. She took a small step out to decide her next move, and a twig snapped beneath her foot. Daniel turned to catch the culprit, and a sharp pain shot through him. His back stiffened, and an obviously painful groan escaped his throat.

Kat stayed out of sight, but peeped back around to see what had happened. She watched on as Daniel lifted the right side of his shirt to reveal a rather large, severe looking bruise that extended from the front of his rib cage to the back.

"Daniel! Are you alright?" she gasped, her voice laced with concern as she emerged from her hiding spot. Before Kat could see any more damage, he dropped his shirt, turned his back to her, then continued his strained labor in hopes she'd keep her distance.

"Hello there, Princess. What brings you here?" He asked, ignoring the distress in her voice. Kat gave the back of his head a queer look. "Your side... What happened to you?"

Kat stepped closer, but the movement of the pitchfork created a perimeter around him, halting her.

"Nothing to worry about Princess, I'm perfectly fine."

"That looked anything but *fine,* Daniel... What happened?"

Her voice half cracked, and Daniel paused at the sound. "I - uh- noticed it yesterday evening when I was changing into some dry clothes... after everything."

It took Kat a moment to understand what he had meant, only to remember the wince of pain she witnessed as he jumped from the carriage the previous evening. *The river.* She took a step forward so that they could talk face to face, but he turned away swiftly, keeping his back to her.

"Daniel, please, it must hurt terribly. You really should have let a healer attend to it."

"I appreciate the concern Princess, but I promise I'm okay."

Kat chewed her lip, contemplating if she should push further for answers, but ultimately realized it was not her place.

"If you say so..." she answered sadly. She had spent most of the morning preparing her apology to him, but now that she was here, she couldn't make the words come out.

Daniel could almost feel the anxiety radiating from her, without even turning around. He didn't understand why she was there, or why she continued to linger. "Was there something I could do for you?" He asked, continuing his work.

Kat snapped out of her small trance at the sound of his voice. "Oh well... I was hoping to talk to you about yesterday," she said, glancing down at her knotted fingers.

"Yesterday?"

"Yeah, you know, when I was a complete jerk to you, and then you saved my life."

"Kat... I thought we'd cleared all that up."

A sense of relief passed through her at the sound of him calling her 'Kat', but she needed to see the look in his eyes to know for certain everything was alright. She took a couple of steps to her right, but he pivoted away; her heart sank. "Then why can't you stand to look at me?"

Had he just been pretending everything was okay? She cringed at the thought that maybe his feelings since the river *had* changed. If he couldn't even look at her, *how could he say everything was fine?* A knot formed in her throat and her eyes watered. She hoped that if he knew the reason behind her outburst, she may actually stand a chance at forgiveness.

"I just... Well, I was hurting... Something your mother said-"

Daniel nearly turned around but caught himself. "My mother?" he asked.

"Nothing bad! She told me I reminded her of *my* mother... that they used to be close and that I could come to her if I ever needed anything," Kat said with a strange sort of melancholy. Daniel sighed.

"Anyway, it just got to me and I missed my mother, and then I was so angry, and I took it out on you... and I had no right to do that. You didn't deserve it." Kat paused. Still, Daniel said nothing. "And then the things about your father and sister... It was absolutely horrible of me and you have to know I didn't mean any of it! Not a single word..."

Kat stood and waited for what seemed like ages for Daniel to say or do something, but nothing happened. She tried to place her hand on his shoulder, but he pulled away. This time, her heart all but dropped into her stomach. She had obviously hurt him more than she thought. She supposed that everything from the previous day was just a show he had put on to save face in front of Jerren and Sir William. Daniel was very important to her and to have offended him so much that he couldn't stand to look at her, hurt her deeply, but after what she had done, she couldn't blame him for hating her.

"That was all I wanted to say..." she mumbled, trying to stifle the oncoming tears.

"Thank you, Princess, but it really wasn't necessary."
Princess?

Daniel could hear the slight sniffle of Kat trying to hide the fact she was crying. He wanted so badly to turn around and say that 'there was nothing to be sorry for' and 'If it meant she felt a little better that she could yell at him anytime'. He wanted to hug her and beg her not to cry, but he knew the second he turned around, they'd have a different conversation entirely. A conversation he didn't think a princess should be involved in.

"I-" Kat's voice cracked. She cleared her throat and collected herself the best she could. "Thank you for listening."

Daniel closed his eyes as though he were in a great deal of pain, though it was far from physical. He hated himself for the obvious stress and worry he knew he was causing her. He could hear the soft tread of her footsteps moving away from him, but he just couldn't let her go. "*Hell...*" he said under his breath. "Kat, wait!"

He turned to face her, but as he did, a voice boomed behind him. Daniel whipped himself around to confront the voice, and hoped Kat had already walked away.

"Slacking off again?! After all the work you left me with yesterday? My first lesson not get through to you, boy? Do I need to give ya another? Come here, you little whelp!"

The stable master marched hard toward him. Daniel bowed his chest out and stood taller, ready for any assault, whether verbal or physical.

"Master Kent," a small voice said from behind Daniel, surprising himself and the man before him. The stable master's eyes grew three times their size, and he took a step or two back. "Excuse me, but please, don't be cross with Daniel. I had a very important matter to discuss with him that simply could not wait." Kat said, stepping protectively between Daniel and the man.

"Oh- of -of course Princess, your Highness.." the man blubbered.

"I apologize for any delay in Daniel's work I may have caused. Though if it's alright with you, *good sir*, may I have just a moment more with him?"

The look on Kat's face made the stable master, who weighed slightly less than a horse, feel as though a feather could have knocked him to the ground.

"Please take all the time you need, Princess Katiana..."

Kat curtsied politely. "You are *very* kind, Master Kent. Thank you so much."

The man bowed clumsily, then disappeared once again into the stables. Kat's blood boiled. It was an outrageous idea to her for someone to speak that way to *anyone*, let alone *Daniel*. "How dare he! I should've beaten that man with my shoe!"

Seeing Master Kent's reaction to Kat's presence made Daniel smirk, and pride filled his chest at the thought that Kat was so willing to protect *him* for a change. "I don't know. I think you handled the situation nicely, Kitty Kat."

Kat turned to face Daniel, and she couldn't stop the horrified gasp that escaped her lips. He had a large, deep cut across his right eyebrow that had obviously stopped bleeding but looked as though it could start again at any moment; a split in his bottom lip, which was swollen and purple. His left eye had swelled, almost completely shut, and evidence of a deep bruise extended from the swollen eye and down his cheek.

"It's not as bad as it looks." he shrugged.

"Oh Daniel…"

Kat took a step towards him, lifting her hand towards his cheek. Her finger tips barely brushed the discolored skin, and yet he winced. She pulled her hand away quickly, mortified to have caused him even more pain. Seeing his wounds made her heart ache, though a part of her wasn't entirely surprised. It wasn't as if she'd never seen injuries like these before, especially after tourney or vigorous training or a random fight that had broken out during a banquet. In fact, it was rare to see Daniel or one of the other squires without some sort of minor injury or another. These seemed different, though. They were more severe looking, almost menacing.

In an attempt to get ahead of the situation, Daniel told her how a rogue horse had bucked, and threw him into the corner of a large wooden post, then thrashed its head against his; but Kat wasn't buying it. To anyone else, the story would have been a convincing one, but Kat knew him well enough to know he was trying to hide something.

"Why are you lying? What really happened?" she asked with narrowed eyes and folded arms.

"I'm not. I've told you what happened." Daniel shrugged, then continued with his work.

Kat rolled her eyes. "It looks really painful. Did you at least go to the healers' tower and let them look you over?"

"It's no big deal, besides I've got work to finish."

"Daniel! Stop! Forget about that for a minute! You look awful!"

"Well, that's just rude."

"Ugh! You're impossible!"

"All part of my charm, Princess," he winked with his non swollen eye, but winced, clearly forgetting about the cut.

Kat was just about to walk away, seeing he was determined to keep whatever had happened a secret, when a sudden spine tingling thought struck her like a bolt of lightning. "You CANNOT be serious!!" Kat grabbed Daniel's arm and jerked him around to face her.

"Ow..."

"That horrible man did this, didn't he?"

Daniel stuttered slightly, caught off guard by Kat's question; His reaction, though, told her she had discovered the truth. "UGH!"

The Princess was livid. She paced back and forth, muttering half to herself, half to no one in particular. She ranted about how horrible Kent was; what she should've said to him had she known; asking what plausible reason he could have for his behavior; all the while scolding Daniel for trying to hide the truth.

Daniel tried to respond to each question or statement. Occasionally, he would just call out her name, hoping to get her attention, but she cut him off as soon as he began. Eventually, he gave up trying to talk altogether. Daniel found it all quite amusing, and rather sweet. Until she said the one thing he had been worried about.

"Why Kitty Kat, I didn't know you cared so much!"

Kat paused finally, taking a breath to calm herself. "This isn't funny Daniel... Just wait until Uncle Will hears about this! I'll go find him."

Kat turned to march away, but Daniel caught her arm before she could make it two steps.

"Kat, stop."

"What is it?"

Daniel sighed. "You can't tell your uncle... *or anyone else*."

Kat paused, unsure why he would be so worried about anyone finding out. "Don't be ridiculous! Of course I can! He'll be furious!"

She turned to walk away again, and again was subdued.

"Exactly! I could've fought back, but I didn't... I brought this on myself. Besides, I've caused enough trouble around here lately, and frankly don't need another reason for your uncle to be even more disappointed in me and potentially send me away."

Kat was stunned at Daniel's revelation and all together confused. "Daniel-"

"No, please listen to me. You can't say anything," he demanded.

"But-"

"*No.* Promise me, Kat."

"How could you-"

"*Promise me.*"

Kat could see how insistent he was and even though she knew he was wrong, she could tell it meant a great deal to him. She sighed. "Okay, Daniel... I promise."

Daniel took a deep, relieved breath. "Thank you."

Kat couldn't stand the amount of hurt she had caused him, and all in less than a day. She hurt his feelings; he had gotten hurt while saving her, and then that abhorrent man beat him, presumably for the work he missed while off with her. She wanted to make things right, and she knew the only way she could was to keep his secret, no matter how badly she wanted to tell her uncle.

She knew he would be furious, but not at Daniel. Sir William had taken Daniel as his ward because Daniel's father had been his best friend, but Daniel had always been, *always meant,* so much more to him. She couldn't understand why Daniel couldn't see that.

Sir William had no wife or child of his own. He spent his whole life devoted to serving the crown. He had dedicated his life to that purpose long before his sister became queen and was determined to continue his service even more after she passed. His niece and nephew had become his world, then after Daniel's father passed, Daniel became just as important to him, if not more so.

Kat had never been more sure of anything than the fact that Sir William saw Daniel as the son he never had. She also knew that if Sir William found out what had truly happened, he would make certain it would never happen again. Which was an idea she wholeheartedly supported after glancing over his wounds once more.

Anger and sadness welled deep within her. She knew the longer she stayed and saw what Daniel had suffered, the harder her emotions would be to contain. She walked away, but Daniel called out to her. The tone of his voice was earnest and contrite, and she couldn't help but look over her shoulder to acknowledge him.

"You can yell at me anytime for any reason. There is *nothing* you could ever say or do that I couldn't forgive… I mean it."

Tears burst from Kat's eyes, and she could contain herself no longer. She ran at him full force and threw her arms around him. He winced at the sudden impact, but made no noise to alert her otherwise.

"You're wrong, you know," Kat said, still holding tight. "Uncle Will would never send you away for any reason. *He loves you…* and he knows nothing that happened yesterday was your fault… And what that man did wasn't your fault, either. You did nothing wrong! You should have never been put in that position, and I'm so sorry he hurt you."

Just as quickly as she had run to Daniel, she released him and ran toward the main gate, leaving him to think about what she had said. She couldn't bear hearing any sort of rebuttal, and desperately wanted to get as far away from the situation as possible. Tears filled her eyes, and she struggled to wipe them away. She was so focused on clearing her face, she bumped directly into Sir William.

"What is it, Princess?" he asked, concerned.

Everything was still too fresh, and before she could stop herself, words came spilling out. "Uncle Will, you can't let him get away with it, you just can't!"

The knight bent down to look his niece in the eyes, now *very* concerned. "Get away with what? Who?"

Kat knew only Sir William could make it right... but then she thought about the look on Daniel's face when he made her promise not to say a word.

"I... I mean..."

"What is it Kat? Please tell me..."

"I can't... I - I promised..."

Before her uncle could get any more information, she took off running into the castle. Sir William watched his niece disappear through the main doors and, for a moment, considered chasing after her. He didn't like the feeling he'd gotten from their interaction and was determined to know more. Instead of following her though, he turned toward the direction from whence she came. To the stables, and presumably to *Daniel*.

The Thistle and the Wolf

Sir William spent years watching over Kat, Jerren and Daniel, and in that time, he had learned a great deal about each of them. Their favorite colors, and foods; the style of clothes they preferred; what songs they liked to sing. He learned their tells and could understand why they were feeling a certain way before they themselves knew. He knew their true feelings towards one another, even if it was not yet obvious to them. In fact, no one knew, or *loved*, them more than he did.

He knew Kat felt guilty about all that occurred the previous day; he knew Daniel had been working all day in the stables to make amends for it; and he knew the lengths both Daniel and Kat would go to protect one another. Seeing Kat so upset, especially after everything she had gone through, broke his heart, and he hoped if he found Daniel, he could find what caused her such distress.

"Good afternoon Toby!" Sir William said, greeting the stable master.

Kent jumped. "A-afternoon, my Lord," he stuttered. "What brings you here?"

Tobias Kent was typically a confident man, and wasn't shaken by much; that being said, Sir William couldn't help but notice how jittery he became at his presence, and how hard he had tried to hide it. Kent's unusual attitude intrigued the knight as much as it worried him. "I was hoping to find my young ward. Is he about somewhere?"

The stable master's eyes widened, and he turned his attention to a nearby mare; the man's expression, and abrupt turn was suspicious to Sir William. He had a sharp mind and an attentive eye, especially in sketchy situations, and the quick shift caught his attention in the worst possible way.

"Last I saw, he headed 'bout the kitchens, perhaps for an early supper, my Lord."

Sir William smiled and clapped the man on the shoulder, making him jump. "Thank you Toby. I hope Daniel didn't cause you too much trouble with his absence yesterday. You know how boys can be."

Kent coughed, choking on his own bile, and Sir William noticed small beads of sweat had formed across his forehead. "No trouble at all, my Lord."

The short time he had spent with Tobias Kent did little to calm the knight's unease. He knew Kent was a rash man, who sometimes reacted much more abrasive than was necessary; a fact that seemed to send a chill down Sir William's spine. As he walked through the stable doors once more, his senses were on high alert.

A noise from the backside of the stables caught his attention, and he followed the sound. As he rounded the corner he found a very odd-looking Daniel leaning against the stable and struggling to stand. The closer he stepped, the more he observed, and the more his niece's plight made sense.

Daniel held the right side of his body, as if trying to shield it from his own movements. He had a blackened eye, and some deep looking cuts across his eyebrow and bottom lip; not to mention half his face seemed at least twice its normal size.

"Alright there, Daniel?"

Daniel jumped and stood to attention at the sound of Sir William's voice. "Of course, my Lord, just finishing up some chores," he said, his voice cracking. He cleared his throat, then hurried back to work as if nothing at all was different. Sir William noted his reaction and followed his lead. "Did you get into a fight? If so, you seem to have lost."

Daniel paused slightly, deep in thought about how to respond, but ultimately delivered the same story he had told Kat about a rogue horse. He knew if it hadn't worked with Kat, it definitely wouldn't work on Sir William, but there was no other explanation for the injuries... Well, no other explanation except the truth, and he was determined to keep that to himself for as long as he could.

Sir William listened closely to Daniel's story, and instantly knew he had been lied to. He assumed the promise Kat made had something to do with her knowing the truth about Daniel's injuries. It would certainly explain how upset she had been; seeing Daniel in such a state upset him just as much.

"Was there something you needed, my Lord?" Daniel asked, curious why Sir William was now lingering.

"Oh yes, I was wondering… have you seen the princess?"

Sir William's question was simple and delivered with such casualness that no one could suspect his true motive. Daniel's shoulders lowered at the mention of the princess, and Sir William knew he was on the right track. The knight continued on, hoping more pieces of the puzzle would fall into place. "I just ran into her. Well, she ran into me and she seemed upset. After everything that happened yesterday, you can understand my concern. I know you all hate the idea of giving each other up, but I was hoping you might help me figure out what happened. You wouldn't know anything about… well, *anything*, would you?"

Daniel kept his eyes low and shifted his weight back and forth as Sir William spoke, but as he finished, it was clear Daniel had made his mind up about how he would treat the situation. He stood tall and lifted his eyes once more. "I'm sorry, my Lord, but I don't." Daniel lied again, though with more confidence.

Daniel hated lying to Sir William. He hated lying at all; the only time he did it was to keep Kat, or sometimes Jarren, out of trouble. It felt odd that this time it was the other way around and he himself was trying to stay out of trouble.

Sir William rubbed the back of his neck and sighed. He knew the only way to find the answers he needed now would be with a bit of trust and patience.

"Well, if you hear anything, you'll let me know, yes?"

Daniel agreed and went back to work. Sir William felt as though he should walk away, but there was a nagging feeling in his gut that wouldn't let him. "You're certain you're alright, Daniel?" he asked once more, his words full of concern.

For a split second, Daniel had wanted to tell him no, he wasn't alright. That he was in more pain than he cared to admit and what had caused it all. He wanted to tell him that Kat acted the way she had because he made her promise not to tell him how Kent beat him; and tell him how sorry he was for lying to him and letting him down. He wanted to tell him everything, and then beg him not to send him away. *But how?*

Daniel chewed his bottom lip, hoping he wouldn't reopen the cut across it, contemplating what he could possibly say next. He lifted his eyes to Sir William, and his heart was beating so hard he thought for sure the knight could hear it. Just as he opened his mouth to speak, a voice rang out behind him.

"Oh good! You've found him!"

A chill ran up Daniel's spine as Master Kent spoke. His voice was smooth and chipper, and it made Daniel squirm.

Kent made his way over to Daniel and put an arm around his shoulder.

Daniel tensed at his presence, and it was clear to Sir William that Daniel felt uncomfortable. He looked as though he wanted nothing more than to push the large, sweaty man away from him. He watched as Daniel's hand fisted at his side, tightening with each passing second until his knuckles were nearly white.

"I often tell him he works too hard for a boy so young," Kent lied with a chuckle, as he jostled Daniel's shoulders. Daniel swallowed his anger at the man, and gave a forced smile to play along.

"I couldn't agree more," Sir William said, watching the interaction closely.

"After that wild beast banged him around, I told him to take some time and get seen after, but good ol' Daniel here insisted he stay and finish the work."

While Kent's performance was a convincing one, Sir William had already begun to piece the puzzle together. Daniel's injuries, why Kat acted the way she did, Kent's nervous behavior. All he needed now was for someone, or something, to verify his hypothesis, though he wanted more than anything for his suspicions to be false.

It wasn't until Kent's right hand fell forward on Daniel's shoulder that he knew for certain what had happened. Kent's knuckles were bruised and puffy; almost as if they had hit something, or rather *someone*, several times. Sir

William bit back the anger that built inside of him; it wasn't the time or the place for it. He put on his best and brightest diplomatic face, knowing he couldn't risk tipping off the son-of-a-bitch that he knew the truth.

"Well, I think you've worked hard enough today, Daniel. Why don't you come with me and we'll get these injuries tended to?" Sir William asked, though his tone suggested it was not a request.

Sir William lifted his cool gaze from Daniel to Kent, and the stable master's eyes grew at the hardening look on the knight's face, and he instantly removed his arm from around Daniel.

"But my Lord-" Daniel began then stopped, having received a warning look from Sir William.

Daniel propped the pitchfork he had been holding against the cart of hay, and stepped away from Kent to stand beside Sir William. The knight put a protective hand on Daniel's shoulder, and Daniel couldn't help but think how the gesture had been much more welcome to him than Kent's had been.

"Thank you so much Tobias for looking after Daniel so well," Sir William said with a smile, though it did not reach his eyes. Tobias Kent said nothing, bowed his head, then retreated into the stables. The knight stood silent, and stone faced, until Kent disappeared from his sight. He took a deep cleansing breath, and squeezed Daniel's shoulder a little tighter than he meant to.

"Daniel?"

"Yes, my Lord?" he answered, hesitantly. The knight's heavy hand on his shoulder sent a ripple of anxiety through him. *He knew.*

"I'd appreciate it, if in the future, you would refrain from lying to me more than you already have, and asking my niece, or even my nephew, to do the same."

Daniel lowered his head, ashamed. *He definitely knew.* "Yes, my lord..."

A new wave of nerves coursed through him, he was about to fall to his knees and beg for forgiveness, but didn't get the chance. Sir William lifted Daniel's chin up to survey each of his injuries. He pressed near his eye and lip to see how badly they had swelled, then inspected the cut on his brow. He tested his vision and even the range of motion in his neck. This wasn't the first time he had done this sort of inspection, and Daniel knew better than to interrupt him.

The more the knight saw, though, the more his anger toward Kent grew into a furious rage. "You'll need some stitches, and it'll most likely scar," he said, pointing to the cut across Daniel's right brow. "It's going to swell a bit more, and the bruising will last a couple of weeks, but it doesn't seem like there's any *major* damage done."

Daniel nodded, unsure how to respond.

"Now, let's have a look at your side," Sir William instructed.

Daniel took a step back, "That's not..."

Sir William held up his hand, not to be argued with, and Daniel gave in with a small sigh. The knight inspected the bruising over Daniel's rib cage with intense scrutiny. The coloring differed from the bruising on his face. It was darker, more set, telling him he had received it well before the other injuries.

"The river..." Daniel said, answering Sir William's silent question, as he winced at a gentle poke. "I was trying to get to the princess, and a current grabbed me and slammed me against a rock."

Sir William sighed, and mentally kicked himself for letting Daniel go uninspected the evening before. "Nothing seems to be broken, but we'll have the healers tend to it as well, just to be sure."

Daniel nodded in agreement and lowered his shirt. Sir William stood, but made sure he was at eye level with Daniel. "Are you alright?" he asked in a fatherly voice.

Daniel nodded slowly, his expression full of remorse and guilt. He felt bad about how he had behaved and what he had done, and a part of him even felt as though maybe he had deserved the punishment he received. After all, he had shirked his responsibilities, then got Kat into danger, then asked her to lie for him. If anyone deserved a good beating, it was him.

"I should have fought back ... But honestly... I- I thought..." His words caught in his throat, and even though he wanted to, he couldn't bring himself to finish the sentence.

Sir William's heart ached, knowing exactly what it was Daniel was trying to say. He placed a firm hand on Daniel's shoulder, hoping to provide him some solace. "Daniel, you did nothing to deserve this... Do you understand?"

Daniel shrugged, and looked back down at his feet, and Sir William let out a heavy sigh.

"Look at me Daniel," the knight commanded, and Daniel obeyed. "I understand why you tried to hide this from me, and I understand why you asked Kat to as well..."

It had been years, but it still surprised Daniel when Sir William seemed to read his mind, and he stared at the knight in awe.

"I can only imagine what kind of trouble that niece of mine would have gotten herself into yesterday had you and Jerren not been there, and I am more grateful than words can express for the sacrifice you were willing to make to ensure her safety." Sir William's voice broke and his eyes watered at the thought of what could have happened. He cleared his throat and shook his head, erasing the dark thoughts that clouded his mind, then continued on.

"You all are young, and carefree, and allowed to step out of line, now and then... But what *he* did," Sir William said, nodding towards the stables. "Is inexcusable on a number of levels." Daniel shrunk inwardly, and it wasn't until he felt the gentle weight of Sir William's hand resting on the side of his neck that he looked the knight in the eyes.

"I am so proud of you for standing your ground, and I promise you, it will *never* happen again."

The sincerity in Sir William's voice caught Daniel off guard. *He was proud?* For a split second, Daniel imagined that Sir William, the man he had looked up to for so many years; the man who, without knowing it, had not replaced his father, but became some extended version of him, cared for him the way he cared for his niece and nephew, maybe even a little more.

He imagined he was like a son to him, and hoped that no matter what he'd done, or taken the blame for, it would never be enough to send him away. He imagined that Sir William would always be a part of his life, and that he could someday express the gratitude he felt for him and all he did; for he couldn't possibly know what he meant to him.

What Daniel didn't know was that at that very moment, Sir William had been thinking and feeling the same thing. Without warning, Sir William put a loving arm around Daniel's shoulders and pulled him into a fatherly embrace. "I'm glad you're alright, and I'm sorry you've had to put up with so much."

The invisible weight Daniel had felt bearing down on him dissipated, leaving him feeling small and vulnerable. It had been so long since he had felt the warmth of a father that it all but broke him.

Sir William tightened his hold for just a moment before releasing Daniel, then stepped back and cleared this throat. "Now, let's get you taken care of, hm?"

"I'd appreciate that, my Lord... I'd also *really* enjoy a nap."

Sir William chuckled, ruffled Daniel's hair, and together they walked to the healer's tower. Sir William stayed with Daniel as the healers tended to him, despite Daniel's claims it was unnecessary. Then, after the healers had finished their work and given Daniel some herbs for the swelling and the ache, Sir William thought it was time for a different type of healing.

"Daniel?"

"Yes, my lord?"

The knight took a deep breath in an attempt to build up the courage he needed to say what needed to be said, but the thoughtful expression on his face confused Daniel, who took his own deep breath hoping it would prepare him for whatever came next.

"Your father... was my greatest friend. We did most everything together... Much like yourself and Jerren, and I see so much of him in you... I know without a doubt, he would be so proud of the man you're becoming... I know I am..."

Sir William paused slightly to gauge Daniel's reaction, and satisfied with his hopeful face, continued on.

"*He* was my best friend... but *you*..." Sir William trailed off, trying to find the right words to articulate how he was feeling. "To see you hurt like this, the way you were, for the reason you were..." Sir William rubbed the back of his neck. The anger at Kent was still too fresh, and he was having a difficult time reining it in.

"Well, let's just say I don't intend to let it happen again... And I know... *I know* I could never replace Trystane. He's impossible to replace... *But*... I hope you know I will always be here for you. In *any* capacity you should need."

Sir William's admission took Daniel by surprise. He wasn't sure what to say, but he had an inkling about how Kat must have felt the previous day while talking to his mother. It was overwhelming to the point of maddening. He was stunned and his voice shook slightly as he spoke. "Tha-Thank you..."

Not sure what to say next or where to go from there, Sir William cleared his throat, and offered a suggestion. "You should get some rest. Take the rest of the day, yeah?"

Daniel nodded in agreement.

"I've got some things to sort out. Do you think you can manage the walk back alone?" Sir William half teased.

Daniel chuckled. "Yes, my Lord."

Sir William ruffled his hair once more. "Go on..." he said, giving him a gentle nudge. "And no detours! I have eyes everywhere!" he quipped, but the stern look in his eyes told Daniel he was serious.

"Yes, my lord." Daniel chuckled, turning away. After hearing what Sir William had to say, Daniel stood a little taller and felt brighter. Even his injuries didn't feel as severe, though he attributed *some* of that to the medicine he'd received from the healers. When Kat told him how she thought her uncle would react, he hadn't believed it; He was more than glad to realize he was wrong.

As Daniel reached the courtyard, he glanced towards the main gate, and for a split second, he contemplated going into the village, to the inn, hoping to spend some more time with his family. *He could rest there, right?* At just the thought, the hairs on the back of his neck prickled. He turned around to see Sir William in the healer's doorway, giving him a stern look and pointing towards the eastern keep. Daniel gave a weak chuckle, and put his hands up in surrender, then hurried toward his quarters.

He'd be lying to say going to the inn wasn't tempting, but he could only imagine how his mother and aunt would react to seeing his injuries. His mother would be worried to see him in this condition, and Aunt Ada, well, she just might storm the castle in retaliation. He suddenly thought that maybe a quiet night in his room was a better idea after all.

The first few minutes of Daniel's seclusion were gratifying, but before long, it became much more daunting; there wasn't much to do sitting in his room, all by himself. His injuries slightly obscured his vision, so reading or sketching was out of the question. He tried resting, but sleep seemed to evade him, so instead, he sat on his windowsill, and gazed out at the late afternoon sky, completely lost in his own thoughts.

He thought about his father and wondered if he would be proud of him. Then, he thought about his sister and how much he missed her. He thought about his mother and two little brothers, who he wished he could be closer to everyday instead of just during the summer. He even thought about Aunt Ada and Tom, and hoped that one day they'd make whatever they had between them official and become a family.

Then his thoughts turned to his extended family. He thought about Jerren, and how he was more like his brother than his friend, or his prince. He thought about Sir William and how glad he was to have him as his mentor and role model, and wondered if he had meant everything he said; but most of all, he thought about Kat.

It wasn't a new thought by any means; over the last few years, he thought about her a lot. He wished he could go back and stop his mother from ever saying anything to her, though he loved her a bit more for what she had said. Or maybe if he had handled things differently after they left the inn, she wouldn't have anything to feel bad about. He knew what it was like to miss someone the way she did, and he couldn't blame her for how she reacted.

The memory of her falling into the river rippled through his mind, and sent a shiver up his back. He had been so scared watching her float away from him, but when he finally got to her and she opened her eyes, all he wanted to do was cry tears of joy. He tried not to dwell on that though, and instead thought about how it felt to hold her in his arms as they walked back to the western gate, and the kiss she had left on his cheek... And then, he thought about how much of a shit he was for making her feel bad after everything that happened.

From his perch, he watched as the night sky rose. He knew he should do *something* for the princess; Something that told her everything was okay, and that he was sorry for making her feel bad; but also to tell her thank you for keeping his secret, even though she knew better. *Maybe some more flowers*; but that didn't seem like enough.

The evening was growing late, and just as he was about to give up on the idea, a thought struck him. Though it was scarcely known, Daniel was a talented artist, and would make sketches of things he'd seen when he traveled, or if he had nothing better to do; with that in mind, he realized he already had the perfect gift for the princess. He pulled a sketchbook from his trunk, tore out the page he had been working on, then tacked it onto a very thin piece of wood. He wrapped the gift, and tied the wrapping with some twine, but thought it needed something a little extra; something that could only be from him. He smiled knowing just what to do, but frowned knowing he could only get what he needed from the field near the stables.

He knew Sir William was serious when he said he needed to rest, and that he had eyes everywhere, *but this was for Kat.* Slowly, Daniel opened his door and peered down the hall; *It was empty.* Hoping to leave undetected, he rushed towards the stairwell, where he ran into Jerren.

"What the hell?" Jerren said, with wide eyes, observing Daniel's injuries.

"I'll explain later." he replied without stopping.

"Hey! Where are you going?"

Daniel sighed, knowing Jerren wouldn't be able to let it go. As he reached the bottom of the stairs, he stepped to the side and waited for the prince to appear. Seconds later, Jerren came barreling out of the stairwell and nearly ran right past him. "Going somewhere?" Daniel smirked.

"What the hell?"

"You said that already."

Jerren rolled his eyes, folded his arms, then waited for a proper response. Daniel chuckled at the prince, but gave in all the same. "I uh - had some trouble earlier today, but it's all taken care of," he said, as if this sort of thing happened every day. Jerren stared at him, waiting for more information, but Daniel just shrugged.

"I haven't seen you all day. Your face is all busted up, and that's all I get?"

Daniel gave Jerren a crooked smile, "*He cares! He really cares!*"

"Come on, seriously... Are you alright?"

Daniel thought it was nice that Jerren seemed so concerned about his wellbeing, especially when he didn't need to be. "I'm getting there," he replied truthfully.

"Will you tell me what happened?"

"Yes, but you'll have to wait."

Jerren accepted Daniel's response and left it at that; but before Daniel got far, the prince called after him again. "Don't let Kat see you like this," he warned. "She'll be out for blood."

Kat's first reaction to seeing his injuries danced to the front of Daniel's mind. *She had been out for blood.* Daniel bit the inside of his cheeks to keep from smiling at the thought, and gave Jerren another sharp nod. "Noted."

Once he parted ways with the prince, Daniel made his way through the corridors and out to the garden. From there, he snuck to the back side of the stables, where he picked a single, full, thistle. He did his best to clear the spiny stem and was about to sneak back to his quarters when he heard a commotion coming from inside the building.

He hid behind a cart of hay, curious to know what was happening. He could hear raised voices, but they were muffled and he couldn't make out what was being said. Suddenly, the stable doors burst open, making Daniel jump and fall backwards. When he looked around to see what had caused the ruckus, he saw Tobias Kent flat on his back, turning and moaning in pain. A tall, muscular figure emerged from the stables and loomed over Kent. The light from the stables was to the figure's back, and Daniel was having difficulty making out who, *or what,* it was. As his eyes adjusted to the bright light, peering through the dark, Daniel could make out the silhouette of a man.

The man picked Kent up by his shirt and hit him hard in the face once, and then again. The second blow was so powerful that Kent's head seemed to bounce off the ground. Daniel heard Kent splutter some sort of apology as the mystery man pulled him back up by the shirt. He watched, stupefied, as the man leaned in close to Kent's face and muttered something in a low, dangerous voice. Kent nodded enthusiastically and pleaded once more for mercy. The man shoved Kent back to the ground, then watched as he retreated into the stables on his hands and knees.

When Kent was finally out of sight, the man dusted himself off, and straightened his shirt. He had only taken a few steps, but Daniel could tell from his stride alone that he had to be someone important. *What had Kent done?* Daniel watched the mystery man, and carefully followed behind to see who it was. The man passed by a torch, and Daniel realized it wasn't just *any* man... It was *Sir William.*

He had never seen Sir William hit someone else outside of sparring, and certainly not in the way he had hit Kent. He was constantly lecturing Daniel about avoiding 'physical confrontations' as much as possible. In fact, Sir William was the most diplomatic person Daniel had ever met. Burning with curiosity, and not caring if he was reprimanded or not, he ran to catch up to Sir William.

"You're supposed to be resting," Sir William scolded. He glanced back towards the stables, and when he saw the thistle in Daniel's hand and the look on his face, he sighed.

"You weren't meant to see that," he said, as he rubbed the back of his neck. "But I did promise you I'd make sure what he did would never happen again."

"But, *why*?"

Sir William cocked his head to the side at Daniel's question. "Why?" he repeated, confused. "Daniel... I've already told you. I don't like to see you hurt... And what Kent did..." Sir William was flustered and wasn't sure how to finish his sentence.

Everything Sir William told Daniel earlier came flooding back; about his father, and him, and what it all meant. Daniel smiled, then flung his arms around Sir William, hugging him tightly, the way he wished he could hug his father. The knight was momentarily stunned, but ultimately gave in to the sweet gesture and hugged him back.

"You're not going to get in trouble, are you?" Daniel asked. Sir William let out a deep throaty laugh, and shook his head. "No... but you might if you don't get your butt back to bed."

Daniel looked down at the thistle in his hand, then up the castle walls, where he could see Kat's balcony. Sir William must have followed his eyes because he began to chuckle to himself. "She's been worried about you all evening."

Daniel blushed and looked at Sir William with wide eyes. "What do you mean?"

"She didn't say so, but I can always tell."

"Oh?"

"She barely touched her supper, and I noticed her eyes kept wandering to where you normally sit."

Daniel blushed a little more. "Why are you telling me this?" he asked, with a crack in his voice.

Sir William laughed lightheartedly. "Because I know my kids."

He winked, ruffled Daniel's hair, then strolled away across the courtyard.

His kids? Daniel smiled to himself and then turned to walk back to his quarters.

"Daniel..." Sir William called.

"Yes, my Lord?"

"You have five minutes."

The grin on Daniel's face broadened, and he raced back to his room to grab his gift, then made his way to the western tower. He had planned on leaving it outside Kat's door, but as he drew nearer, he saw the door was open. He turned away, ready to abandon the whole idea, not sure what he would say to her, but he didn't make it far.

"Daniel? What are you doing?" Kat asked.

Daniel's nerves ruffled; he took a deep breath to calm them, then turned back to face her. "I was going to deliver this."

Kat's brow lifted slightly confused, and Daniel extended the gift to her. She blushed when she realized the delivery was for her. "Oh!... What's this for?"

"I just wanted to say, I'm sorry for being a jerk earlier and, uh, thank you for... you know."

"Daniel... I should be the one-"

Daniel held his hand up to stop her. "That's all done, Princess. No need to go over it again." He smiled, and she returned his warm gaze.

Increasingly curious about the small package, Kat carefully pulled the thistle from the binding, smelled it, stuck it in her hair, then pulled at the twine.

"Oh, you don't have to open it now. It's really not much," Daniel said, a little embarrassed, though his words did not dissuade her. In fact, they intrigued her all the more. When the image was revealed, she looked from it to Daniel, in awe.

"*You* did this?"

Daniel scratched his forehead nervously and shrugged. "I mean you don't have to sound *so* surprised."

"Daniel, this is beautiful!" Kat smiled as she traced the outline of her family crest. "It looks just like the one in-"

"The throne room.. Yeah," he finished for her.

"Thank you! Thank you so much."

"You're very welcome, Princess," Daniel said, swelling with pride.

"How did I not know you could draw like this?"

"What else is there to do during court?"

Kat laughed, and Daniel thought it was the most wonderful sound he had ever heard. He caught himself staring a little too long, and shook his head to refocus his train of thought. "I guess I should... go get some rest."

"Me too," Kat said with a shy smile. "You look much better than, well... before," she added quickly.

"I feel much better."

"Good!"

"Oh, and before I forget... you were right," Daniel admitted. "About your uncle... He found out, all on his own and, well, let's just say he handled the situation."

Kat smiled smugly. "Well... I'm glad it all ended the way it should."

"Good night, Princess," he chuckled as he turned away. He made it a few more steps when Kat called to him.

"Yes, Princess?"

She sashayed towards him, but her expression was stern. "First of all, if you keep calling me *Princess* with no one else around, I will never speak to you again."

Daniel chuckled and put his hands up in surrender. "Alright, I promise."

Kat paused slightly as she contemplated what to say next.

"Was there a second of all?" Daniel asked with a smirk.

"As a matter of fact there is," she began. "You never answered my question."

Daniel gave Kat a confused look. "What question was that, Prin-"

Kat's look hardened, making Daniel laugh. "Kat," he corrected.

"Yesterday, when we were out by the stables, before *everything...* I asked you if I still reminded you of your sister, and you never answered."

"Oh!" Daniel half squeaked, quickly looking down. He rubbed the back of his neck anxiously, not sure what to say; then, shifted nervously from foot to foot. Finally his eye's met Kat's, and he watched as a wide grin spread across her lips; almost as if she knew something he didn't.

Daniel's mouth went dry. "What?" he asked.

Kat made no response, but instead reached up on her tiptoes and lightly kissed Daniel's cheek. "Good night, Daniel."

Daniel watched, a little shocked, as Kat strolled happily back to her room and closed the door behind her. The cheesy grin on his face was so wide, the split in his lip threatened to reopen. *Had that really just happened?*

He let out a long sigh, then nearly floated back to his room. When he finally reached his destination, he closed the door behind him, then flung himself backwards onto the bed, and softly touched his fingertips to where Kat's kiss lingered on his cheek. He felt incredible, like nothing in the world could ever bring him down. His injuries were all but forgotten, his heart filled with hope for what tomorrow would bring, and his head filled once more with thoughts of his princess.

Seasons Change

As Daniel crossed the western bridge, a shiver ran down his spine. It had been just over three years since the day Kat fell into the river, but each time he crossed there, the memory came flooding back. It was early fall; the leaves on the trees had already changed, and the slightest chill whirled in the air.

Daniel paused for just a moment and took a deep breath in. Autumn had always been his favorite season. He loved the rich colors of the changing leaves; He loved the cool days and even cooler nights, especially those spent around a warm fire with good friends. His absolute favorite part of fall, though, was returning to Eraduun.

Daniel's annual trip home for the summer was a tradition he truly treasured. He knew the importance of the time he was able to spend with his mother and brothers; but the older he got, the more he questioned its value. Not because he didn't love them, or his home, but because he loved his life in Eraduun just as equally.

Over time, the castle became his second home; being there more than Nocfeynir, *how could it not?* He loved his life in Eraduun *so much* that choosing one place over the other left an uneasy imprint on his heart; and leaving either place was always bittersweet. The only thing that made the trip back to Eraduun in the autumn tolerable, was the accompaniment of his mother and brothers traveling with him to attend the Harvest Festival.

The Harvest Festival was a two week-long celebration held in Eraduun, marking the founding of their great nation. There would be parties, and competitions, and vendors of every variety that would come from all corners of the continent. It was Daniel's favorite time of the year and he felt a little guilty he hadn't come back sooner to help prepare.

As Daniel neared the western meadow, a booming voice greeted him. "Young master Daniel, I see you've finally returned. We were beginning to wonder if you'd made the move permanent this time."

Daniel dismounted his steed and placed the reins into the hands of the man before him. "Not just yet, Master Kent, though the older I get, I have to admit it gets a bit more tempting."

The man gave a slight smile, and a quick nod, then led the horse into the stables to be tended to. It had been years since 'the incident' between Daniel and Kent occurred, but since then, they had come to a sort of understanding with one another. Kent had apologized, of course; though Daniel knew the 'conversation' Kent had with Sir William had encouraged it more than genuine remorse.

After that day, Sir William would only allow Daniel to work in the stables when absolutely necessary, or under extreme circumstances. In fact, Sir William cut Daniel back on his more mundane duties all together. Before, if he had not been under direct orders from Sir William, Daniel would go wherever he could be of use. After what Kent had done though, Sir William found it necessary to keep him at his side.

Essentially, Daniel became Sir William's shadow. He attended more council meetings, ran important errands, and even trained with the other knights. On the odd occasion, Sir William would even send Daniel as his proxy to attend an event, or settle a dispute among the squires. It was a notion that took Daniel a while to come to terms with; and though it was a great honor, it came with an enormous amount of pressure and responsibility. He always did his best to represent Sir William, but he couldn't help but feel he often fell short.

"Well, it's about time!" a familiar voice called out. "Your last letter said you'd be here two weeks ago!"

Daniel smirked and bowed dramatically at a nearby apple tree. "I apologize for my tardiness, your Highness. Had I known how you yearned for my presence, I would've arrived sooner."

Jerren dropped from his perch with a scoff, then shoved his friend's shoulder.

"It's good to see you too," Daniel chided.

The boys chuckled, then exchanged a quick embrace. Daniel loved being around his little brothers, but nothing compared to the time he spent in the company of his best friend.

"So, what news from the northland?"

As Daniel and Jerren walked the grounds, Daniel filled the prince in on the summer and everything to do with his family. Each topic was more trivial than the last, but he knew Jerren would want every detail.

"I don't care how tall Archer is, I'll see him tomorrow! Did you do anything fun? Beat the shit out of anyone? *Meet any gorgeous women?*"

Daniel laughed and shook his head.

"Oh, come on, you mean to tell me there isn't a single pretty girl in the north?... *besides your mother.*"

Daniel rolled his eyes and gave the prince a pointed look that told him not to push his luck.

"Tell me I'm wrong!"

Daniel groaned with annoyance. "Yes, your Highness, there are *scores* of pretty girls in the north."

Jerren raised his eyebrows expectantly.

"*No*, I did not spend my entire summer vexing them as *you* did."

Jerren released an aggravated groan. "You have got to lighten up and live a little!"

"I know *you* think chasing after every attractive scullery maid and page boy you come across counts as living, but my feelings on the matter tend to differ."

"At least I know how to have fun… though you'll be happy to know my days of careless romance are over," Jerren said. The tone of his voice was almost convincing, but not quite convincing enough.

"HA!"

Daniel's sardonic outburst offended the prince, so much so that he swiveled in place just to glare at him.

"I'm serious. I met the love of my life this summer!"

Daniel laughed long and hard and maybe a bit overly dramatic to make a point.

"Are you done?" Jerren sneered. Daniel cleared his throat, leaned against the castle wall, and crossed his arms, preparing himself to hear the latest chronicled tale of Prince Jerren Scarborough's new sworn love.

"I'm telling you, she's the one! She's the most beautiful girl I have *ever* seen!"

Daniel scoffed.

"Look, I know I've said that before, but I really mean it this time! … And let's not even get into this debate about the qualities of a beautiful woman. I *know* your type and I'm wholly unimpressed," Jerren smirked, and it was Daniel's turn to roll his eyes.

A movement off to the side caught his attention, and he smiled. "Speaking of which," Daniel said, more to himself than to the prince as he stood a little taller.

"Daniel! You're back!"

Kat ran at him, smiling, then threw her arms around his neck and hugged him tightly. Daniel lifted her from the ground, and quickly spun her around. She giggled, and the sound warmed his heart.

Since her fall into the river, and the resulting experiences, Kat and Daniel had rekindled their friendship, forming an irrevocable bond. They spent more time together than they did apart. Though, with their increasing time together, it became much harder for Daniel to ignore his growing feelings for her.

"Kitty Kat! You get more lovely each summer."

Kat pushed away from him, then playfully whacked him with the book she held in her hand as a reprimand for the use of a particular nickname.

Daniel laughed and shrugged. "Old habits."

"You're forgiven, but *only* this once and *only* because you were kind enough to write to me so often *and* just told me I was pretty."

Jerren was just about to make a comment about the ridiculously goofy smile on Daniel's face when he realized something. "Wait, just how often did you write to her?"

Daniel and Kat quickly glanced at one another, exchanging a telling look at the Prince's expense.

"I'm supposed to be your best friend!" Jerren half whined.

Daniel chuckled and put an arm around Jerren. "You are my best friend," he quipped. "But... she actually writes back to me... Not to mention, she's just so damn gorgeous." Daniel winked at Kat, who rolled her eyes at his bold flirtation, but smiled all the same.

It never ceased to amaze Daniel how much Kat seemed to change over the summer. Each year he came back, she was smarter, stronger, and, truth be told, much more beautiful than he could remember. She was blossoming into a fine young woman in *every way*, and Daniel had more than noticed.

"Why don't you just kiss her, and get it over with already," Jerren muttered in a low voice only Daniel could hear. Daniel gave the Prince a swift jab to the ribs to shut him up and was glad Kat didn't seem to notice.

"Oh, don't be bitter, brother. It's not Daniel's fault you're such a snore... Besides, he just likes me better, always has, right Daniel?"

Kat fluttered her eyelashes, and Daniel grinned in response, Jerren however made a retching noise at the display.

"Princess?" Mara called from the front courtyard. Kat scrunched her face together. "Well, I guess duty calls," she sighed, then hugged Daniel once more. "I'm glad you're home! Promise we'll talk later, okay?"

Daniel agreed and watched as Kat pranced toward the grand hall. The very moment Kat was out of sight, Jerren clapped his hands together, batted his eyelashes, then leaned into Daniel's shoulder. "Oh Daniel! Promise we'll talk later and I'll tell you how much *I loooove you*."

"Oh, shut up," Daniel said, shoving him away.

"I mean, honestly, it's nauseating watching the two of you sometimes," Jerren quipped. "One of these days, one of you will have to make a move, so I don't have to witness all the giggles and blushes. Plus, when she finally rejects you, maybe you'll start having a little more fun."

"Hark, I think I hear Sir William calling for me," Daniel said, changing the subject.

"Except he's in the village working on preparations for the harvest festival... Which you *would have known* had you bothered to write to *me,* as much as you wrote *her Highness*," he mocked, then copied Kat's curtsy.

Daniel laughed. "Aw, someone's a *wee* bit jealous. How cute."

The boys took turns mocking one another, then began a faux sparring match, which led to a chase towards the main gate. So far, not much had changed since early spring, and Daniel was more than grateful for that. If he was being honest with himself, he hoped nothing would ever really change, though he knew that was impossible.

Between Sir William entrusting him with more responsibilities, his brothers growing like weeds, Ada and Tom married with a baby on the way, and he, himself being on the very precipice of manhood, everything was already changing too quickly. Part of him wished it could all just slow down.

In the past year, Sir William talked only of Daniel's future, and plans he had for it. Every spare moment they had together, he spent preparing Daniel to become a knight; An idea that seemed to terrify Daniel as much as it excited him.

Becoming a knight meant more, *everything*. More responsibility, more accountability, more time away from the people he loved, and more people to potentially let down. And though it would certainly bring more positive things to his life, he wasn't entirely sure he was ready for it.

He still had so many questions. Would he have to leave the castle? Would the crown ship him off, somewhere far away, to fulfill some duty? Or would they send him back to the north to oversee the land and title of his father? Would being a knight mean he'd have to leave Jerren and Sir William? *Would he be forced to leave Kat?*

Admittedly, there were certain aspects of Daniel's life he was not yet ready to part with, and he saw knighthood as the catalyst that would push him away from them all.

"I suppose you'll be entering the tourney again this year?" Jerren probed as they walked into town.

Daniel shrugged. "Do you really think it's fair to the others if I do?"

Jerren scoffed. "If they would allow me to compete instead of spectate, you'd be the first I'd knock out of the running."

Daniel laughed, and Jerren rolled his eyes. "You know I am the prince, right? I could have you tossed in a dungeon or sent to the far reaches of the kingdom, and no one could stop me."

"My apologies once more, *your Highness,* though I dare say you'd miss me too much."

"Doubtful," Jerren said, but then gasped, having some sort of epiphany. "You should enter *the big competition!* I'd love to see Sir Cardon knocked on his ass!" Jerren said with a bit too much enthusiasm.

"I'm not a knight," Daniel admonished.

"Pah, technicality."

"Says the prince."

"Exactly! I've said you could, so you can! Problem solved."

Daniel snickered and momentarily wondered what it would be like to have that kind of power.

"It could be like your 'rite of passage' to prove yourself worthy to serve the crown and protect the royal family!" Jerren exclaimed.

"No pressure or anything…"

"I'll even let you fight me!"

"So tell me about this girl..." Daniel said, ready to move the conversation along. The prince's eyes lit up immediately, and Daniel smirked.

"Odette," Jerren sighed. "She's the niece of Lady Breken."

Daniel lifted a curious brow; he had met Lady Breken before and remembered her to be quite plain, to put it benevolently.

"She looks *nothing* like her aunt!" Jerren defended, reading Daniel's doubtful expression.

"Her hair is long and curly and darker than the night sky. Her eyes shine and sparkle as brightly as golden coins in the sunlight... *and her skin!*" The Prince melted at the thought. "It's the most perfect shade of bronze and as smooth and iridescent as a pearl..."

Daniel eyed his friend with skepticism, trying his very hardest not to burst into laughter at his dramatic description. Jerren, though, wasn't amused in the least bit, he narrowed his eyes at him, then marched ahead in a huff. Daniel chuckled to himself and caught up. "I'm sorry, I'll stop... She sounds like a goddess."

The growing smirk on the prince's face told Daniel he thought she was *so much more.*

"So... what happened?" Daniel asked. A fleeting look of sadness flashed in Jerren's eyes that Daniel didn't quite understand.

"Nothing happened." Jerren shrugged.

"What'd you mean?"

"The whole month I spent in the east with her, we were inseparable. Every moment together we spent laughing and talking and flirting. Then the day I left, she was nowhere to be found... I didn't even get to say goodbye..."

Daniel's heart ached a little for his friend. He could tell he was serious about his feelings for this girl and he was well aware of how it felt to care for someone so far out of reach.

"Do you think you'll see her again?" Daniel asked.

"I don't know... I've written to her several times, but I haven't gotten anything back..."

The tone of the prince's voice was hopeless, and pathetic, and Daniel knew in an instant, his feelings must have been true. After that, a melancholy sort of mood seemed to loom over the boys. They walked, at least a short distance, in silence, with Jerren mourning the loss of his would-have-been love, and Daniel commiserating along with him.

"Maybe she'll attend the festival, hardly anyone misses it. She could be on her way here as we speak!" Daniel said, attempting to cheer his friend up.

"Yeah, and then I won't have to spend the entire festival watching you pine for my sister!"

Daniel scoffed and shook his head. "Prince or no, I'll still kick your ass."

Jerren was seconds away from retaliating when Sir William interrupted him. "Ah Daniel! Good, you're here!

After your letter last week, I was hoping you were still going to make it in time for the festivities."

"*LAST WEEK?!*" Jerren interjected. "Do you write to all the members of my family so frequently while you're away, or am I the only one to get snubbed?"

Daniel shrugged. "I hadn't the time to write to the king *this summer*, though I suspect if I had, he would've been far too busy to reply."

"Hilarious, you're just hilarious…" Jerren said. Though his unimpressed attitude swiftly shifted to an eager one. "Well! I have done my duty and delivered you to my uncle, the *honorable* Sir William. Now, I must bid you both adieu, for I have… *other matters* to attend to."

Jerren swaggered back up the path, but before he got far, Sir William called him back. "There'll be no pubs today, nephew. Your father is expecting you back any minute… Something about a fitting for a new tunic… and maybe ask about a matching bib to keep this one clean."

Daniel laughed at the knight's playful suggestion, while Jerren groaned, rolled his eyes and marched back towards the keep; knowing better than to spar with his uncle.

Sir William chuckled at his nephew's reaction, then turned his attention back to his ward. "Now, Daniel, there is still much to be done before the festival next week. There will be many dignitaries in attendance and-"

"And it is our responsibility to make sure they are as comfortable and well taken care of as ever." Daniel said, finishing the knight's sentence with a flourished bow. Sir William abruptly put Daniel into a loose, and obviously playful, head lock, and ruffled his hair. Daniel hardly protested, but instead laughed along with his mentor.

"Still as ornery as ever I see," Sir William teased.

"I wouldn't want to disappoint you, my Lord," Daniel chuckled.

"Well, in that case, you should have these to wear for the tourney."

Sir William pulled a small package from the cart beside him, then presented it to Daniel. Carefully, Daniel unwrapped the package only to reveal a set of new, extremely expensive looking bracers. His eyes shot immediately up to Sir William, then dropped back down to the gift.

The leather used was supple, yet obviously durable, and was of the finest quality of light armor. What had really caught Daniel's eye, though, was the pattern stamped into the soft leather.

A thistle bud stretched vertically across the leather, with spiny veins encircling it. But the addition of a crescent moon cradling the bud, and a howling wolf at the heart of it all, is what Daniel had cherished the most. The image combined Sir William's sigil and his own family's sigil seamlessly—almost as if it should have always been that way.

Daniel smiled as his fingers traced the design with a sense of reverence. "Are... Are you sure?" he asked in disbelief.

Sir William rubbed his neck, unsure how to feel about Daniel's reluctance. "Well, I had hoped, but if you're not comfortable with them, of course I understand."

"No! I mean yes! I am… I want to wear them!" Daniel stumbled out.

Sir William smiled at Daniel's excitement, then cleared his throat. "Good, you've more than earned it, I think."

With some help from a more than willing Sir William, Daniel fitted the bracers to his arms. He said it was to break them in before the tournament began, but, admittedly, he had been far too excited to wait.

This gift meant more to him than any other he had ever received. The sigil you bear is something that is given, passed down from father to son for generations. Sir William had honored not only his own legacy, but Daniel's as well. It was like a physical manifestation of Daniel's two homes becoming one, and he was proud to wear it whenever and wherever he could.

❖ ❖ ❖

Over the next week, Daniel worked relentlessly from dawn to dusk. When he wasn't sleeping, or stopping for the occasional bite to eat, he was running errands, training with the knights, or helping in some other capacity.

He chopped extra wood for whomever might need it, went on hunting trips, carted goods to and from town; he even found time to help Tobias Kent prepare the stables. No one had asked him to do any of these things, but if he could do anything to make the festival as enjoyable for anyone else, he would do it.

Daniel had just unloaded another bundle of wood for the kitchens and sat on a nearby cart for a quick break when Kat found him. She stood outside the kitchen door, holding an apple, and stared at him.

"Enjoying the view, Princess?" he said with a raised brow as he wiped away the sweat that beaded on his forehead.

Kat let out a laugh, then wrinkled her nose. "The view would improve immensely, if it were not so sweaty."

Daniel chuckled at her response, then shrugged.

"Here, you look like you could use this more than me." Kat took a few steps forward and tossed her apple to Daniel. He caught it, lifted it to her with gratitude, then took a large bite.

"You know, there are plenty of people around here that could do these things. You can relax a little." Kat said, taking a seat beside him.

"*Relax?* Yes, I think I've heard that word before. Your brother 'relaxes' often, doesn't he?" Daniel smirked. "I assume that's why he's so bad at everything."

"Well, at least you'd smell better," Kat teased.

Daniel grabbed at his chest as though his heart were giving out; too wounded by the princess's words to go on any longer.

"Stop it." She giggled, nudging him with her shoulder. Daniel chuckled, then slowly his mouth lifted into a wicked grin.

"What?" Kat asked suspiciously, recognizing the glint in his eyes.

"You've hurt my feelings... and I think I need a hug."

Kat's eyes grew large. "Daniel, don't. You. Dare!"

She knew what Daniel was up to and there was no chance she would willingly let it happen. Daniel's smile widened at the challenge. He nodded his head, then jumped from the cart to block her path. Kat scooted herself back on the cart, then stood, putting as much distance as she could between them.

"I'm serious Daniel..." she said, trying her very best to keep a straight face.

Daniel pulled himself back up into the cart, and stood, arms opened wide. "Come on, Kat, give it up. Where are you gonna go?" he smirked and took a step forward. Kat leaned back as far as she was able and put her hand out in warning, but suppressed a laugh.

Seconds before Daniel embraced her, she looked past him, and her face fell. Daniel's brow furrowed at her troubled expression, and he dropped his arms, then turned his head to inspect their surroundings.

The moment he turned away, Kat jumped from the cart. The sudden jolt of her jump caused Daniel to lose his balance. He slipped, but caught himself at the last second. Kat let out a taunting laugh, and her eyes glimmered with amusement. "Catch me if you can!" she goaded as she raced into the orchard.

"Oh... it's on Princess!" Daniel said, leaping after her.

Kat only made it halfway down a row of apple trees when Daniel scooped her up from behind and swung her around. She squealed at the sudden impact and giggled. Daniel squeezed her tight, then rubbed his sweat soaked hair on the back of her neck.

"*Ew!!!* Okay... *OKAY!*" she protested, as she laughed.

When Daniel finally set her down, she turned and playfully pushed him away. "You're disgusting!"

Daniel laughed and took a deep bow, but Kat only rolled her eyes. "Oh, don't be that way... you know you liked it," he winked, giving her a broad grin. Kat pushed him again, but this time, he grabbed her hand and pulled her into another embrace.

"*Daniel!!!*"

Kat laughed, and tried to push him away, but her struggle only made him hold tighter. "You are impossible!" she said, grinning from ear to ear.

"Having fun?" Sir William asked, startling them both.

Daniel released Kat, practically pushing her away from him. Then, they each took an extra step away from each other for good measure; though the blush on their cheeks wasn't fooling anyone. Sir William chuckled to himself, then waited for his answer.

"I was just escorting the Princess back to the castle," Daniel said, rubbing his neck.

"Yes, I just needed a bit of fresh air and thought a stroll in the orchard would do me some good," Kat added.

Sir William concealed a smile with his hand, nodding along to their responses, his eyes full of humor. He cleared his throat. "Well, I believe Madame Mara was looking for you," he said to Kat.

"Right, of course."

Kat marched past her uncle, leaving Daniel with a small smile. About half way down the row of trees, and out of Sir WIlliam's vision, she turned around and stuck her tongue out at him. Daniel laughed, but quickly tried to hide it with a cough. He tried to stay focused on Sir William, but his gaze kept drifting to Kat, who every few feet would glance over her shoulder back at him. Her expression was giddy and warm, and each time he saw it, he stood taller and smiled brighter. He had almost forgotten Sir William was standing there, until the knight cleared his throat once more, snapping him back to attention. "I'm sorry, my Lord, did you say something?"

Sir William hadn't said a word, he had, however, watched the exchange between Daniel and his niece carefully, and found it more amusing than he dared to admit. He began to laugh, long and hard, no longer able to conceal his mirth.

"What?" Daniel asked, a bit confused.

Sir William smirked, patted Daniel on the shoulder, then turned away, chuckling to himself. Daniel looked around, confused for a second, not understanding what was so funny, but quickly put it out of his mind. He sighed, put his hands on the back of his neck, then strolled happily back toward the castle. If he accomplished nothing else today, at least he made Kat smile.

The Festival

The first day of the Harvest Festival was, in actuality, just a big party. Knights, noble families, vendors, and entertainment from across the kingdom paraded through the village to the jousting grounds. There, the royal family hosted the opening ceremonies, welcoming all who had traveled to join in the celebrations, as well as announcing everything planned for the following days.

  Competitions of every kind began almost immediately after the opening ceremonies concluded. Cooking contests; eating contests; knife throwing; archery; rock toss; and every day brought more. But the biggest event; The Tourney, began on the third day and had been known to sometimes last as long as the festival itself.

  Each night there were feasts and little parties at the castle, and throughout the village, but none that compared to the celebrations the evenings of the opening and closing ceremonies. *Those* were the best and biggest parties of the entire year; they were also Daniel's favorite parts of the whole festival.

He couldn't quite explain why, but this year, everything seemed a little more exciting. The music was more upbeat; food was more flavorful; people were more lively; and the women, without a doubt, were more beautiful. Even the wine tasted sweeter, which made Sir William's warning about drinking too much seem rather insignificant.

The first evening's feast was in full swing, and both Daniel and Jerren were feeling *much* braver than usual. They crooned along with each tavern song they knew; and flirted brazenly with serving girls and the young women of the court. They received several warning looks from Sir William, but were too immersed in the festivities to mind them.

At one point, Daniel noticed Kat receiving more attention than he cared for, from *several* young noblemen. The notion made him squirm, but with the help of his newfound bravery, he thwarted any advances he could.

He spilled a goblet of wine 'accidentally' on one boy. He introduced pretty girls to a few others, and he asked the princess to dance any chance he got, knowing she wouldn't refuse him.

"What are you doing?" Kat asked, narrowing her eyes at him during one dance.

"What a silly question, Princess. We're dancing," he replied, with a slight smirk.

"You never dance this much... even with *me*."

She was right, of course, and Daniel wasn't sure how to respond. "I just don't want these thickheads getting the wrong idea about anything."

Kat laughed. "*Thickheads*? Really? And pray, tell, what *ideas* do you think they have?" she asked, rather amused.

"I know all too well what ideas, and it's much too improper to discuss with a young, impressionable princess," Daniel replied, only half joking.

Kat laughed once more. "Oh please! My first suitors feast is in just a few months."

"Yes, and until then, it is my job to keep those handsy bastards at bay."

"I can handle myself, you know?"

"I'm well aware of that, Princess, but if I wasn't over here bothering you, I'd have to sit around watching your brother drink himself into a stupor, and this is just so much more fun." Daniel winked, and Kat let out a soft giggle.

"Why Daniel Enid... What *has* gotten into you?"

"The world may never know."

The dance ended, and Daniel offered a deep bow, then kissed Kat's hand. The two exchanged a small smile as they parted ways across the dance floor, but when Daniel looked back, he groaned seeing a new swarm of would-be suitors surrounding Kat. What disappointed him more was that she seemed to rather enjoy their attention.

The extra dancing and wine had clouded his head; The room was too warm and too full, he needed air. He half stumbled into the garden, and when he looked down the outer corridor he saw Sir William and a woman — no, not just a woman... *his mother.*

They were talking, laughing, no doubt reminiscing about their childhood, and overall seemed to be enjoying themselves. Daniel thought they looked rather happy together; In fact, the closer he looked, the more he noticed just how happy. There was a certain glint in Sir William's eye; he had never seen it on *him* before, but was most definitely sure of the sentiment behind it.

Sir William stopped suddenly, and took his mother's hand. He said something with a sincere, almost hopeful face, and Daniel could've sworn he saw his mother blush as Sir William brought her hand to his lips and gently kissed it.

It was an odd sight to be sure, but Daniel hadn't minded seeing them together that way. He wouldn't have minded in the slightest if they were even closer still. In his mind, they both deserved an extra bit of happiness, and if they could find it in one another, that would be even better.

Daniel retreated further into the garden, hoping his presence would go unnoticed and their moment uninterrupted. He smiled to himself at the thought of the two of them together. He had the sudden urge to seek out Jerren in hopes that they might devise a scheme to ensure the outcome, but a pair of low voices coming from the other side of a bush distracted him from his mission.

"*Please* don't make me do this, Ro-"

"This is the only reason I allowed you to come with us, Odette... now be a good girl and do as you're told," a young man said.

Odette? Daniel paused at the name and wondered whether it was the prince's Odette.

"I don't think-"

"You *will* do this!" the man demanded.

Daniel could hear the fear in the girl's voice against the man's harsh tone, and he didn't like the way the conversation was going. He walked to the other side of the bush to investigate and found the young man not only had a harsh tone, but a solid grip on the arm of the young lady.

Daniel could only see a fraction of the couple's images in the dim light, but from what he could see he made note of. The boy was tall, muscular, not unhandsome, with blondish hair and an air of self importance about him; undeniably eastern nobility. The girl seemed about Jerren's age and was absolutely *gorgeous*; every bit the beauty Jerren had described *his* Odette to be. He noticed she was well-dressed, but not as well as her counterpart.

"But uncle said-"

The boy scoffed. "Come off it already. He's not your uncle, and mother's not your aunt. Why are you still trying to pretend you're something you're not?"

Odette seemed to wilt. "I just thought..."

"Oh please, you're *nothing* and you'll always be nothing," the boy cackled, throwing his head back just enough to allow Daniel to see his face. Daniel hung his head and groaned when he realized who he'd snuck up on. Regardless of the status the boy held though, Daniel had seen and heard more than enough.

"Sorry to interrupt," he said, startling both parties.

The boy looked him up and down, then scoffed. "Piss off, mutt."

Daniel ignored the arrogant boy, and kept his attention on the lady in front of him. "Is everything alright, my lady?"

The boy, Rollin Breken, the only child of Lord and Lady Breken, turned to face Daniel, putting himself strategically between Daniel and Odette.

"I said... *Piss. Off.*"

Despite the nasty glare he was receiving, Daniel stood his ground. He wasn't keen on the idea of fighting a nobleman's son, but over the years, he had seen how pompous and rude little Lord Breken had been. Not to mention all the stories he'd heard about him, none of which were flattering. So, with Daniel's enhanced sense of bravery, lack of self-control, and the current look on Odette's face, he would've felt justified about whatever happened next.

"Let's not be rude, my lord... I was speaking to the lady," Daniel said, taking a step forward.

Breken's eyes burned. "And *now* you're speaking to *me.*" He replied, squaring himself with Daniel, but Odette caught his arm.

"Rollin, please."

Daniel stood tall, eyes locked, refusing to back down, but Breken's glare was equally intense. Daniel thought for sure he would swing at any second, but he didn't. Instead, he shook off the rather weak grasp Odette held on his arm, smirked and walked away, leaving Daniel with an ominous message. "I'll see you on the tourney field... *Mutt*."

'*Mutt*.' The word echoed in Daniel's mind. It wasn't a brilliant ridicule by any means, but one he had heard often enough over the years. *But then again, what else would you call someone trying to be something they're not.* He glanced down at the wolf on his bracers, and a surge of boldness, or recklessness, overcame him. "Aren't you a little too old to be competing in the squire's competition?" Daniel asked, turning to taunt the sour young Lord.

Breken paused, and though Daniel could only see his back, he knew he struck a nerve. He didn't know what possessed him to pick a fight, but he could not help but goad Breken further. "What? Not *man* enough to try your hand at an actual competition?"

Breken squeezed his fists, then marched straight back to Daniel. "Why chance defeat?" He said, looking Daniel up and down once more. "When victory is incontrovertible."

Breken stormed past Daniel, hitting his shoulder as he did, then stopped once more in front of Odette and whispered a warning; Daniel couldn't be sure what Breken said, but he knew by the look on Odette's face, whatever he had interrupted was far from over.

Together, Daniel and Odette watched as the all important Rollin Breken disappeared from their semi-secluded spot in the garden, and into the bustling of the great hall. Odette sighed in relief, then turned toward Daniel. "I'm so sorry to have troubled you, my Lord."

My lord? Daniel turned around, thinking she had been addressing another, then blushed, realizing she meant *him*. "It was no trouble at all, my lady, as long as you're alright... and just to clarify, I'm no lord."

"My apologies... My *cousin* and I were just having a disagreement of sorts, but thank you for your kindness."

"Well, it's hard to pass up a chance to rescue a damsel in distress, especially when the damsel is as pretty as you."

Daniel smiled, a sincere and dashing smile, and Odette turned a deep shade of red. "I'm Daniel Enid," he said, extending his hand to her; her eyes grew large with recognition, and she placed her hand in his. Daniel brought her hand quickly to his lips, causing a soft coquettish giggle to escape her throat. "I've heard much about you, my Lo- I mean... Daniel."

"Don't believe a word the Prince says about me... Unless it was good, then it's all true."

Daniel gave her a wink, and Odette blushed one more, though there was a certain surprise in her eyes she couldn't hide at the mention of 'the prince.'

"How did you-"

"Prince Jerren told me, not a week ago, he had met the most *beautiful* girl in all the kingdom and described her in great detail. I see now it wasn't his imagination after all," Daniel said, gently running the pad of his thumb across her knuckles.

The wine had gone further to his head than he realized; He wasn't typically this bold and wondered what Jerren would have to say about his advances. The sudden sound of someone clearing their throat behind him made him jump. He turned to find a rather irritated Kat, and a stunned Jerren.

"*Odette?*"

Jerren stepped forward in pure wonderment, completely ignoring Daniel's existence, and Odette followed suit, freeing her hand from his. "Your Majesty," she replied shyly, as she curtsied.

Their mouths weren't moving, but Daniel could see exactly what they were thinking and feeling. Hoping he wouldn't intrude on the silent moment, he took a step back to be level with Kat and gave her his most charming smile. "It's beautiful tonight, don't you think?"

Kat scoffed, and rolled her eyes, but then took a possessive step in front of Daniel, putting just a little more distance between him and *her*. Jerren, though, seemed to be in another world entirely, one that included only himself and the lovely Odette.

"I'm so glad you're here! When you didn't say goodbye, I thought I'd never see you again," Jerren said, taking both of her hands in his. She was about to respond, but looking back at their company made her shy. Jerren turned to see what had pulled her focus, and watched a disgruntled Kat swat Daniel's hand away from her face. She narrowed her eyes at him, but he only smiled. Jerren assumed Daniel had tried, and failed, to tuck a stray hair behind Kat's ear, and grew suddenly annoyed at their presence. Feeling the glare of the prince on them, Kat and Daniel turned in unison to face him.

"Well don't be rude, brother. Aren't you going to introduce us?" Kat asked with a small smirk, as she stepped forward a little more. Jerren rolled his eyes, and stepped to the side to present Odette to his sister, all the while keeping hold of one of her hands.

"We've already met," Daniel said, winking once more at Odette, who giggled.

"*We know.*" Jerren and Kat said in unified displeasure, making Daniel jump.

"Odette Gerrard, may I introduce my younger sister, Princess-" Kat scoffed, and stepped between Jerren and Odette, effectively severing their physical connection.

"I'm Kat," she said with an inviting smile.

"It's a pleasure to meet you, your Majesty."

Odette curtsied, but Kat waved the unnecessary formality away, then hooked her arm around Odette's and began to stroll her around the garden, leaving Jerren and Daniel behind.

Jerren threw his hands up in frustration at his sister, and Daniel laughed.

"Oh, shut up," Jerren muttered, quickly following behind the girls. The boys strolled close enough to be a part of the group, but far enough behind to not interrupt the conversation, only half listening as the girls chatted about the festival and made plans for the rest of the week. Jerren was too focused on his own thoughts to pay Kat's dribble any mind, and Daniel, well he was having a hard time focusing on anything other than Kat.

"How'd you come across her here?" Jerren asked Daniel in a low voice, his eyes not leaving the silhouette of *his* lady.

Daniel had been so distracted, he nearly forgot about the somewhat troublesome conversation he had overheard. "We need to talk later," he insisted. "Little Lord Breken is up to something."

"What'd you mean?" Jerren asked, pausing to look at him. Daniel was about to tell the prince all he had overheard when Kat suddenly stopped and turned to the two of them.

"Don't you two have anything better to do?" Her voice oozed softness, but her eyes burned with annoyance.

"Then follow two stunning ladies around the garden on a gorgeous night? *What could be better*?" Daniel cooed with a smile.

Kat let out a small, unamused huff, and it was obvious Odette was slightly uncomfortable. Jerren clapped both Daniel's shoulders hard with a tight squeeze, giving him his cue to 'shut up.'

"We'll just be on our way," Jerren said quickly. He grasped Odette's hand and his, and gave it a tender squeeze. "Miss Gerrard, I hope to see you again soon."

Odette smiled sweetly, then bowed her head, but Jerren was having none of that; gently he lifted her chin and left an affectionate kiss on her cheek. She sighed slightly, and delayed the release of his hand as long as she could. Once their moment had ended, Jerren turned to Kat, and his soft expression changed to indifference as he gave her a curt nod. "Sis."

When it was Daniel's turn to offer his farewell, he bowed his head to Odette first. "My Lady," he said with a flirtatious grin. Then, mimicking what he had witnessed Sir William do, he gently lifted Kat's hand to his lips, and let them linger there a moment before finally leaving a light kiss against her knuckles. *"My Princess,"* he crooned.

Kat did her best not to change the unimpressed expression on her face, though it was hard to hide the creeping blush she felt rising in her cheeks. Daniel's eyes were fixated on hers, and Jerren had to physically pull him away for him to look anywhere else.

"You are completely hopeless!" The prince sighed as he pushed Daniel out of the garden and into the breezeway.

Daniel shrugged and swiped two goblets of wine from a serving tray they passed on their way back to the hall.

"Well, at least we know one thing," Daniel said, standing a little taller.

"And what's that?" Jerren scoffed, turning to take one last look back at the girl of his dreams.

"*Odette Gerrard* clearly likes me better," Daniel smiled, though Jerren failed to see the amusement. "You've definitely got some competition."

Daniel raised his cup to his friend, then drained it with one breath, and Jerren followed suit. "Don't let *my sister* hear you saying things like that. She'll have you dropped to the bottom of the southern sea."

Daniel chuckled. "At least you'd have a chance with Odette then."

Jerren pounced on Daniel's shoulders, weighing him down as much as possible, but Daniel leaned slightly so that Jerren's weight was even across him, then used the momentum to re-enter the great hall with the prince on his back. The boys let out a cheer, and the surrounding crowd responded in kind.

The next morning, as Daniel lay unconscious in his bed, a sudden surge of frigid water brought him to life. He jumped up quickly, only to find a soaked Jerren standing beside a furious Sir William.

Both boys had slept through breakfast, the morning festivities, and well past lunch. After a rather lengthy lecture about setting a proper example, and not shirking responsibilities, Sir William sent Jerren to spend the remainder of the day entertaining various noblemen and their families; and Daniel to chop wood from midday till dusk, breaking only to relieve himself or vomit.

When Daniel's punishment had ended, he all but crawled back to his room, and collapsed onto his bed. His body ached, his head pounded, and all he could think of was sleep.

Hours later, his body jolted awake as the remaining contents of his stomach lurched from their resting place. He quickly grabbed a pail that someone had left on the side of his bed, and let the purge take its course. After what seemed like an eternity, he lifted his head from its hanging position, and found a tray of food, along with two large pitchers of water set up near his fireplace. The idea of eating, *or drinking*, anything made his stomach churn once more, but the folded note beside the tray got the better of his curiosity.

Daniel rose from his bed, and lazily dragged his body across the floor to the small table. He grimaced at the smell of the food, and quickly picked up the bit of parchment.

Eat it all; small bites. Drink both pitchers. Trust me.
-WH

An unsure groan escaped his throat, but he followed the instructions left by Sir William all the same. And, to his surprise, after he had eaten every bite as slowly as possible and drank all the water, he felt much better; physically at least.

He gathered the dishes back onto the tray, then set it, along with the soiled bucket, out into the hall, then began to clean himself up. When he was presentable once more, he grabbed the bracers Sir William had given him, and walked down the hall to the knight's chambers. He stared at the door for a minute, trying to find the courage to knock. He knew how disappointed Sir William was, and even though what he was about to do was the *hardest* thing he'd ever done, he knew it was right.

Daniel hung his head, let out a heavy sigh, then timidly wrapped his knuckles against the heavy wood door and waited. But, there was no answer. Hesitantly, he opened the door, and found the room empty. He hung his head once more, and sulked over to Sir William's desk; taking a moment to look over the bracers one last time, and sadly tracing the carved image they held. After the way he behaved, *how could he possibly keep them?*

He had just come to terms with the outcome of his actions and set the bracers on the desk, when a voice called out from the door making him jump.

"Hello?"

Daniel turned quickly and watched as the door opened a little more, revealing his mentor.

"Daniel?" he asked, then quickly scanned the room. "Where's Jerren?"

Daniel shrugged in response to Sir William's question, and the knight's brow furrowed. The only reasons he ever found Daniel in his room were either at his request, or in an attempt by him and Jerren to hide from a social gathering. But he hadn't sent for him, and Jerren, or any of the subsequent provisions, was nowhere to be found.

"What are you doing? I was just coming to check on you," he said, scanning the room once more. His eyes traveled from Daniel to the bracers laying on his desk, and his face fell. "Oh, so you've decided not to wear them?"

"I just thought you'd want them back."

"Want them back? Why?"

"I don't deserve them… I acted like such a fool at the feast, and I missed a whole day of events and responsibilities you were counting on my help for."

Sir William couldn't help but chuckle to himself. "Daniel, sit down." Daniel obeyed, flopping himself down onto a nearby chair.

"Stop being so hard on yourself. You're young, and meant to have a little fun; to make mistakes! With all the mischief you and Jerren have caused, I thought you knew that already."

Daniel shrugged again, and Sir William sighed. "I remember a couple of nights before my first official tournament as a knight; I was slightly older than you are now. My nerves muddled from exhilarated to petrified to undeserving, and back again. I had way too much wine and ale the evening before, and I'm still not sure how I even made it back to my room. My father was so angry at me! Especially after he found several unexplained chickens in my wardrobe." Daniel and Sir William laughed together.

"And do you know what my father did?"

Daniel shrugged.

"He woke me up the next morning with a bucket of freezing water and made me run the perimeter of the manor until I could no longer stand... You wouldn't believe the number of times I got sick."

"Yes, I would."

Sir William stifled a laugh at Daniel's expression, then continued on with his story.

"After that, he told me to get some rest, brought me two pitchers of water and a tray of food, with a few instructions. Well, I did what my father asked, ate the food, drank the water, and cleaned myself up, and I felt better... until I didn't."

Daniel recognized all the parallels of his story with the actions of the day, and though he could hardly meet his gaze, his curiosity buzzed with anticipation, wondering what Sir William would say next.

"Later that evening, I went to my father and told him to pull me from the lists. He asked me if I was still feeling poorly. I told him I wasn't. He asked me if I had injured myself somehow. I told him I hadn't. 'Then why can't you compete in the tournament?' he asked. I looked my father straight in the eye and told him I didn't think I was worthy enough... I missed my first event, I made a fool of myself and I didn't deserve the honor." Sir William paused, to give Daniel a pointed look, knowing exactly how he was feeling. "Do you know what my father did, then?"

Daniel shrugged again, still unable to really look at him.

"He stood me up." Sir William pulled Daniel out of the chair. "Put one hand on my shoulder and pointed at me with the other," he continued, mirroring the actions of his story.

"And he said, 'Son, you have worked too hard for too long to just give up now. There are going to be a lot of times in your life when you don't feel ready for something or like you don't deserve something, and you're going to make a lot of mistakes. The only thing that is for sure is that *tomorrow is a new day*. All you can do in this life is try your very best, and as long as you do that, nothing else matters. Sometimes you will fail, sometimes you'll succeed. Either way, I'll be right by your side to tell you how proud I am of you and how much I love you."

Sir William placed a firm hand on the side of Daniel's neck and used his thumb to push up his chin; forcing him to finally look him in the eye. "So... *Son*, you have worked too hard and too long to walk away now," Sir William smiled. "And no matter what you do... I will always be proud of you and I will always love you."

Daniel's eyes watered, and a large lump formed in his throat. He tried to look down, to blink away the oncoming tears, and clear the lump the best he could, but Sir William's unshakable grip anchored him in place, and when he finally focused in on his gaze all he could see was pride and the love of a father.

Daniel choked back his emotions, and offered a swift nod, as if to say, *I love you too.* Sir William pulled Daniel into a tight embrace, which he held for sometime; not that Daniel was complaining in the slightest.

"Now," Sir William said, finally pulling out of the embrace, and clearing his throat, while blinking back a couple of tears of his own. "Get those things off of my desk and get your butt to bed," he ordered. "You have a tournament to win tomorrow!"

Daniel chuckled, wiped his face, then grabbed the bracers from their resting spot. "Yes, Sir!"

Daniel felt much better, *in every way.* His physical ailments were all but forgotten, and had been replaced with feelings of renewed ambition; and his typically light hearted demeanor had been restored, and with it came a burning question from the previous evening.

"Before I go... Can I ask you something?"

"Of course," Sir William smiled.

The corners of Daniel's mouth rose into an impish grin, knowing he had finally gotten the upper hand on his teacher. "Just *how long* have you carried a torch for my *mother*?"

Sir William hung his head in defeat, feeling caught, but let out a chuckle. "*Good night, Daniel,*" he said dismissively, ushering Daniel quickly to, and out the door.

"I really feel like we should talk about this…" Daniel said, using his weight to delay the exit. "Just give me a rough estimate… Couple of years? Decades? You can tell me!" Daniel teased as Sir William gave him one last shove into the corridor.

"I'll tell you what, Danny," Sir William said with confidence, as he leaned against his door frame. A slow smile crept across his face, and his eyes danced with glee. "I'll answer *your* question, when *you* tell *me* just how long you've 'carried a torch' for my *niece.*"

Daniel took a quick breath in, holding it for a moment, while deeply contemplating how to respond to the accusation. *He wasn't wrong, but like hell was he going to tell him that.* Sir William smirked at Daniel's delayed reaction; knowing full well he had uncovered the truth he's always known. He folded his arms, raised his brow, and with an expectant tilt of his head waited patiently for Daniel to say, or do, *anything*.

Daniel opened his mouth to speak several times, but words would not come out. Finally, a pathetic sort of squeak escaped his throat, and unable to withstand the torture any longer, he made a hasty retreat. "Good night, my Lord."

"Just an estimate? A couple of years? Nearly a decade? *You can tell me!*" Sir William teased, using Daniel's own words against him.

Daniel didn't bother turning around or saying another word; he just held up the bracers, and waved them slightly in acknowledgement as Sir William's laughter filled the empty hallway.

The Tournament

The next morning when Daniel awoke, the effects of the alcohol had long since worn off, but he could still feel knots forming in his stomach. He didn't understand why he felt so nervous; it was far from his first competition, and he had faced many of the same competitors in the past and won. This competition felt different, though; more important, like he had something to prove.

The closer Daniel walked to the tournament field, the more his hands shook and his stomach bubbled. He knew he was a skilled and talented fighter; the best had trained him, after all. But despite everything Sir William had taught him, he knew there could always be someone better, someone quicker, or someone more underhanded; he prayed to the Gods, he would not meet that opponent today.

As he entered the small preparation tent Sir William secured for him, he found Jerren and Kat. "Surprise!" they said in unison.

Daniel smiled. "Shouldn't you two be up in the stands by now?"

"We couldn't very well watch you get your ass kicked without wishing you luck first," Jerren teased as he punched Daniel's arm. Kat let out a small scoff and gave her brother a rather perturbed look. "Oh, don't even listen to him! You're going to do great, as always!"

A shy smile crept across Daniel's face. "Thank you, Princess. It'll be nice to have *someone* cheering me on."

"That reminds me," Jerren said, interrupting what would have otherwise been a tender moment. "Uncle Will invited your family to sit with us."

The prince gave Daniel a certain knowing look, one that told him he was privy to the same information Daniel had verified the night before about Sir William and his mother.

"Can't say I'm surprised," Daniel said, exchanging an understanding grin with the Prince.

Kat gave the two boys a curious look, obviously not understanding what they meant. "Am I missing something?"

"Nearly always," Jerren answered, dismissively. Kat tsked and made a mocking face, but Jerren ignored his sister's taunt, wished Daniel luck once more, then went on his way. Daniel turned to ready himself, expecting Kat to follow her brother, but she was surprised to find she didn't, and before either of them could say anything, a voice called from outside the tent.

"Hi Danny! It's me, you in there?"

Daniel looked from Kat to the door, then cleared his throat before answering. "Yeah, I'm here, Seydi. Come on in."

Seydi entered and was stunned, or maybe a little embarrassed, to see Kat, and vice versa. Both girls looked at each other, exchanged a rather formal greeting, then quickly directed their eyes towards their feet.

"I didn't mean to interrupt," she said. Daniel stood awkwardly, looking from one girl to the other, then back again.

"You're not interrupting anything..." Kat said softly. "I was just wishing Daniel the best of luck."

"Oh... me too..."

Hesitantly, Seydi walked over to Daniel, lifted on her tiptoes, and kissed his cheek. "Good luck, Danny," she whispered, turning his face a light shade of pink.

"Than- thank you, Seydi," he sputtered out. She smiled at him, turned around to curtsy to Kat, then quickly retreated from the tent.

Daniel stood dumbstruck for a moment, unsure of what to do or say. He raised his fingers to the spot on his cheek Seydi had kissed, then shook his head, snapping himself out of the small trance she had left him in.

"Was there something I could do for you, Princess?" he asked, half startling Kat who was obviously deep in thought.

"Oh, umm... right." She blushed and looked down at her feet once more.

"Are you alright?"

Kat cleared her throat and attempted to steal her nerves. "Well, I just wanted to... wish you luck, I guess."

There was so much more she wanted to say, but couldn't seem to get it out.

"Thank you, Princess," Daniel said, lowering his head, a little disappointed at the awkward encounter.

Having completely lost her nerve, Kat cleared her throat and began to retreat.

"Kat, wait!" Daniel called. She turned to face him, but kept her eyes cast down.

"About the other night..." he began. Kat looked up and was visibly confused.

"I owe you a massive apology for the way I behaved... I was brash and senseless, and I - well, I may have had a little too much wine," he admitted, rubbing the back of his neck.

Kat's gaze softened instantly. "Maybe just a little," she agreed. "But... You have nothing to apologize for, Daniel."

Daniel met her warm gaze, and his heart skipped a beat.

"I- Well, I made this for you... for today... for luck," Kat said as she pulled a bit of cloth from the pocket of her cloak. Her heart raced as she passed the small token to him, but she did her best to conceal her nerves.

The handkerchief she gave him had a ring formed by a thistle, with the bud nestled into the center of the crescent moon stitched onto it. Daniel smiled as he rubbed his thumb across the stitch, knowing what had prompted the design.

"I wanted to recreate the bracers Uncle Will gave you," she said, turning Daniel's forearm to compare the pictures. "But my wolves never seemed to come out right," she continued, obviously frustrated with herself.

"And I would've given it to you sooner, but... I don't know, I guess it seemed like an old-fashioned, silly thing to do."

Kat shrugged, and her cheeks colored, but Daniel's warm smile lifted her spirits, and erased any hesitation she previously had. "Thank you, Princess... It's perfect, and I'll treasure it always."

"I really hope you're the one I get to present the trophy to." Kat smiled.

"With this on my side, how could I not be?" he said, proudly examining her token once more. Before Daniel knew what was happening, Kat rested her hand on his arm, leaned up, and kissed the opposite cheek Seydi had, then turned away shyly, leaving him alone and stupefied once more.

The flap of the tent closed, but Daniel couldn't help pulling it back to watch as the princess walked away. She paused just before climbing the back stairs of the stands, and must have felt his stare; she glanced over her shoulder towards him, and the smile she sent back to him nearly stopped his heart.

When she finally disappeared from sight, Daniel let the canvas flap close and moved his thumb over the stitch in the cloth once more. He felt ten feet tall. This really was his chance to prove himself, and gods be damned if he didn't do absolutely everything in his power to win... but it wouldn't be for him; *It was for her.*

The squire's tournament comprised three separate events: archery, the joust, and close combat. To be named champion, one young man alone would need to master all three events. Because so many young men had entered the tournament, the presiding knights divided the contestants into two groups. Once each group had a solitary victor, they would compete against each other in three rounds of close combat to determine the overall champion.

As the young men lined up before the crowds, Daniel swiftly sized up his competition. To his dismay, they placed Rollin Breken in the other group, so the only way to beat him would be for each of them to come out as victors, and he thought that highly unlikely... for Breken at least.

Archery was first, and quite an easy victory for Daniel. Sir William had always praised him for being a natural marksman; it made Daniel proud to prove him right. Then came the joust. Daniel rode hard and fast, sending blow after blow to each young man he faced; knocking a few of them off their horses altogether, until, at last, he was victorious.

"Two down. One to go," he whispered to himself as Sir Cardon awarded him his second victory.

There was a minor break between each event that allowed the young men of one group to rest while the other group competed. Because Daniel was in the second group, he could watch the first group with scrutiny, looking for tells or signs that would allow him an advantage over any victor should he face them.

For the close combat event, the competitors were permitted any weapon they preferred, as long as it was blunted or hollowed, and inspected before the match began. While Daniel had practiced with many weapons, he was by far a better swordsman than anything else. Typically, he would try his hand with an unfamiliar weapon to challenge himself, but he couldn't risk losing now, when he was so close.

He was half disappointed, half emboldened seeing Rollin Brecken stand victorious over the first group. Breken gave Kat a wolfish grin, and kissed her hand, as she pinned a golden medal to his chest; sending a chill up Daniel's spine. Kat, though, blushed a deep red and smiled shyly back, and it was enough to ignite a jealous fire within Daniel. There was no question about it; he *had* to win. *He had to beat Breken.*

Each match Daniel entered and won gave him more confidence and less humility. Feeling a little more cocky than usual, he began to peacock, flaunting his skills whenever he could; But his overconfidence made him sloppy and distracted. During his last match, knowing he was ahead and close to victory, he goaded the young squire opposite him. For his efforts, he received a hard strike on the wrist of his dominant hand with a hollowed out hammer. He couldn't help the anguished groan that was released as a reaction to the impact, but he also couldn't let it stop him. He took a deep breath in, and with all the strength he could muster, delivered a finishing blow.

Daniel had to bite the inside of his cheeks to keep from groaning as the referee held his hand up, declaring him the winner. He looked up at the stands, and the first thing he saw was the obvious disappointment on Sir William's face; he lowered his eyes instantly.

As Kat stepped forward to pin a medal to his chest, she leaned in slightly.

"Are you okay?" she asked, glancing down at his wrist.

"Never better, Princess," Daniel lied. He gave her a winsome grin and a small wink; she grinned back, and he knew she had believed him. He lifted his eyes once more towards the stands, only to see the back of Sir William's head as he left the bleachers. Suddenly, the pain in his wrist seemed secondary to the emptiness he felt in his chest.

He gritted his teeth and bore each congratulatory handshake as if nothing at all was wrong, but he knew he couldn't take much more. As he meandered through the crowd, hoping to return to his tent as quickly as possible, he found himself face to face with Rollin Breken.

"Congratulations, Enid," he bellowed with a smirk. Breken extended his arm out to Daniel, who tried hard to hide his contempt. "Same to you, my lord," Daniel said as cordially as possible.

He extended his injured arm towards Breken, who gripped Daniel hard at the wrist and pulled him slightly forward. "See you out there, Mutt," he sneered in a low voice only Daniel could hear. Breken's grip on Daniel's wrist tightened, sending a rippling sensation up Daniel's arm; and though his wrist began throbbing with pain, he stood strong, doing his best to contain the ache he felt. Breken smirked once more, then walked away, chuckling.

"Shit." Daniel mumbled under his breath. He only had so long to prepare himself for the final event and it was obvious Breken would take full advantage of his injury. He marched back to his tent, ignoring all other 'congratulations' along the way. Anger and humiliation coursed through him. He whipped through the canvas door, pushed over a weapons rack, swept his small table clear of all its contents, then all but threw himself down onto a chair.

He huffed and cursed under his breath as he unlaced the bracer around his injured wrist. With his wrist finally free of the compression the bracer had given, it pulsed with pain. Not long after, it began to swell and color. Gritting his teeth, Daniel slowly opened and closed his fist, trying hard to stretch and exercise his aching muscles. In a fit of frustration, he slammed his fist down onto the table, which he realized instantly had been a mistake. He grunted loudly at the impact, then pulled his fist to his forehead, taking deep, angry breaths, till the sudden pain ebbed. The canvas flap fluttered behind him and he swiftly stood, hiding his injured arm behind his back.

Sir William glanced around the tent and seemed to note the overturned weapons rack, as well as the mess on the floor. Then he looked back at Daniel, who refused to meet his eye.

"A minor storm seems to have burst through your tent," Sir William said in a disapproving tone. Daniel remained silent.

"I'm surprised you're not strutting about the grounds, continuing your parade of tricks..."

Daniel's shoulders sank at the accusation, but his fists clenched.

"What are my most important rules of combat, Daniel?"

"Honor, humility, mercy," he mumbled to his mentor.

Sir William stepped forward, trying hard to contain his own anger. "*Like a man, Daniel*," he growled.

Daniel lifted his fiery gaze to meet Sir William's. "Honor. Humility. Mercy. *My Lord*."

The knight's nostrils flared, and his mouth formed a hard line, but Daniel refused to back down. Sir William shook his head at his young ward's show of disrespect, then sighed as he rubbed the back of his neck.

"The best way to see the measure of a man is to watch him fight," Sir William said, as he paced back and forth in front of Daniel. "Does he prance and preen? Boast or taunt? Does he take cheap shots or show unnecessary brutality?" he paused in front of Daniel. "Or does he show respect for the life before him? Is he humble and gracious? Is he honorable enough to show mercy when required?"

Daniel's temper softened as the knight continued his lecture, knowing his own foolishness may have very well cost him his victory.

"You are more skilled than every other boy that I saw compete in this tournament." Sir William admitted, surprising

Daniel. "But I hoped you would be a better man than them, too."

Sir William's words were like a knife to Daniel's heart; he lowered his head once more in shame.

"Now, let's see that wrist…"

Knowing the sight of the injury would only fuel the knight's disappointment further, Daniel took a step back.

"Daniel." Sir William warned.

Daniel slowly lifted his hand towards Sir William, who shook his head as he observed the injury.

"Grasp my hand as tight as you can," he instructed. Daniel obeyed.

"Good. Now, advance." Daniel pressed forward, gritting his teeth, as Sir William doled out more commands. "Retreat. Lunge. Guard. Slope. Shed. Fade. Advance."

He obeyed each command with sharp, concise movements, treating Sir William's hand as his hilt and his arm as his blade. Over and over they repeated these steps, and the more commands Sir William gave, the less Daniel focused on his pain.

"Good." Sir William said, halting the exercise. He reached down and grabbed two training swords from the jumbled pile of weapons and tossed one at Daniel.

"Now, block."

The knight swung down hard, and Daniel barely had time to raise his sword to block the blow. Sir William pressed harder and harder, waiting for Daniel to give in. Daniel put his other hand on the blade to support himself, and as he tried to push back, pain rippled once more up his right arm.

"Don't think about it. Breathe Daniel," Sir William ordered. "Push me back!"

Daniel took a deep breath in and pushed with all his might, until finally the knight stumbled back, giving Daniel a small smirk. Daniel raised his head with confidence, spun the training sword in his injured hand, and, returning the knight's smirk, assumed his stance.

"There's the Daniel I know," Sir William beamed. Daniel relaxed his stance, pointed the blade of the training sword toward the ground, and fidgeted with the pommel.

"I guess I got a little carried away."

"And paid the price for it," Sir William said, pointing to Daniel's wrist with his sword.

Daniel rubbed the back of his neck, unsure of what to say next.

"Come, let's get this properly cared for."

Sir William tossed his training sword aside, pulled another chair up, and sat across from Daniel. From a small satchel, the knight pulled a jar of salve, a long strip of cloth, and a thin wooden splint with a curved end.

Sir William lifted Daniel's hand and surveyed the injury once more. "Well, it's not broken."

Daniel let out a small sigh of relief.

"But I can't imagine going a round or two against Rollin Breken is going to help it."

Daniel wilted. "I thought as much."

Sir William rubbed the salve over the swollen area on Daniel's wrist, then paused. "The splint will help keep it still, but you'll have a hell of a time using your sword."

Sir William eyed his ward carefully, and waited for his response. Daniel took a deep breath. If he was going to have any chance of beating Breken now, he'd need as much movement as his wrist would allow. "Leave it off."

Sir William chuckled at his response, but nodded in agreement. He wrapped the strip of cloth around Daniel's hand, down his wrist, and back up again, securing it with a small, flat knot. Then, he strapped the bracer tightly back onto his forearm, making sure he'd have the support he needed.

"How's that feel? Range of motion alright?"

Daniel twisted and turned his wrist; opened and closed his hand; and tested his grip on the training sword he hadn't yet put down.

"It'll do," Daniel smirked. Sir William chuckled at his cheek, then stood, placed a heavy hand on Daniel's shoulder, and gave him a pointed look.

"Be *better*."

"Yes, my Lord."

Sir William ruffled Daniel's hair, making him chuckle. Then, placed his hand on the side of Daniel's neck. "And remember... Win or lose... yeah?"

A small smile crept across Daniel's face, and he nodded, understanding the sentiment behind the statement. The knight patted the side of Daniel's neck, but as he turned to leave, he noticed a bit of cloth protruding from Daniel's vest. The familiar design intrigued him, and he pulled on it.

"Wait-" Daniel began, but it was too late to stop the knight. Sir William inspected the token, then chuckled.

"That's some pretty fancy stitching," he said with a raised brow. Daniel snatched the cloth from his hands and tucked it back into his vest, making Sir William chuckle even more.

"It was a gift!"

"From who, I wonder."

"A friend."

"Must be an excellent *friend*... If I'm not mistaken, I Believe *my niece* had been working on a similar design just the other day."

Sir William smirked at him, but Daniel ignored his taunt and began to straighten up the mess he made. Sir William chuckled, patted him on the shoulder, and left him in peace. The brief interaction with the knight had lifted his spirits and renewed his determination; though, when Daniel emerged from his tent, the sight before him left his stomach in knots all over again.

By the steps of the bleachers, he saw Kat and Rollin Breken, closer than he would have liked. Daniel tried to get a better view, but didn't want to risk getting too close. He watched on as Breken pulled a rose from behind his back and presented it to the princess. Even from where he stood, Daniel could see the effect Breken's flattery had on her. He reached out his hand to hers, then left a small kiss against her knuckles, causing Kat to blush a deep pink, just before scampering up the steps. Daniel felt like an iron ball had dropped in the pit of his stomach when he saw her glance back towards Breken and giggle. Breken stood tall and triumphant, but no sooner did the princess disappear; he turned and cast his eye elsewhere. Anger flared once more in Daniel, and he marched through the crowds till he came face to face with Breken.

"Stay away from her," Daniel sneered. Breken chortled as Daniel put himself between the young Lord and the stairs that led to the princess. Breken scoffed slightly, then took note of where Daniel stood.

"How sweet, the mutt has a crush on the Princess," he laughed harder still.

Daniel's fists clenched, and before he could stop himself, he pushed Breken hard, causing him to stumble back. Breken's amused expression turned deathly cold, and he marched hard towards Daniel, stopping mere inches from his face.

"Listen here, you little shit," Breken began in a dangerously quiet voice. "No one tells me what to do. Certainly not some rag dog wannabe... And after I beat your ass to the ground, your pretty little princess will have no choice but to entertain me. Gods know *I* could certainly *entertain* her... for a while at least." Rollin Breken winked, and Daniel saw red.

He lunged hard at Breken, who had already braced for the impact. They began pushing and swinging at each other as hard as they could. Once Daniel got a decent punch in, it took three full grown knights to separate them. Breken spit out a bit of blood, then wiped his mouth. "I'm going to kill you, mutt!" he yelled, fighting against the men that restrained him. Daniel lunged forward, but a solitary voice halted him.

"Daniel!" Sir William barked.

Breken smirked, then howled like a dog as another knight urged him away. Daniel's nostrils flared with rage. Sir William put a hand on his shoulder, but Daniel shook it off, twisting away from him. As Sir William went to pursue him, the warning bell for the final match rang out above them. Daniel groaned, then marched towards the gate.

He couldn't recall a time he'd ever been this angry, and it was a thought that only drove his wrath harder. As he paced back and forth in front of the gate, like a taunted bull itching to be released, he could hear the vague sound of Sir William's voice warning him not to let anger lead him, and to enter the fight with a clear mind; but the idea of doing that seemed impossible. Breken had disrespected him, and the Princess, and Daniel could not, *would not,* stand for it.

Daniel and Breken were called forward and introduced to the crowd once more. As Daniel looked up into the stands, he saw Jerren give him a confident nod. His mother smiled proudly at him, and beside her, his brothers cheered loudly. The love and support they were giving him had almost been enough to blink him out of his blind rage, until his eyes fell on Kat, who was smiling as she smelt the rose *he* had given her.

Sir Cardon released Daniel and Breken to choose their first weapon, they turned to face each other, and at the sound of a horn, the match was under way. They circled the perimeter, each waiting for the other to make the first move. Breken's eyes lifted to the stands above Daniel's head, then back to Daniel, and he smirked.

Daniel lunged forward, but Breken blocked him. He winked, and Daniel lunged at him once more. Again and again, Daniel advanced, swinging as hard and as fast as he could. Breken sneered and blocked each blow, only fueling Daniel's frustration. Daniel swung hard at Breken's side, but he ducked, and with a sweeping kick sent Daniel to the ground. Before he could even try to get up, Breken was on top of him with his blade to his throat; and so the first round and point went to Breken.

Daniel marched back to his starting station, where Sir William stood just behind the gate and called him over before the next round began.

"You've got to calm down! You're playing right into his hand. Whatever happened before, forget it. Take a deep breath, and clear your mind."

Daniel had wasted too much energy in the first round, and he knew Sir William was right. He closed his eyes and took a deep, calming breath. The shouting of the surrounding crowd faded into muffled noise until finally it was silent. All he could hear was the sound of his heart beating too fast. He took another deep breath, and the beats slowed.

A horn blew, signaling the start of the second round, and this time Daniel would not fall into Breken's trap. He planted his feet firmly on the ground, lifted his sword so that the blade was flush with his face, and inhaled. He could hear Breken's advancing footsteps, yet kept his back turned. Breken lifted his sword above his head and just as he swung down to strike, Daniel dodged the blow, sending Breken stumbling forward.

The crowd cheered, and just as he had in the tent with Sir William, Daniel spun his sword in his hand, and readied himself for the next strike, only this time it was *he* who wore the smirk.

Daniel moved quickly and seamlessly. He blocked and advanced at just the right moments. He matched Breken blow for blow and refused to let up. Finally, Breken stumbled back, and Daniel seized his opportunity. He spun hard into his opponent, and in one fluid movement, captured his sword and sent him to the ground.

Second point, Daniel.

From the stands he heard monstrous cheers, and as they rallied back to their corners, Sir William shook Daniel's shoulders proudly.

"That's my boy!" He roared.

A wave of pride coursed through Daniel, and he knew victory was within his reach; he couldn't let it pass him by.

The final horn blew, and the determining round began. The boys circled the perimeter of the enclosure once more. Two hungry predators stalking their prey. Breken lunged first, but Daniel fortified himself. Daniel had blocked the blade, only for Breken to spin around and elbow him hard just below his ribs. He grunted and stumbled slightly back, but regained his composure quickly. He advanced, nearly catching Breken's arm, but he moved too quickly.

Again they went around, and again they took turns lunging at one another. Breken would swing, and Daniel would pivot. Daniel would slash and Breken would spin. Back and forth they went until suddenly there was a clash. Daniel blocked a half attempted swing at his torso, and a battle of wills ensued. Their swords locked in a cross, and neither boy would dream of backing down. They pushed harder and harder, until they heard a crack.

Seizing his moment, Daniel pushed back, then swung hard at his opponent's blade, which broke into several pieces on impact. Daniel raised his sword to Breken's throat, but just before the referee called the match, Breken spun hard into Daniel, grabbed his injured arm and slammed the pummel of his broken sword down on Daniel's wrist. Daniel cried out in pain, as Breken twisted the injured arm, securing it behind Daniel's back.

Breken's grip on Daniel's wrist tightened, making Daniel's grip on his sword weaken, until finally it fell from his hand. Daniel was completely at the mercy of Rollin Breken, who pulled Daniel's arm back until he heard a pop. To add insult to injury, Breken lifted the broken blade to Daniel's throat, then swiped it across the corner of his jaw, leaving a deep cut.

Sir Cardon named Rollin Breken champion of the tournament, as Daniel sulked towards the healer's tower, with a swollen wrist, a dislocated shoulder, and a cut that was sure to leave a scar.

How to Say Goodbye

"I just hope Daniel is alright… I didn't see him at all after the tournament, and before I even get the chance to speak to him, he's off on another errand… I'm a little worried about him." Kat admitted to her partner as they strolled through the gardens.

"As am I, Princess. I felt awful about how banged up he got during our match… Gods know tournaments can get rough," Rollin Breken said with a certain glint in his eye. "I just wish there was something I could do to make it up to him."

The sincerity in young Lord Breken's voice warmed Kat's heart, as had the time she had spent with him since he won the tournament. It would be a lie to say that she hadn't enjoyed the attention he showed her. He was handsome and charming; witty and clever; but it was the freedom to do and say as he pleased that intrigued Kat most of all.

"Princess Katiana, how lucky to have stumbled across you here," Sir William said, appearing out of thin air. His sudden appearance startled both Kat and Rollin Breken, though that had been his plan.

"Is everything alright, Uncle?" Kat asked, concerned.

"Of course! But I believe Mara was looking for you… something about a dress fitting."

"Oh gods! I'd forgotten! Please forgive me, Rollin, but I'm afraid I must leave you," Kat said in a fluster.

"No trouble at all, Princess," he said with a suave smile. "Our time apart will only give me more time to miss you."

Breken winked flirtatiously at Kat, who let out a girlish giggle; and while Kat seemed smitten with the young lord, Sir William remained vastly unimpressed. Daniel's attitude towards Breken alone would've been enough for Sir William to form an unfavorable opinion, but after the stunt the young lord had pulled at the tournament and the slimy scene he had just witnessed, he was determined to keep Breken well away from his niece. He could see Rollin Breken for exactly who he was, even if Kat couldn't.

"Lord Breken, may I have a word?" Sir William asked, stepping forward to obscure Breken's view of the princess.

"Of course. I'm never too busy for an audience with a man such as yourself," Breken cooed. His words sounded sincere enough, though Sir William could see the coldness in his eyes as he spoke.

"Forgive me if I'm out of turn, but I wonder what an experienced, well groomed, young man, *such as yourself*, means by spending so much time with a girl my niece's age? She seems rather young for you."

Breken smirked at Sir William's comment, but remained cordial. "Forgive me, my Lord, but I'm afraid you misrepresent your niece in a most unflattering manner. *She's a young woman.* One who is soon to hold her first suitors feast, and as a *well groomed*, *experienced*, *young man*, I would be a fool not to want such a beautiful prize... and as far as ages go, I'm not much older than that ward of yours, I wonder if you've had a similar conversation with *him*."

Sir William kept a straight face at the attempted jab towards Daniel, though his blood pressure rose slightly. "As you say... But I wonder if you are entirely suitable for the princess."

"And why is that?" Breken asked, though it was obvious he did not care to know the answer; his indifference on the matter only furthered Sir William's disdain towards him. "If I may be candid, I believe you lack certain qualities that a man by her side ought to possess."

"What qualities would those be, *my Lord*? Dark hair, blue eyes, and a shambled estate?" Breken quipped. Sir William's fists clenched with anger at the boy's impertinence. "No, *my Lord*. Qualities such as humility, kindness, respect, integrity, *intelligence*, and *honor*."

Breken's smirk dissipated, and his jaw clenched. "I have to disagree, *Sir*... Though, I can see now where Enid's backwards ideas of strength come from. Maybe if he had a better teacher, he would've stood a chance against me."

Sir William took an assertive step forward, and glared hard, allowing his presence to loom over the arrogant youth. His anger was too hot, and he could no longer contain it. "I will say this one time, *boy*. As long as I live, *you* will go nowhere near Princess Katiana… Are we clear?"

"Unequivocally, *old man*… But who, I wonder, will stop *her* from coming near me?" Breken sneered.

Sir William and Rollin Breken stood locked in a staring contest, knowing if looks could kill, neither would survive. The only thing that had saved them was the interruption of a steward.

"Sir William."

"What?!" he barked, turning to face the voice.

"Pardon me, my lord. Lord Greggory has requested to be taken on a hunt."

Sir William groaned.

"I'll be right there. Thank you," he replied, dismissing the steward.

"Lord Breken, you are more than welcome to join as well," the steward said. Sir William shot Breken a warning look, one that told him he had better refuse; Breken, though, smirked, and it was clear he had every intention of ignoring the not so subtle hint. "Count me in."

Sir William flared his nostrils and walked away before he ended up doing something he may later come to regret. He walked the grounds, attempting to cool his temper, and caught sight of Daniel delivering yet another load of freshly cut wood to the kitchens.

"You ought to rest that wrist and shoulder... They haven't properly healed yet," he said with a pointed look.

Daniel could hear the displeasure in the knight's reproach, but gave him a sheepish shrug. "Just trying to help as much as I can..."

Sir William sighed. The pride he had in Daniel restored his good humor instantly, he laughed and shook his head. "You've been working hard these last few days. When's the last time you took a break?"

Daniel said nothing as he rubbed the back of his head, answering Sir William's question.

"Sir Greggory requested a hunting trip... But I think we can manage with one less... Take a day to relax and enjoy the festival."

"But my Lord..."

"Daniel, go have some fun. You've earned it... Why don't you go rescue my niece and nephew from whatever dull gathering they've found themselves in, and take a trip into the village?"

Daniel's face lit up at the idea. "Truly, my Lord?"

Sir William chuckled once more at Daniel's obvious excitement. Truthfully, the only highlight of the hunting trip would have been having Daniel along with him, but Sir William knew Daniel's days of careless frivolity were numbered, and wanted to give him as many chances as he could to enjoy them. "Go on," he urged. "Just try to stay out of trouble!" he called after Daniel, who had already begun to race towards the keep. Daniel looked over his shoulder and offered the knight a mischievous smile as he disappeared into the main hall.

When Daniel met up with the Scarborough children, Jerren was more than grateful for the rescue, though Kat, for whatever reason, and much to Daniel's dismay, stayed behind. He tried to hide his disappointment, and settled on the fact that one Scarborough was better than none. Once the boys reached the center of town, though, the minor setback had been all but forgotten.

The whole village was alive. Shops were full to the brim, the square hosted all kinds of vendors, and a few side streets had stages set up for various performances; every other block held some kind of competition, and it seemed as though the whole country had come to Eraduun to celebrate.

It was still early in the day, but there was so much to do. The boys tried their hand at a few of the games, and some vendors asked Jerren to judge different competitions. They tasted new foods, and drinks, and even caught a couple of shows. A little after noon, they stopped at the inn for a quick lunch, where they took Declan and Archer off the hands of Daniel's exhausted mother and pregnant aunt. They took the boys all around; bought them too many sweets; and even picked up a few gifts and trinkets along the way.

It was just after dusk by the time Daniel and Jerren slumped back to the castle, but their spirits were high; it had almost been the perfect day. They had just made it to the main hall when a commotion in the courtyard caught their attention. "Bit early for a brawl, isn't it?" Jerren laughed. They turned around to investigate, and were horrified by what they found.

The small hunting party Sir William had organized had returned in an uproar. Daniel and Jerren were shocked to see a majority of its members covered in blood, some obviously their own, others it wasn't quite clear. Several of them began shouting orders to squires and castle guards to fetch healers for the wounded.

Daniel searched for Sir William amongst the chaos, thinking it was rather odd he wouldn't be at the forefront of the party; but when he found no sign of him, a sinking feeling grew in his gut. He scanned the courtyard once more, and his attention was suddenly pulled toward the game cart, where he could see nothing but a pair of boots extending outward. The hairs on the back of his neck prickled, and fear gripped his heart as he watched blood trickle through the wooden planks of the cart. Daniel glanced over to Jerren and found his instincts seemed to be conveying a similar message. In a synchronized motion, the boys rushed towards the cart, only to be pushed back by several very somber looking members of the hunting party.

"Daniel. Your Majesty, please," one man said, halting them. The pained look on the man's face only confirmed their suspicions.

"Make way for the healers!" someone called. The path cleared, and the boys seized their opportunity. They rushed to the cart, and to their horror discovered it didn't hold just any man, but a mess of blood, and the mangled frame of a hardly breathing Sir William.

Jerren took one glance and had to turn away. Daniel, however, stood frozen in time with his eyes locked on Sir William's. Tears sprang to the knight's eyes as he reached out to Daniel as well as he was able; he opened his mouth to say something, but only blood sputtered out. Before Daniel could even react, the gathering crowd pushed him out of the way.

"What happened?" the head healer asked.

"One of the young lords wandered too far from the party and found himself face to face with a starving family of bears... Had Will not been there, the beasts would have torn the boy to shreds."

The head healer quickly doled out instructions and Sir William was rushed into the tower. Jerren followed the cart, but Daniel was in shock. Everything seemed to slow down around him. He couldn't move, he couldn't breathe, and the world around him seemed to muffle and blur. He had a hazed vision of Jerren calling his name, and Kat running into the courtyard, but he couldn't make sense of it. At some point, he just turned away from it all.

He meandered through the chaos, not sure which way he was going, and walked aimlessly until he found himself at the base of the old western tower. He turned around, and his focus was pulled to the lights of the healer's tower that twinkled in the distance. The constant movement within, told him the healers were working tirelessly. He stared at the dancing shadows for what seemed like an eternity, but then, they stopped, and everything was still; One by one, the shadows disappeared, telling him all he needed to know.

From the top of the tower, the healers unfurled a black banner, a sign that there had been a death in the castle. Seconds later, another black banner was released; this one had silver and gold trim, and as the bottom of the banner unrolled, the silhouette of a silver wolf baying at a golden crescent moon appeared.

Daniel reached down, grabbed a stone, and hurled it at the old tower, releasing a painful but cathartic howl from deep within. He fell to his knees and tears flowed from his eyes. He looked up at the old tower, and a flood of memories came to life. Memories of him and Jerren climbing up it, using it for target practice, or just training in its shade. Memories of him and Kat chasing each other around the base while having a picnic, then laying and watching clouds disappear behind its thick walls. Each memory that flowed into his mind included Sir William. The man who had taken him in, the man that had cared for him and taught him everything he knew; the man who had become a second father to him... *Now he was gone, too.*

Tidal waves of anger and sadness overcame Daniel as he tried, and failed, to make sense of everything. He stood, picked up another stone and threw it at the tower. Then another, even harder, then another and another; releasing all of his pain into each throw. He walked closer to the tower, as hot tears streamed down his cheeks, and blurred his vision. He continued the assault until he was out of stones, and his shoulder ached. Still not content with the attack, he punched the old stone, then finally surrendered to his grief and slumped to the ground. He covered his face and let out another pained cry, though it was not entirely for his now aching hand.

After some time, Daniel's tumultuous emotions subsided, leaving him feeling hollow. He sat at the base of the tower and stared into the sky, feeling as though the heavens themselves would crash down on him at any moment. It was dark and cool, and the stars had begun to glow. A soft melody of a mourning tune drifted on the wind from the village, and from the distant north, he could hear the howl of a lone wolf echo across the sky; Daniel imagined the wolf was calling out for Sir William, and the thought made his chest ache. He wiped his tear stained cheek against his shoulder, then returned his gaze to the sky. He closed his eyes to stop another bout of tears from falling, when a sound from the other side of the tower caught his attention.

The clank of wood against stone rang out again and again; the reverberation of the assault was all too familiar, and Daniel knew whoever had instigated the attack had been hurting the same way he was. He stood quickly, and snuck around the base of the tower hoping to catch sight of its aggressor. A light sob broke through the darkness, and Daniel stopped in his tracks. He contemplated turning back, not wanting to intrude on anyone else's grief, but curiosity got the better of him. Carefully, he peered around a large column, and with the light of a full moon shining overhead, he could make out the slender frame of a woman. But it wasn't any woman, *it was Kat.*

The Princess stood at the base of the tower, hacking away at it with an old training sword. Daniel hid himself behind the column, pressing his body into the stone, hoping she hadn't seen him. He rapped the back of his head against the column, feeling incredibly stupid and selfish; he hadn't given Kat, or Jerren, a second thought. As much as Sir William meant to him, *they* were his actual family.

The clanking of the training sword finally ceased, and Daniel could hear the soft sobs much clearer. "Oh Kat," he sighed. He stole a glance at her, but as he shifted his weight to look around, a bit of stone from the column crumbled, giving away his position.

"Who's there?!" Kat ordered, wiping her face and raising the wooden sword. Daniel lowered his head, frustrated with himself.

"I know you're there! Come out!"

Daniel crept out from his not so secret hiding spot, with his hands up in surrender. "It's just me..."

He knew Kat never wanted to be perceived as vulnerable; she didn't cry in front of anyone, if she could help it, anymore at least. He thought maybe seeing him may comfort her somehow, or at the very least allow her to lower her guard, but his presence seemed to have the opposite effect. Kat's eyes burned with anger, and her grip on the sword tightened.

"Kat, it's me, Daniel," he said, thinking maybe she couldn't see him in the faded light.

"What do you want? Why are you here? Go away! I don't want to see you!"

Kat's brusque rejection filled Daniel with unexplainable anger. Everything was still too fresh, and his emotions were not his own. *Why was she being so hateful? Didn't she know how much he was hurting too?*

"What's your problem?" he spat back.

"You! *You* are my problem!" She screeched.

"Listen here, you spoiled little brat!"

Daniel took a heated step forward, narrowly dodging the training sword that was flung deliberately at his head. He looked back at the sword in shock, only to turn just in time to catch the flying fists of the angry Princess.

"You should've been there! Why weren't you there?" Kat screamed at him, trying to hit anywhere she could. Daniel caught her by the wrists, but struggled to hold back her assault. "Kat, stop!" he yelled. "Kat!"

He shook her slightly until she stopped fighting, and her eyes met his. Her green eyes sparkled in the moonlight beneath the film of tears that coated them, and the longer he stared into them, the easier it was to see her fiery expression melt into unbridled grief.

"He was asking for you! You were supposed to be there..." Kat said, releasing a strained sob. His heart dropped. "I'm sorry..." he choked out, pulling Kat into a tight embrace. She gave in immediately, collapsing into him. Guilt spread through Daniel as though it had been seared into his blood, and he held onto the princess feeling like if he let go, he might just crumble into nothing. He stroked her hair and tried to calm her as she sobbed into his chest; hoping if he focused on her grief, he could bury his own. "I'm so sorry Princess... I'm here," he whispered, kissing the top of her head. "It's going to be alright, Kitty Kat."

Daniel sighed, hoping his sympathy, and compassion would be enough to soothe her, but before he knew what was happening, Kat had pushed him to the ground and struck him hard several times.

"Don't call me that!" she yelled, desperately trying to break through the faceshield Daniel's forearms formed. "Don't you ever call me that!"

Kat fought hard, and though Daniel was trying his best to get her off of him, he didn't want to risk hurting her.

Then suddenly, as if through an answered prayer, an outside force lifted her off of him. "Kat! Stop!" Jerren called over his sister's wild screeches. He wrapped his arms around hers and lifted so that only the tips of her toes were touching the ground.

"Let go of me, Jerren!"

"I will- when you- st-"

Kat slammed her elbow into Jerren's ribs, forcing him to release her, then ran off towards the castle. Daniel sighed, feeling half relieved, half defeated, and let his body sink against the cold ground.

"Are you alright?" Jerren asked, extending a hand out to Daniel.

"Are you?" he asked, noticing Jerren wince as he helped lift him from the ground.

"I'm swell," the prince replied, rubbing where his sister elbowed him. The two boys stood in silence for a minute, watching as Kat disappeared into the distance.

"I'm sorry I wasn't- I mean I didn't-" Daniel began, not even sure what he was trying to say, or how to finish it. Jerren let out a soft snort, and put a hand on his shoulder. "I get it. You have nothing to apologize for... It was for the best that you weren't there... He wouldn't want you to remember him that way."

The haunted look on Jerren's face told him the scene had been horrific, and though it was a nice thing to say, it was too little, too late. There was already a vision of Sir William's maimed body etched eternally into Daniel's mind.

"I should've gone with him," Daniel said, lowering his head in shame. "I was *supposed* to go with him..."

"Don't."

Daniel lifted his eyes to the prince, stunned by his harsh tone.

"Don't sit there and beat yourself up thinking you could've changed anything that happened."

Daniel shrugged, feeling as though his friend was wrong; he could have changed it, *he should have*.

Jerren knew exactly what Daniel was thinking, and frankly it pissed him off. He glared hard at Daniel, then shoved him, nearly sending back to the ground.

"What the hell?!"

"I said... Don't." Jerren demanded. "All that would've happened is you would've gotten yourself killed too... and then where would we be?" The thought was heartbreaking enough that Jerren had to turn away to wipe a stray tear from his cheek.

"Jer, I-" Daniel said, taking a step forward to console his friend.

"Just... don't do that," the prince said softer. "You don't deserve that kind of guilt and he wouldn't want that for you either."

Daniel thought maybe Jerren had a point, and knew nothing else needed to be said on the subject, though it didn't erase how he felt. "You didn't have to get all deep on me..."

Daniel waved an imaginary flag of surrender, trying to lighten the mood, and to his surprise it worked. Jerren chuckled, and then tilted his head towards the keep. Daniel nodded in agreement, and together, he and the prince began their slow stroll back to the castle.

"She got you good," Jerren said, pointing towards Daniel's lip.

Daniel raised a brow, then lifted his hand to a surprisingly tender lower lip. When he pulled his fingers away, he was surprised to find a decent amount of blood on them. "Yeah, I guess she did... Kent's got nothing on her right hook."

"Don't worry, I won't tell anyone you got beat up by the Princess," Jerren teased.

Daniel smiled a little and shook his head. It appeared Jerren had developed a similar comedic coping mechanism for grief, and a part of Daniel was grateful for that. "Thanks buddy, I appreciate that," he said, knowing Jerren was also full of shit, and wasn't likely to let him live it down, *ever*.

"What'd you do, anyway?"

Daniel sighed heavily. "I called her Kitty Kat."

"HA! You are stupid, aren't you?"

"Evidently."

Jerren shook his head, a little amused. "I know an excellent cure for that."

"No you don't."

"I meant the lip, and the hand you obviously smashed on a rock, you jackass."

Daniel gave him a rather pathetic smile, then swung his arm to rest on his friend's shoulder. "My apologies, your Highness. I wasn't sure what ailment you were referring to," he quipped. "By the way... Did you know about your sister's superhuman strength?"

"I do now.." Jerren said, rubbing his still throbbing ribs.

"She threw a training sword at my head."

"Oh..." Jerren said, realizing something. "Uncle Will..." he sighed. "Father finally agreed to let her train with a sword, and uncle Will is-" he stopped himself. "... *was* teaching her."

"Oh," Daniel said sadly. Jerren nodded, then let out a small laugh. "Do you remember when we first started training? I couldn't lift my arms above my shoulders for two weeks!"

Daniel chuckled.

"You can't swing a sword if you can't hold it straight!" the boys said in unison, sharing a small, sad laugh. The memory was enough to send them each into their own cluster of thoughts, and they remained silent the rest of the way back.

When the boys entered the main hall, a hush fell across the room and all eyes were on them. Jerren grabbed two goblets of wine, handed one to Daniel, and raised the other. "To Sir William Henery!"

The whole of the hall echoed the name and together they toasted Sir William. After that, the indistinct murmur of the hall continued. Jerren turned around and nodded to Daniel. They grabbed a few provisions, the most important of which being two full pitchers of wine, and snuck away unnoticed. Not thinking, Daniel instantly scanned the crowd for Sir William to give him 'the nod' that said they were leaving. He sighed in frustration at his mistake and followed closely behind Jerren.

As per their little tradition, the boys stood outside Sir William's chamber door. They stared at the door in silence, both wanting to go in, but neither willing to.

"My room?" Daniel suggested, and the prince nodded in agreement. Daniel placed what provisions he had on a nearby table, and immediately began to clean his wounds, as Jerren downed several cups of wine. "I don't think this is going to last us as long as we had hoped," the prince said, nearly halfway through one pitcher. Daniel chuckled slightly and shook his head.

The mood in the room changed perpetually. One minute they'd laugh about a time Sir William had scolded them for doing something ridiculous; and before they knew it, they'd be secretly wiping away tears. Then, they'd sit in jarring silence, trying to wrap their heads around what they had just lost. The cycle continued on for hours until Jerren finally broke it. "Come on," he said, getting up from his place on the windowsill.

Daniel gave him a quizzical look as he crossed the room. He looked out the window to see it was obviously very late, or maybe very early. "What are you doing?"

"*We* have somewhere to be."

Jerren's response perplexed Daniel, but he followed along anyway. "Where are we going?" Daniel asked in a hushed voice, not wanting to disturb the sleeping castle. They arrived at Jerren's chambers, but to Daniel's surprise, Jerren walked further down the hall towards Kat's bedroom. As they drew nearer, Daniel noticed her door was slightly ajar and there was still light coming from inside. Jerren smiled sadly, then approached the door, only to have Daniel quickly pull him back.

"I don't think I should be here…"

Jerren rolled his eyes and pulled forcefully on Daniel's shirt. "Just come on, you big baby," he whispered, approaching her door once more. He knocked lightly and poked his head in.

Kat was leaning against her balcony door, looking out at the night sky, and hugging one of her pillows. Still awake, and still crying. When she turned to find her brother in the doorway, she didn't seem surprised in the slightest, but instead looked at him with grateful eyes. The corner of his mouth raised slightly, and he shrugged.

"I hope you don't mind… I brought some company." Jerren opened the door a little more to reveal a hesitant looking Daniel. Daniel was too embarrassed to meet the princess's gaze, and so kept his eyes low. Jerren, on the other hand, walked in as casually as possible, sat on the sofa next to the balcony door, then waited for his sister to sit beside him. When she refused to move, he pulled on her arm until she gave a weak smile, and sat next to him, giving in to his silent demand. He held out his hand expectantly, and she instantly took it. He nudged her slightly with his elbow, then leaned back on his free arm, propped his legs up and closed his eyes.

Daniel watched the display carefully, unsure of what he should do, or if he should even be there. Even after what happened between them earlier that night, he wanted nothing more than to curl up next to Kat, hold her and tell her everything was going to be okay, but he knew it wasn't his place.

He looked from Jerren, who could have easily been asleep, to Kat, who looked… *empty*. He couldn't just walk away, but how could he stay? "I'm so sorry about earlier," Daniel said, hoping that his words carried at least some significance.

"Shut up and come sit," Jerren demanded. Daniel rubbed the back of his neck weighing his options. *This was not his moment.* He turned to walk away, but to his surprise, Kat called out to him. "Please stay," she said, in a delicate voice.

Daniel looked back to see fresh tears streaming down her cheeks and his heart broke all over again. Unable to refuse her plea, he sighed, then slowly crossed the room and sat down on the other side of her.

The room was silent. They didn't speak, or move, or even glance at one another. The only sounds that could be heard were the crackling of a fire, the wisp of the wind, and an occasional sniffle from Kat. Between the stillness of the room, and the heavy toll the day had placed on him, Daniel caught himself drifting in and out of consciousness, until the lightest touch on his hand caused him to jump.

"I'm sorry," Kat whispered, a little embarrassed she had startled him. Daniel turned his body to face her; her eyes, cheeks and nose were red and blotchy from crying all evening and her hair was frizzy, but Daniel still thought she looked beautiful.

He took a breath, like he was going to say something, but Kat shook her head, stopping him. She took the pillow she had been hugging and propped it up on the back of the sofa, just behind his head, and lightly patted it with her free hand, telling Daniel to lie back. He gave her a weary look, but then hesitantly obeyed.

"I'm sorry about earlier, too." Kat whispered

Daniel sat up quickly and shook his head. "You have nothing to apologize for…" he said, wiping a tear from her cheek. Kat leaned into his hand, and his pulse quickened. A moment later, her eyes lifted to him. "You look tired…"

Daniel shrugged, finally lowering his hand from her cheek. Kat reached out, intertwining her fingers with his, then pulled slightly, so that he laid back once more.

In the darkness of the early morning, green and blue eyes locked on one another; full of pain and heartbreak, but also so much more. Daniel sighed and gave his princess a sad smile. Kat returned the weak smile, then rested her head against his shoulder. Slowly, Daniel brought her hand to his lips, lightly kissed it, then placed it on his chest. Kat sighed then softly nuzzled into his shoulder, letting Daniel rest his head against hers, and before long they both drifted to sleep.

Legacies

Daniel woke just before sunrise, feeling stiff and a little cold. He pried his eyes open, and it took him a moment to realize where he was, as he blinked rapidly, trying to filter the growing daylight into his eyes. He needed to stretch his muscles, but when he realized Kat was fast asleep on his shoulder with her right arm wrapped around his own, he didn't dare move. The image of the princess's tear-stained face hours before flooded Daniel's mind. She had looked hopeless, and distraught then; but *here*, cuddled next to him, she looked peaceful, carefree, and more beautiful than he had dared to realize.

A few loose strands of hair cascaded across her face, and hoping to get a better view, Daniel carefully tucked them behind her ear, and as he lowered his hand, he couldn't help but let his thumb brush against her cheek.

"I saw that," Jerren murmured, making Daniel jump. Jerren opened his right eye just enough to see Daniel's aggravated expression; he chuckled to himself, then closed it again. Daniel carefully took the pillow out from behind his head and gave his friend an easy thump across the face. Kat stirred at the movement, and the boys held their breath, hoping they had not completely woken her.

Without opening her eyes, Kat snuggled a bit more into Daniel so that her head was in the crook of his neck. She pulled her hand from where it laid near Jerren and slid it up to rest on Daniel's chest; Daniel froze. Her breath was warm against his neck, and his heart raced as his face filled with color. Kat muttered something sleepily, then sighed, catching the boys off guard once again. The only word either of them could make out was a name. *'Daniel.'* Daniel's eyes grew large, and his breath caught in his throat.

"I guess next time I'll just send you," Jerren snorted, unable to contain his amusement at the situation. Daniel shot him a warning look, and Kat's eyes fluttered open.

"Good morning Princess," Daniel half stuttered. Kat pulled away quickly, realizing just how close she had been to him. She sat up straight, and attempted to tidy herself, all the while desperately trying to hide the deep blush that crept across her cheeks. "Sorry..." she muttered.

Jerren laughed, causing Kat, and Daniel, to give him a hard look. "I should go," Daniel said, standing abruptly.

"I think that's a good idea," Kat replied, standing with equal abruptness. Daniel's shoulders fell slightly at her hasty reply. "That's not- I didn't-"

"It's alright, Princess," Daniel said, giving her a forced smile. Kat lifted her gaze to his, and when their eyes met, whatever embarrassment she felt before was replaced by gratitude. She threw her arms around him, and was glad he seemed to welcome her embrace. "Thank you for staying with me," she whispered.

Daniel's heart swelled, and he held her tighter. "Always."

They took a bashful step apart, letting their fingertips brush against one another, but said nothing more as Daniel turned to make his way out to the hall. He glanced back at the princess and watched as she glared at her brother, who wore a wickedly amused smile. Jerren chuckled at her expression, then pulled her forward and wrapped his arms around her. Kat sighed, giving in once more to her brother's charm, and Daniel watched as the smallest of smiles crept across her face when Jerren leaned in to kiss her temple.

"Love ya, sis."

"I love you too."

"We're here... Yeah?"

Kat nodded tearfully and gave him one last hug. Daniel smiled to himself, then turned away, allowing the siblings a final private moment, and he made it about halfway down the hall before Jerren caught up to him.

"So... how'd you sleep?" Jerren smirked. "I'll give you all the time you need to commemorate the moment, but please be sure to include me in your diary entry."

"Oh, shut up," Daniel quipped back. Jerren laughed as he was shoved towards his room, but before he disappeared behind the door made a point to mimic the way Kat had uttered Daniel's name.

Daniel shook his head in response, but couldn't erase the grin on his face. He made his way towards the eastern wing, engraving the picture of Kat asleep on his shoulder into his memory; and though he would never give Jerren the satisfaction of being right, he couldn't stop thinking about the way she had said his name. He knew it didn't really mean anything, but it gave him hope all the same.

Daniel stood a bit taller, and his heart was full, and just when he thought nothing could bring him down, he found himself in front of Sir William's door. Reality suddenly came crashing down on him, and his mood darkened. He let out a hard sigh, then hurried down the hall to his room, slamming the door shut behind him.

He had hoped to catch up on a couple hours of sleep, but the walls around him felt suddenly confining, and he couldn't stand the idea of being there much longer. He quickly freshened himself up, donning a new shirt, and the bracers Sir William gave him, then emerged from his room. He wasn't sure where to go, or what to do next, but before he could even try to figure it out, he found himself face to face with the King. "Ah Daniel, you're still here, good."

"Yes, your Majesty," Daniel said, a little surprised to see him, but also confused by his comment. *Why wouldn't he be there?* He shook his head to snap himself out of his stupor, then quickly bowed.

"I was wondering if you wouldn't mind accompanying me on my morning stroll. There are a few things I'd like to speak to you about."

A million thoughts raced through Daniel's mind. Was he in trouble for something? Had he done something wrong? *Why in the world would the king want to speak to him?* The sudden thought of someone seeing him and Jerren sneak into Kat's room in the early hours of the morning hit him, and any color that might have been in his face drained.

"Are you alright Daniel?" The King asked, concerned.

Daniel shook the idea from his head and cleared his throat. "Yes, your Majesty... It would be an honor."

The King spent a moment looking him over, trying to discern his hesitation, but seemed to ignore whatever thought that may have vexed him. "I understand last night was... well, to say it was *difficult* would be a monumental understatement."

"Yes, your Majesty," Daniel replied, reflecting the King's solemn tone.

"I apologize for catching you so off guard, though if you're sure you're up for it, I'd very much like to discuss your future."

"My future?"

A whole thicket of new thoughts tangled in Daniel's mind. Where he had been nervous before, he was now slightly terrified. Terrified that the King, knowing he served no true purpose, would send him away. He'd have no choice but to go back north. *What would he do there? What could he possibly become?* They would force him to leave the castle, to leave his whole life. Daniel took a deep, slow breath, trying hard to maintain his composure, as well as quell the sudden urge to vomit.

"But first," the King said, halting Daniel's internal spiral, only to release an emotional gut punch. "I want to tell you how very sorry I am for your loss."

The hand the King placed on Daniel's shoulder as he spoke seemed to weigh thousands of pounds, as did the empathetic expression on his face. "You meant a great deal to my brother-in-law, and he had such grand plans for you; to him, *you were utterly irreplaceable*."

Daniel's mouth went dry, and a lump formed in his throat. "Tha-thank you, your Majesty," he stuttered, unsure of what else to say. "I know you meant a great deal to him as well."

The King chuckled, surprising Daniel. "I'm not so sure about that. Seems he fought me at almost every turn, but he put up with me to be sure, gods love him."

Daniel made no response other than a rather queer expression, making the king smirk. "He was a much better man than myself, and I think he knew it from the moment he laid eyes on me, many, many years ago."

"I can't see him thinking that at all, your Grace. You are the beacon of the kingdom. There could be no better."

A sad smile spread across the King's mouth. "And that response leads me to our next item of discussion… You are very young," the King began. Daniel braced himself for the impending reprimand, but none came.

"And yet, despite your young age, you have proven yourself and your loyalty time and time again. To Will, to my children, to the realm, and even to myself."

There was a twinkle of admiration in the king's eye that filled Daniel with pride, though he wouldn't dare to acknowledge it.

"It was Will's dream for you to become a knight one day soon, and in time, a lord. That you would serve the crown alongside him, and eventually replace him in his duties."

Daniel's eyes grew wide, and his brow furrowed. Sir William had always hinted at having *'grand plans'* for him, but Daniel had never imagined just how grand.

"For many years, he's seen your great potential. He knew you would rise to the occasion when given the chance. In fact, he came to me earlier this week, just before the tournament began," the King paused once more, trying hard to suppress some rising emotion. "He asked me if I'd be willing to grant you knighthood within the year."

Daniel choked on his own spit in disbelief, but the king ignored any insecurities he might have witnessed and continued on. "Is it still your wish to follow in the footsteps of your father, and lord master?"

"More than anything, your Grace."

The King smiled slyly, the way Jerren always did when he had gotten some clever idea. "Then it's settled."

"Your Grace?"

"The council and I have decided the festival will continue as planned, and at its conclusion, we will hold a celebration in honor of William. There... you will become the knight he hoped you to be."

Daniel was in such a state of shock, the slightest breeze could've swept him away.

"And once I have knighted you, I would like you to take over some of the lighter responsibilities Will left behind serving as his proxy; and of course in time, with a bit more experience and proper training, stepping in to his full responsibilities and a title of your own."

"Your Grace, I- I don't know what to say," Daniel replied, completely dumbfounded. He wasn't sure he had heard or understood correctly. How in the name of the Gods was he supposed to step into *that* role? *His role.* And why in the hell would the King choose him of all people?

The King remained unbearably nonchalant about the whole situation. To him, the matter seemed decided, and impossible to alter; and as flattered as he was by the King's confidence, Daniel seemed far less sure of his own abilities. He was young, impulsive, and immature; he still felt like such a child. A helpless, clueless, lost child. How could the king expect him to do... *anything?*

"This must seem like such a great responsibility for someone your age," the King said, reading Daniel's mind. "But I am confident in this decision. It will not all land on your shoulders, and you will have my council at your disposal to help guide you. Will knew you could do it and I promised him I would do all I could to fulfill his wishes for you... Though this is all moot if it is not your wish as well."

Daniel was at a complete loss. Did he want it? Of course! *But was he ready?*

"You should also know, any assets or wealth Will has left behind, he named to you. You can have whatever life you choose to have, Daniel."

"*But why me?*"

The corner of the King's mouth lifted into a half smile. "Like I said, he had grand plans for you. He saw the man you have the potential to be. I see it too... and it is my selfish hope that one day you may serve my son as loyally as my dear brother served me; And though the idea of honoring you alongside him at the end of the festival felt right to me, I will grant you whatever time you need to decide."

The King clapped Daniel on the shoulder, snapping him out of a daze, then walked away. Though he had not gotten far before turning back.

"Oh, and Daniel... Whatever decision you come to, I want you to remember two very important things."

"Your Grace?"

"Number one, you will always have a home here. The friendship and guidance you have shown my children over the years is irreplaceable, and I realize they may need you now more than ever."

The corners of Daniel's lips curled with pride at the compliment he had just received; not to mention the knowledge that he wouldn't have to give up anything *or anyone.*

"Number two... You were the most important piece of his life, his pride, *his legacy...* You were very much the son he never had." The king cleared his throat. "The last words Will spoke to me were of you, and how his only regret in leaving this world was that he could not see the man you would become."

Tears sprung to Daniel's eyes, though he tried hard to suppress them. "Thank you, your Grace."

Daniel bowed his head, and the King nodded in recognition, then continued his stroll down the hall. The moment the king disappeared from sight, Daniel crumbled to the floor, the wall alone keeping him upright. He pressed his palms hard against his eyes to keep the oncoming tears at bay, then shook his head and took a deep breath.

It was hard to wrap his head around everything the king had said to him, but he knew he couldn't break down; not now, not here. He rose from the floor, dusted himself off, and then proceeded forward with his head held high.

As he walked the long halls, he saw that the stewards and maids had already draped the castle in black veils; the memorial for Sir William had begun. The longer he walked, the more people he passed and the harder it became to ignore the stares and comments.

One man offered him a concerned "How are you doing?" Then another a sorrowful condolence. One maid gave him a wistful, "he was a great man." And so on and so on, until he could no longer stand it. By the time Daniel reached the western corridors, he wanted to scream. He needed space to think, to process, to cry, and he knew he could never find that space within the walls of the castle.

His first instinct was to seek out Jerren, but his room was empty. The sudden sound of glass breaking mixed with raised voices coming from down the hall, near Kat's bedroom, distracted him from his mission, and he raced toward the ruckus. He was about to reach for the door handle, when a panic stricken Mara emerged quickly from the room, shutting the door behind her.

"Is everything all right?" Daniel asked, as the sound of more glass breaking made the hairs on his neck stand tall. He reached for the door, but Mara blocked his path.

"It's not a good time, Daniel."

He ignored Mara's suggestion and reached out again, but the nanny put a gentle hand up, halting him.

"I just want to check-"

"She's grieving."

"But what if-"

"She'll calm down in a moment, and *I* will go check on her."

Daniel was skeptical but knew better than to test her, and so backed off. The sound of breaking glass finally subsided, and soft sobs echoed through the hall. Mara sighed, half relieved, half heartbroken. When she opened the door, Daniel could see Kat on the ground, crying and hugging herself. He was ready to rush in behind the nanny, but she closed the door quickly, leaving him on the other side.

Having no other choice, he put his ear to the door, hoping to hear what was being said. He listened carefully, only catching a few words of apology between Kat's sobs and the sound of glass being gathered together. As much as Daniel wanted to burst in, hold Kat and tell her everything was going to be okay, he knew exactly how she was feeling and thought she was in much better hands with Mara.

With a heavy heart, Daniel turned away and slowly made his way to the main entrance, where he found Jerren standing outside a dark coach. The Prince looked as worn and ready to get away as he did.

"There you are! I've been looking everywhere for you. I thought maybe you'd gone to the inn."

The inn?...His mother. Daniel sighed and lowered his head. She had known Sir William most of her life. He knew they had been close as kids, and then there was whatever he had witnessed between them earlier in the week. The thought that his mother had once again lost someone dear to her hurt him in a way he could not explain.

"I suppose I should…"

"Let's go," Jerren said, opening the coach door.

"I think I'd rather walk."

"Suit yourself, but if one more person offers their condolences or if I have to sit through one more story about uncle Will, I'm gonna snap," Jerren grumbled. "I couldn't make it out of my bedroom without six different people saying something or offering to do something or feed me."

Daniel sighed, knowing the feeling well. "Yeah, okay," he agreed as he climbed into the coach.

The boys sat in silence as the coach pulled out of the castle's entrance; both too tired and emotional to think of anything to say. Daniel glanced out his window and watched as the banners hanging from the healers' tower flapped in the autumn breeze. "I'm worried about Kat," he said, breaking the silence.

Jerren lifted his head towards Daniel; he didn't say anything, but the look on his face told Daniel he needed to hear more. Daniel sighed knowing he was about to add to his friend's grief, then told him all he had seen and overheard moments before.

"Damn it!" Jerren cried as he punched the panel between the door and window of the coach; the force of his strike had been so powerful that the footman leaned his head in to make sure everything was okay.

"I'm a little worried about you now too," Daniel remarked. Jerren scoffed, shook his hand out, then leaned back in his seat, feeling rather defeated.

"When our mother died... We were young, you know... Of course she was sad, but we had father, and we had Uncle Will. He was everything to her, and I'm just not sure if she is going to get over this one."

Daniel couldn't help but think of his father. He was old enough to remember how it felt when he died. It had hurt him so much, but how he felt now was far different and seemed so foreign. "I'm not sure any of us really will," he murmured.

The closer they got to the village, the more people they heard outside the coach. The surrounding streets flooded with cries of "To Sir William" and "May he rest in peace." Jerren hung his head in misery, while Daniel tried his best to block out the noise with his own thoughts. But just as his mood took a turn, a sudden realization hit him, and he began to chuckle.

"What's funny?" Jerren asked, confused by his friend's outburst.

"You wanted to take the coach to avoid hundreds of people giving you attention, and talking about your uncle and feeding you."

Jerren still looked very confused. "And?"

"You wanted to be left alone; *no fuss, no bother, no food*!"

The Prince gave Daniel a perturbed 'obviously' sort of look, but Daniel only grinned. He raised his eyebrows and looked hard at his friend, urging him to find the answer on his own. Jerren looked back, still confused and a little annoyed... and then *it hit him.*

"Oh, Gods!" Jerren put his hand over his mouth and the two broke into a fit of laughter. "We're about to walk into the lion's den!"

"And, it's gotten so much worse now that she's pregnant!"

Jerren fell back into his seat, smiling and rubbing his head. "We'll gain 30lbs just walking in the door."

Daniel sat back a little and sighed.

"Gods bless Aunt Ada," Jerren said, chuckling still. "Do you remember the time Uncle Will tried to replace the horse you killed?"

"*For the last time... I* did not kill it!" Daniel exclaimed.

"The look on your face when it keeled over, though! And when Ada found out that uncle Will had bought a new steed to replace it, she fed him so much, he couldn't button his trousers right for two entire weeks!"

The boys laughed even harder at the memory until the melancholy mood snuck back in.

"He had such a habit of cleaning up our messes," Jerren said, lowering his head. "I suppose we'll finally have to straighten up a bit."

Daniel said nothing, but nodded in agreement as the words the king spoke echoed in his mind. The boys sat in silence once more after that; each deep in thought, staring out their respective windows, reflecting on how their lives were sure to change.

As they neared the inn, Jerren signaled the driver to park towards the back alley to avoid any gathering crowds. The two boys quickly and quietly hopped out of the coach, entered through the backdoor, then snuck up the stairwell that led to the private quarters, desperately hoping to avoid any contact with people, *or Aunt Ada.*

They entered the room Daniel's mother and brothers typically occupied, and found Declan lounging on the cushioned bench reading a book. From the dressing room, they could hear Archer whining about the outfit his mother had picked out for him.

"That's enough Archer Enid. You *will* wear these clothes and if I see so much as a speck of dirt on them, *gods help you!*"

Daniel and Jerren snorted at Leanna's scold, and Declan jumped at the sound, nearly dropping his book. He rose from the bench, but Daniel held up his hand and shook his head, halting him.

"Dec, are you ready to go?" Leanna called, with the smallest of cracks in her voice. Daniel's heart constricted.

"Yes, mum, but I don't think we'll need to…"

"How could you say such a thing?" she half scolded, gently patting her cheeks free of tears as she entered the room.

"He's here already," Declan said, nodding towards the door. "They both are."

Leanna sighed and swiftly crossed the room to Jerren and Daniel. She placed one hand on Daniel's cheek, and the other on Jerren's. "My darling boys," she said, with tears welling in her eyes. "I am so sorry."

She pulled them into a warm embrace, and though they had both had their fill of condolences for the day, the sweet embrace meant more to them than they could put into words.

"We're alright, mum," Daniel said, trying to cut the moment short.

She pulled away, but kept a hand on each of them to look them over. "No, you're not," she said, almost sternly. "And I don't want either of you trying to convince yourself otherwise... *You can be strong, and still hurt.*"

The boys each responded with a small nod, silently agreeing with her. She pulled them into a warm embrace once more, then released them to wipe the tears from her eyes and cheeks. Then, she turned to Jerren. "I imagine you are already sick of hearing this, but your uncle really was one of the greatest men I ever knew. He was my dearest friend, and I will miss him every day."

Jerren cleared his throat and tried desperately to conceal the single tear that fell down his cheek. "I appreciate that, my Lady."

It was all becoming too much again, and Daniel was desperate to change the subject. "Where were you going?" he asked, though he already knew the answer.

"We were coming to see you. Both of you, well, all three of you. Where's Kat?"

The boys exchanged a sad look and hung their heads slightly. "She's- um.." Daniel tried and failed to clear the lump that caught in his throat.

"I see," his mother said, seeming to understand. "I assume you've not run into Ada yet?"

Jerren's eyes grew and Daniel shook his head.

"I thought not... She's sent poor Tom all across the village this morning in search of ingredients and all kinds of treats to send with us for each of you. I fear by the end of it all, I'll hardly be able to fit my arms around you."

The boys chuckled, but then a noise clamoring up the back stairwell caught their attention.

"Lena dear- I'm bringing up the first load! There should be an empty chest in the closet we can use!"

Leanna sighed and directed her younger sons to help their aunt. Declan and Archer begrudgingly made their way to the entrance, but Daniel and Jerren had already had the situation handled.

"Thank you, dears," Ada said, handing the armloads of gifts over to Jerren and Daniel without realizing it was them she had handed it to. "Just set that stuff over on the beds so I can wrap and pack it properly."

Daniel and Jerren smiled and shook their heads.

"Ada, I could have sent them down for all that. You shouldn't be overdoing it the way you are," Leanna said sternly.

"I'm fine, dear. I'm more concerned about my poor darlings at the castle."

Daniel and Jerren stood behind Ada, arms still full, and couldn't help but chuckle. She turned around and gasped the moment she realized who was standing before her. She grabbed the load in Jerren's arms and deposited it unannounced into Archer's, making him stumble backwards. Daniel and Declan laughed, and Leanna covered her mouth to hide her amusement, but Ada had ignored the situation and focused only on Jerren.

"Put those down this instant!" she said to Daniel. He obeyed, and she pulled both him and Jerren into a snug embrace.

"Oh, you poor things. Grief has turned you to skin and bones, and who could blame you?" She released them and dabbed her eyes with her apron. "Well, don't you worry one bit. Aunt Ada is here to fix it!" Without another word, she grabbed Jerren's hand and drug him down the back steps. From the room Daniel and his mother could hear the polite, but clearly futile, declines of Jerren trailing behind a very insistent Aunt Ada.

"Gods help him," Leanna said, shaking her head. "Declan, Archer, please try to rescue the Prince, will you?"

The younger boys obeyed, leaving Daniel alone to talk to his mother. "I'm glad you came to see us. I have been so worried about you. And what's happened to your lip? That wasn't there yesterday evening."

Daniel hugged his mother, knowing that if there was anyone in the world that could help him, it was her. "I was worried about you, too... How are you doing?"

Leanna sighed. "My heart is hurting, and living in a world without someone like him will be hard."

The tearful expression on his mother's face broke Daniel's heart. "Mum-" he began taking a step towards her, but stopped when she waved him off.

"I don't want you to worry about me, darling. I've faced much harder things in this life... So enough about me, come sit and tell me what's really brought you here."

She sat on the bench her middle son had vacated, then patted the spot beside her. Daniel obeyed her suggestion, then told her everything that had happened; from the moment he and Jerren reached the castle grounds the previous evening, to the moment they entered the inn. Excluding, of course, the gruesome last vision he had of Sir William, and the somewhat intimate moment he shared with the Princess earlier that morning.

"Oh my darling, that is so much to take in all at once. I'm so sorry you've been through all that," she said as she stroked his back. "Will you accept the King's offer?"

Daniel sighed, hunched over and put his face in his hands. "I don't know, mum," he murmured. "What if I'm not ready? What if I'm not who he thought I was?"

Leanna hugged her son's shoulders, trying to offer what comfort she could. "And what if you are?" She lifted his chin until their eyes met. "It is a great deal of responsibility, and if you're not ready for it, I certainly understand. But... Will... He *knew* you were ready for it. He never doubted it for a second and I hope you know I never will either."

Daniel tried to choke back his rising emotions, but failed. "Why did this have to happen?" he asked with tears building in his eyes. "Why did I have to lose- *Again*..."

Leanna's heart broke for her son. She understood his pain well. She pulled him close to her and cradled him as though he were still a small boy. "I don't know, my love," she said, tears filling her own eyes. She held him close and rocked him gently back and forth. Safe in his mother's arms, Daniel could fall apart, just for an instant. She was warm and forgiving, and more than anything, she understood. He let himself have this one last moment of complete and total vulnerability, and then, when he was ready, he sat up, wiped his face, and cleared his throat.

"I keep trying to think of something I could do for Jerren and Kat... Especially Kat. But I don't think there's anything that can be done..."

"Oh Danny! Of course there is... Just be there for them, the way you always have been."

"I'm not so worried about Jer, but Kat... She's devastated, mum. The look on her face last night and then this morning..."

Just thinking about it pained Daniel greatly. He looked down and watched as his mother fidgeted absentmindedly with the charm on the bracelet she had been wearing.

"Danny, even the smallest actions can have a monumental effect, especially when done by someone who truly cares for you. You know that."

Daniel looked at his mother, then back at the charm she had just released. The corner of his mouth lifted slightly as he rolled the small piece of gold between his fingertips, the way he had as a child when she told him stories.

At a sudden thought, his small smile turned rather large; and he grinned as though a spark had reignited in the dark. He stood abruptly, pulling his mother up with him, hugged her, then kissed her cheek. "You're a genius! Thank you!" he exclaimed, as he rushed out the door and down the steps.

He had just hit the bottom landing when he met his aunt. Before she could say anything, he wrapped his arms around her, kissed her cheek, then rushed out the back door.

A very confused Aunt Ada looked up the stairs to her sister-in-law. "What's gotten into him?"

Leanna smiled and shrugged. "I'm not sure, but he's got that Enid twinkle in his eye."

The Pendant

$\mathcal{K}$at spent the whole day locked in her room; crying, sleeping, or yelling at anyone who dared to enter. It was dusk now, and she had just woken from a short nap. She glanced around her room, and her gaze wandered over to the couch; where the memory of waking up cuddled into Daniel filled her heart and mind. Her cheeks warmed at the thought, but she quickly whiffed it away. *How could she be thinking about a boy at a time like this?*

Losing Sir William had reopened old wounds she had from losing her mother. He had been the last bit of her mother she had left. More than that, though, he was like a second father. Her confidant. Someone she could always count on to be there when she needed him. Knowing he was gone; that she'd never see him again; that he'd never be there to hug her, to calm her, to call her 'Kitty Kat'; it left her broken. She wasn't sure what to do… So, she did nothing.

A sudden knock at her door pulled her from her desolation. It was so soft that had she not been laying still, she wouldn't have heard it. Milliseconds later, the sound of something sliding across the stone floor caught her attention.

She peeked over the end of her bed, and in front of her door, she saw an envelope.

"Hello?" she called out. *Nothing.* Feeling increasingly curious, she climbed from her bed and walked toward the door. She stared at the envelope for a moment, hoping something on it would give away its secrets; but there was nothing there. It was just a plain envelope.

Kat's brow furrowed. She reached to pick it up and something inside shifted; she shook the envelope and heard a soft rattle. The princess turned the envelope over in her hands, desperately searching for clues. There was a seal, but no stamp; and no sign of who it was to or who it could be from. Carefully, she broke the seal and opened the mysterious gift. Inside was a scrap of parchment and a necklace. She pulled the necklace from the envelope and placed the parchment to the side.

At first glance the necklace was simple, and unremarkable; just a gold and silver pendant on a golden chain. The closer she looked, though, the more remarkable and beautiful it became. It was not an ordinary necklace at all. She knew, whomever had crafted the piece took great pride in their work. The gold used to make the chain was thin, and twisted to look like rope. The pendant, which housed a silver wolf howling inside a golden crescent moon, was so intricately carved that the wolf seemed almost lifelike. She placed the pendant in her palm, and tears welled in her eyes as she traced the image. She closed her fist around it and felt a sharp poke.

Kat opened her hand and turned the pendant over to find a… *flower?* etched into the back of the wolf.

At first, she thought it had been the maker's mark, but it was not a stamp, and its simplicity didn't seem to match the elegance of the piece. The edges of the carving stuck out a bit, making it jagged and rough, where the other side had been smooth and seamless. She thought the mark looked familiar, but couldn't quite place it in her mind. She turned the pendant over again and smiled. It wasn't the finest piece of jewelry she'd ever received, but it already meant so much to her.

She held the pendant firmly in her hand once more, ignoring the rough markings on the back; then picked up the parchment that accompanied it. In very clear, neat writing was a little poem.

When light is fading and hope seems gone,
Remember me, hear my song.
I am with you.
Through darkest night and wildest storm,
Hold me close darling, never let go.
I will guide you.
No matter the distance, below or above,
Listen to these words, feel my love
I am right beside you.
I give you my strength; I give you my heart.
Close together or far apart.
I will always love you.

Tears streamed down Kat's cheeks. She turned the parchment over, hoping there was more, but instead of more poems, she found a note.

Kitty Kat-
    Within this pendant, I've left a small piece of me. Wear it always, and you will never be alone.

Kat read and reread each side of the parchment. She had so many questions; *Where did it come from? Was this some gift her uncle had been saving, tucked away in some drawer? Or some attempt by her father to lift her spirits?* She read the poem again, and something stirred in her. Her thumb brushed over the delicately carved pendant, and she settled on the fact that maybe not knowing where, or who, it was from was for the best. The pendant bore her uncle's sigil, and whoever had given it to her had included his pet name for her; it was clearly meant to serve as a reminder of him, as a piece of him, and that's the way she wanted it to stay. Kat fastened the chain around her neck and walked to her balcony to watch the last bits of light fade from the sky.

It was official. A whole day had passed since her uncle's death, but it already felt like he'd been gone for an eternity. Kat grazed the pendant with her fingertips and sighed. She was so fixated on the horizon she hadn't even heard the door behind her open.

"You're awake."

Her father's deep voice made her jump. She turned to him and saw he was holding a small chest. She gave him a quizzical look, but he only shrugged. "I found it outside your door... with this." Her father placed the chest on her bed and handed her a bit of parchment.

Princess,

    We are all thinking of you in this difficult time. We hope these small tokens will bring you some small bit of joy along with all our love.

                  -Your second family at the Spear and Thistle.

Kat smiled at the note, then placed it on the stand beside her. She opened the chest to find its contents wrapped in a purple and gold threaded throw blanket. Her eyes lit up as she unwrapped the throw to find a few small gifts and a variety of sweets. Each gift had a brief note attached and had been from a unique member of the Enid family.

Archer had given her a small paper bird he had folded, and obviously refolded, several times; On it in sloppy writing, he wrote, *'Smile'*. Declan gave her a small book of songs, *'to help her find joy, when there seemed to be none.'* Lady Leanna sent a beautifully embroidered handkerchief with the royal crest surrounded by wildflowers. In her note, she reminded Kat to be hopeful always, and that she would always be there for her. Tom even made her a miniature wood carving of the inn's sign, to show her she *'always had a place to come to.'*

She uncovered Aunt Ada's gift, and found a handcrafted bakery box with the words *'Take a piece of home with you wherever you go'*, carved into the lid. She smiled, then opened the box. Inside, she found a whole Lemon pie, and a card with Ada's coveted recipe scribed on it. Each of their gifts touched Kat deeply; her heart swelled and stopped all at the same time. *It was too much.*

Her head clouded, her eyes blurred, and her hands shook; she couldn't think or speak, or breathe. Her sobs grew louder and louder, until her father enclosed his arms around her, holding her as tight as he could. She pushed, and clawed, and struggled against him, but each time she did, he only held tighter. "Hush now, Katiana... you need to calm down."

But she couldn't. She needed space; she needed air. The world around her seemed to cave in, and the knife that had pierced her heart the night before twisted in its open wound. Her breaths were shallow and unsteady, and the only force holding her together now was her father's arms. He grabbed her hand and put it on his chest. "Feel my heartbeat, focus on me, breathe with me."

Through her blurred vision, she could see her father taking slow, deep breaths. She tried her hardest to obey his instructions, but the air seemed to catch in her throat.

"It's alright, Kat. Try again," her father urged. She tried again, and her voice quivered. Her father cradled her head against his chest, letting his steady breaths lift it up and down; up and down until finally her sobs ceased. Slowly, her head cleared, her chest felt lighter, and she could breathe again.

"I'm sorry," she sniffled.

"Oh my darling girl, you have nothing to apologize for," her father cooed. He kissed her hair, and though he relaxed his firm hold, kept his arms around her.

"Are you hungry?"

Kat shrugged.

"That lemon pie sure smells delicious."

Kat couldn't help but smile a little, knowing just how delicious it was.

"There's my Kat," her father said, finally releasing her. He watched as she lifted the pie from its box, and set it on the small table in front of the fire. In the chest, under all the other gifts, Kat saw Aunt Ada had also sent along utensils, plates and a few napkins; she smiled to herself at the thought of Ada making sure everything was 'just so' before sending it off and wondered how many times it had been done and redone. She pulled the dishes from the chest and set the small table near the fireplace, then cut the pie into even slices, and offered her father the first piece.

The King thanked his daughter, then watched as she pulled the somewhat tattered looking throw from the chest of goodies, and wrapped it around her. She lifted the corners of the blanket to her nose and inhaled its scent. Her resulting smile puzzled him, but he thought better than to question it.

His gaze stayed with her as she selected her own slice of the pie, then curled up in the large cushioned chair beside the fire.

Feeling his stare, Kat lifted her head towards her father. His warm expression confused her and made her slightly anxious. Out of necessity, she did her best to turn his attention elsewhere. "It's even better than Mistress Hilda's," Kat said matter-of-factly, describing the pie. Her father seemed doubtful, but the moment he took his first bite, his eyes lit up. Kat chuckled at his reaction, then took a bite of her own piece.

Kat and her father sat nestled beside the fire until they both had their fill of Aunt Ada's pie and all the other sweets she had sent along. She was grateful for his company, and that she was able to share another part of her life with him. She was even more grateful that Aunt Ada had the foresight to send along everything she had to make the moment possible.

Kat sat in a comfortable silence with her father, watching the flames in the fireplace dance, but before long could feel her mood shift. She didn't necessarily want to be alone, but she knew it would be better if she were. She told her father she was tired, and he seemed to understand what was actually happening. Just before he left the room, her father turned to look back at her, still nestled in the large chair with the old throw wrapped around her. "I love you, my Katiana."

Kat smiled, as she choked back the tears waiting to break free. "I love you too, father."

Once her father shut the door, Kat took a large breath, and emerged from the chair. She had spent too much time crying and was completely over it. Hoping to distract herself, she took turns admiring each of the gifts her 'second family' had given her. It warmed her heart to know how much they all seemed to care for her, and she hoped one day she could repay their kindness. She reached for the book of songs Declan had given her and thumbed through it until she found a song she recognized. She hummed along as she read the words, and hadn't quite made it through the first verse before tears welled in her eyes, and then fell once more.

"Kat?"

Kat's focus shot towards the door at the sound of the unexpected voice. She wiped her face, and put the book behind her back, as though it were something that should be kept secret.

"I'm sorry Princess, I should have knocked," Daniel said, feeling rather guilty for disturbing her.

"No, it's alright..." she replied, filled with relief that it was Daniel, and not someone else.

Daniel rubbed the back of his neck a little nervously. "I just wanted to make sure you got the gifts my family sent."

Kat smiled shyly, tightened her hold on the blanket, then pulled the book from behind her back. Daniel gave a weak smile and a slight nod, then turned to excuse himself.

"I wouldn't mind a little company," she admitted suddenly, and she wasn't sure if she or Daniel were more surprised by the words.

"Oh," Daniel squeaked.

A part of her had secretly hoped Daniel would've stopped by. She had been so horrible to him before and hadn't gotten the chance to *properly* apologize. Though she wasn't sure she could keep her mood swings at bay long enough to follow through with an apology at all.

They stood in an awkward silence for a moment until Kat directed Daniel over to the sofa. She absentmindedly rubbed her new pendant between her thumb and forefinger as if the action would give her the confidence she needed; and though she couldn't explain why, she suddenly felt lighter. Maybe it was the rest she had gotten; the gifts; the time with her father; or maybe it was just that Daniel was there. Whatever the reason, in that moment, she felt a little less… hopeless and a little less forlorn.

Kat and Daniel sat beside each other on the sofa, neither sure what to say or how to begin. Their eyes wandered around the room until finally landing on one another. They both opened their mouths to speak, then stopped, seeing the other had something to say.

"You first," Kat insisted. Daniel shifted nervously in his seat, then cleared his throat once more. "This may be the dumbest question I have ever asked, but… how are you doing?"

Kat said nothing, but gave a sad smile and shrugged. Then, looked down, and continued to fidget with her pendant as she thought about how to answer his question.

"I miss him already…" she said finally.

Daniel exhaled loudly through his nose and lowered his gaze. "Me too," he said, returning her somewhat pitiful smile.

Kat placed her hand on his and gently squeezed it, hoping to offer him a bit of comfort. Daniel sighed, then turned his hand over and intertwined his fingers with hers. A warmth spread through her at the sensation, and she leaned her head against his shoulder, grateful for his company; Grateful, they shared the type of friendship that allowed them to have these sweet and meaningful moments.

She was comfortable and at ease, and here, in this very moment, almost felt... *happy.* "I'm sorry about yesterday. I shouldn't have attacked you the way I did."

Daniel chuckled. "I'm surprised you hadn't done it long before then. I've more than deserved it."

Kat knew he was trying to lighten the mood, but needed him to know she meant what she was saying. She looked up at Daniel through long eyelashes. "I mean it Daniel, I'm sorry," she half choked out, tears welling in her eyes again.

Daniel inhaled sharply, then cradled her cheek with his free hand. "You have nothing to be sorry for, Princess." he said, letting the pad of his thumb skim across her cheek the same way he had earlier that morning.

Kat closed her eyes and leaned into his hand. Daniel swallowed hard as she did, closed his eyes, then pressed his forehead against hers. Kat lifted her hand to his; they were so close together, each trying to quiet the storm brewing in the other, but it couldn't last.

Kat's chest tightened as a new flood of emotions attempted to sweep over her. She stood, breaking contact with Daniel, then walked to her balcony door and hugged herself, Hoping Daniel wouldn't see her in such a vulnerable state.

Daniel frowned. "Would you like me to leave, princess?"

Kat shook her head. "No."

She didn't want him to go, but couldn't stand to turn and face him. She screwed her eyes shut, trying desperately to halt her tears, and just as she was about to give up and send him away, she heard him sing.

Her whole being froze at the sound, and she listened intently as he sang the very song she had been humming; His voice was low, smooth, and warm, and the soft melody seemed to soothe her very soul. She had heard him sing before, but only loud, abrasive, tavern songs; it surprised her to hear how well he sounded singing something so formal.

Her heart fluttered as he rose from the couch and walked towards her. He leaned on the door frame opposite her without missing a note. His voice, and just his presence, was so inviting that without hesitation, she began harmonizing with him. The corner of Daniel's mouth curled up as she sang, and he reached his hand out to her. She took his hand gladly, and by the time the song ended, Kat's heart was light once more.

"I didn't know you could sing like that," she said a little shyly.

Daniel smirked. "You're not so bad yourself Kit-" he stopped instantly, nearly making the same mistake he had the night before. He cleared his throat and quickly dropped Kat's hand. "Princess," he corrected.

Kat frowned, feeling suddenly guilty. She knew when he had called her 'Kitty Kat' before it hadn't been to mock her, or put her down, but was a sweet, comforting gesture. Hoping to amend her previous actions, she reached out and took his hand. When he looked up, obviously surprised by the action, she could see the panic in his eyes.

"I'm sorry, I didn't mean-" he began.

Kat stepped closer, and pressed her forefinger against his lips to keep him from saying anymore. "You have nothing to be sorry for."

She pulled her finger away, then nervously tucked a stray hair behind her ear, and cast her eyes downward. "I know you weren't trying to be rude or anything when you said it. It's just... it was like..."

She sighed and looked around, feeling flustered, struggling to find the right words. "I couldn't bear hearing it, knowing I would never hear *him* say it again."

A single tear slid down her cheek, and she began to pull away, but Daniel held her in place. He gently lifted her chin until she was looking at him, and wiped the tear from her cheek with the ad of his thumb. "Please don't cry, Kat..."

Kat instinctively stepped into his embrace, and he welcomed her gladly. They stood at the doors of her balcony, watching the night sky and holding each other for what seemed like ages. The longer they stood there, the more Kat wished time would stop, and they could stay in that moment forever. *Just her and Daniel.*

"I don't think I could stand never hearing it again," Kat admitted, breaking the silence they had formed. Daniel let out a soft snort. Hesitantly, Kat lifted her gaze to him, and saw he was smirking with the slightest twinkle of mischief in his eye.

"What?" she asked, feeling rather anxious.

"Does this mean I get to call you Kitty Kat from now on?"

Kat gave him a stern look she couldn't quite maintain and took a step back. "That is *not* what I said."

"Oh, but that's what I heard."

"Daniel," she warned.

"Yes, Kitty Kat?"

"Daniel, I mean it."

"What's the matter, Kitty Kat?"

A small giggle escaped Kat's throat, and Daniel's eyes lit up. "Stop it," she warned again.

"Stop what, Kitty Kat?"

Kat rolled her eyes lightheartedly, and shook her head, while Daniel smiled.

"Oh, Fine!"

"Finally!"

Daniel turned dramatically towards the balcony and lifted his hands as though he were making a grand announcement. "My lords and ladies! May I present, her royal highness, the lovely *Princess Kitty Kat*!"

Kat pulled him away from the balcony and into the room, shutting the door behind them, shushing him all the while. "You're impossible!" she said as she giggled.

"All part of my charm," Daniel said with a dramatic bow. Kat giggled once more. Suddenly, all her troubles had melted away and she couldn't help but smile. She pushed on Daniel's right shoulder, urging him to stop, but the unexpected action cost him his balance. He stumbled back, then quickly steadied himself. It was a minor mistake, but Kat could see the embarrassment in his eyes. She had to bite her lip to keep from laughing, but it seemed impossible.

"Oh, you think that's funny?" Daniel asked. Kat pursed her lips and tried her hardest not to give in, but there was no use. She turned her back to him and burst into laughter.

"I'll show you funny, Kitty Kat!" Daniel lunged towards her, lifted her from behind, and spun her around. Kat laughed and squealed with delight until somehow the clasp on her necklace came undone and her pendant flew from her neck. "Stop!"

The urgency in her voice halted Daniel, and he put her down immediately. Kat dropped to her knees and frantically searched the floor for the pendant.

"What is it Kat?" Daniel asked, concerned. Tears filled Kat's eyes. "My necklace..."

Daniel placed his hand on her shoulder, only to have it swatted away. By the way Kat was acting, he knew the necklace must have great value. Out of the corner of his eye, he saw a slight shimmer near the vanity. He walked over and bent down to pick it up, elated at what he found.

"Is this it, princess?"

Kat turned to examine the item and let out a clear sigh of relief. "Yes, that's it!" She took it greedily from him and tried to fasten it around her neck. Maybe it was the clasp or just her nerves, but she couldn't quite get the ends to connect. Daniel watched her struggle for a moment, trying to hide the sense of pride he felt, knowing his gift had served its purpose. Then, he stepped forward and took either side of the chain from her hands. "Let me help."

Kat blushed. "Thank you," she muttered.

Daniel made his attempt to close the clasp, but realized it had been bent. His brow furrowed. *'damn cheap clasp,'* he thought.

"The clasp is bent, princess. May I try something?" he asked, taking the chain from around her neck.

"Just be careful, okay?" she said, feeling unsure. Daniel gave her a reassuring smile, then pulled a dagger from his boot and pressed the clasp back into the correct shape.

"That should do it... May I?"

Daniel presented the necklace to her. Kat smiled shyly, turned around, and moved her hair away from her neck. Daniel's hands shook slightly as he fastened the chain around her; He couldn't believe the charm had actually worked, and he couldn't stop himself from trying to figure out just how well.

"I don't want to sound rude or anything, but this doesn't seem like a necklace fit for a princess. What's so special about it?"

Kat, though, couldn't help but feel somewhat slighted by Daniel's words. She stepped just out of reach and gripped the pendant in her fist. "That's really none of your business."

"I'm sorry... I didn't mean to upset you. I'm just so used to seeing pearls and jewels and this just seems so-" he stopped, unable to find the right word. He felt like the biggest ass in the kingdom. "I'm sorry," he said again, lowering his head.

"It's much more special than any pearl or jewel," she half whispered. Daniel's breath hitched in this throat, and he lifted his head.

"I can't explain it... It's just a feeling I have."

Kat shrugged, feeling a little stupid, until she saw Daniel was giving her the warmest, most compassionate smile she had ever seen. "Did you see the pendant?" she asked. "It's a-"

"Wolf in the crescent moon," he smiled. "I saw."

"I'm not sure how or why, but when I put it on, something happened. It made me feel different, not so sad; maybe even a little hopeful. And just... warm. It was almost like magic."

Kat looked up and couldn't tell if Daniel believed her or thought she was crazy. "I know it sounds stupid," she said, embarrassed by her own words.

"I don't think that sounds stupid at all."

Kat gave Daniel a hopeful smile, and he knew she was waiting for an explanation. "I remember when I was little, my mother had this bracelet I would always sort of play with as she told my sister and I a bedtime story."

Kat saw a flicker of sorrow cross his face at the mention of his sister, and her heart ached a little. "Then after... well, when they- my dad and sister..." Daniel couldn't quite get the words out. He never really talked about his losses, and on those few rare occasions he did, Kat noticed it was painful for him. Daniel seemed lost in thought; Kat was about to say something, *anything*, to rescue him from his uncertainty, but to her surprise, he continued on. "Anyway, my mother seemed to be a bit more protective of her bracelet after that, and when I asked her about it, she said she didn't want it to lose its magic."

"What did she mean by that?"

Daniel frowned, and a wave of guilt coursed through Kat once more. "I'm sorry," she said. "It's none of my business... You don't have to tell me."

Daniel rubbed the back of his neck, contemplating whether he should continue; and the look on the princess's face gave him his answer. "My father had given it to her the day my sister was born," he said after a long pause.

"Oh."

"She told me the birth had been difficult, and my father had to leave the next morning to come, well here... He gave her the bracelet, hoping it would provide her with some comfort... I guess it had, because years later... after everything, my mother told me how it made her feel as though they hadn't truly left her at all."

Hope swelled in Kat's heart at the thought, and she coveted the idea that maybe her pendant could serve a similar purpose.

"I hadn't quite understood what she meant when she said that, but then she told me a story about two lovers and a very special trinket."

Kat was unsure how a story could provide clarity, but couldn't seem to hide the slight blush she felt when Daniel looked at her and said 'lovers', and craved more.

"Oh... Could you maybe tell me about it?"

The Story

Kat felt suddenly foolish; like a child asking for a bedtime story. But just Daniel's presence made her feel better, and she wasn't ready for him to leave.

Daniel gave her a small smile and shrugged. "If you'd like."

Kat smiled and gave him an eager nod. She walked towards the fireplace, wrapped the purple and gold threaded blanket around herself and curled up in her favorite chair. When she was settled, she looked up at Daniel and gave him an expectant grin. Daniel looked down, trying to conceal the tinge of pink that crossed his cheeks and the small smile on his lips.

"What?" she asked, seeing his expression.

He shook his head, but maintained a proud grin. Kat followed his gaze, and it seemed to land on the blanket that was sent along with the other gifts from the inn.

"It was in the chest of things your family sent," she said with a sheepish shrug.

Daniel chuckled. "I know..."

Kat gave him an odd, questioning look.

"I'm the one that put it there," he admitted.

"Oh!" Kat exclaimed. A light blush ran across both their cheeks. "Well, thank you... It's very cozy."

Daniel smirked. "Take good care of it, okay?... It was my favorite."

Kat blushed a deeper shade of pink. "I promise."

Daniel stood awkwardly for a moment, unsure of what to do next. Kat moved her eyes from Daniel to the table where her father had sat, and then back again. "Do I still get to hear the story?"

Daniel looked down and shuffled his feet a little, then made his way to the table. His heart pounded as he walked. He was a little upset with himself for even bringing the whole thing up. He pulled a chair out from the small table, but before he sat down, he gave Kat a nervous sort of look. "I should warn you, I'm not the greatest storyteller, and... Well, it's been a long time since I've even heard the story..."

He knew the story like he knew his own name, each word engraved into his memory, but wasn't sure he wanted to risk sharing it. Daniel glanced at the pendant around Kat's neck, and his nerves rose knowing the story he was about to share was the whole inspiration behind the secret gift; He chewed his lip, hoping Kat wouldn't make any connection between the two.

"I understand," she said, trying to hide her disappointment in his reluctance.

"No- I'll still do it," he said, noting the sad expression on her face. "I just don't want you to be disappointed by my lack of *theatrics*," he said, most theatrically.

Kat let out a tiny, almost half giggle and rolled her eyes. "I promise I won't be," she grinned. Daniel smiled, turned the dining chair around to sit more comfortably, and began his story.

"Once upon a time, in a faraway kingdom, there lived two lovers."

"So far, so good," Kat smiled, and Daniel lightheartedly shook his head, then continued.

"The man was a great warrior, who was often called on by his king to fight in his name. He was a fierce and noble man that never failed or hesitated to answer the call, until he met a fair maiden."

Kat listened intently as she watched the flames dance in the fireplace.

"To the warrior, the maiden was the most beautiful woman in all the land; and it didn't take long for him to discover she was more than beautiful. She was brilliant, kind, generous, and so much more than she first appeared; and because the maiden was all those things, the warrior found she had many suitors that sought her hand."

Daniel paused as his thoughts wandered. *Beautiful, brilliant, kind, generous, and so much more* — everything Kat was. His heart dropped at the idea that in just a few short months, she would have suitors lined up to fall at her feet. Kat met Daniel's lingering gaze and became confused by the diminished hope it seemed to hold. Daniel cleared his throat, then quickly looked anywhere else he could.

"Despite having many suitors," he continued. "The moment the fair maiden's eyes met the proud warrior's, she knew destiny had brought them together."

Their eyes seemed to find each other once more, causing something to stir, and Kat's mouth to dry. "Then what happened?" She choked out. Daniel smirked slightly at the question.

"The maiden and the warrior were deeply and hopelessly in love and married soon after they met. They lived in utter and complete bliss... for a time. But, as most good love stories go, they had no way of knowing the challenge they soon faced.

The day finally came that the warrior was once again called on by his king. His new bride begged him not to leave, for she was certain if he did, she'd never see him again. She knew in her heart that she had married a proud warrior, but that didn't stop her from trying to persuade him not to leave. As the time grew nearer to her husband's departure, and seeing that her persuasions had failed, the maiden slipped into a deep depression, distancing herself from everyone and everything.

The warrior's heart ached for his love. How could he leave knowing how distraught she was? He thought long and hard about what he could do to bring her some peace." Daniel glanced at the pendant around Kat's neck, though she didn't seem to notice.

"The warrior sought advice from those in his village, and it wasn't long before he caught wind of a rumor about a woman that lived in a neighboring town who had a talent for mending broken hearts. He was not sure what help the woman could offer, but was desperate to try anything that might make his wife smile once more.

The morning before he was to make his voyage, he traveled to find the old woman. He told her of his wife's suffering and asked if there was anything she could do to ease it.

The old woman told the warrior to pick a trinket from the collection laid out before them. The warrior picked up a small but beautiful stone. She then instructed him to whisper to the stone all he felt and hoped for his love. The warrior hesitated, thinking it was a foolish idea, but as he began, the words seemed to flow freely out of him. He poured every hope, dream and ounce of love and strength he had into his message."

Kat instinctively grasped her pendant.

"The woman told him the only way to bind the magic of the trinket was to add a piece of himself to it. The warrior thought hard for a moment, then took a thin strip of leather from the hilt of his sword and tied it around the stone. Finally, the woman told him that his wife must wear the trinket for its powers to be effective.

When the warrior returned to his wife, it surprised him to see that she seemed angered by his gift. The maiden, being well versed in other knowledge, did not believe in such magic, and was quite angry that her husband had wasted so much of their last day together away from her.

The warrior, disappointed in himself, placed the trinket into a drawer beside their bed. He hoped one day, should his love need it for any reason, she would know where to find it.

The following morning, the warrior kissed his wife goodbye and reminded her one last time to hold the trinket close until he returned."

"Did he?" Kat asked. Hope brimming in her eyes.

Daniel gave her a confused sort of look.

"Did he return?"

Daniel's shoulders dropped slightly, and it told Kat all she needed to know.

"Oh," she frowned, then turned her attention back to the fireplace.

"Do you want me to stop?"

Kat looked up at him and slowly shook her head. "I want to hear the end," she said in a small voice. Daniel gave an understanding nod and continued.

"Just as the maiden had predicted, she would never again see her love." Daniel paused and watched as Kat quickly wiped away a single tear from her cheek.

"Kat..."

She stood and walked toward the balcony, and Daniel followed behind her.

"I'm sorry..." she said in a voice that told Daniel more tears were falling. "Please keep going."

Daniel took her hand in his. "We don't have to finish it right now."

Kat freed her hand from his and quickly wiped her face. She took a deep, cleansing breath, then turned to him. "Please, Daniel."

Her plea, both spoken and unspoken, tugged at Daniel's heart strings. He sighed and gave a small nod. Kat took his hand in hers and led him over to the sofa. They sat down and the memory of being curled up next to him earlier that morning came rushing in. Slightly embarrassed at the thought, Kat released his hand and shifted to the opposite side. "So... what happened to the maiden?"

"Days turned to weeks, and weeks into months; the maiden had gone mad with grief. Each day, she drifted silently through the town; a ghost of the woman she once was. She never spoke and hardly ate. She spent her days watching the road, waiting for her lover's return, and spent her nights mourning his loss.

One day, though, she came across the trinket her warrior had left behind. She carefully picked it up and ran her fingers across the strip of leather. As the maiden did this, she closed her eyes and pictured her lost love.

She thought about how much she missed him. She thought about how much she still loved him and all she had hoped they'd one day have together. When she opened her eyes again, the slightest of weights had lifted. It was so small, in fact, that she had hardly even noticed it. The maiden used the small bit of leather to tie the trinket to her finger. Thinking, if nothing else, it could serve as a daily reminder of him. Though she still missed her love, each day the maiden woke up wearing the trinket, she felt lighter, less lonely, less forlorn, less heartbroken. Then, one day, out of curiosity, the maiden sought out the old woman that had given her warrior the trinket. The old woman recognized the stone in an instant. She smiled and looked just to the left of the maiden and spoke as if she were speaking to someone beside her.

'Why have you been hiding for so long?'

The maiden looked at the woman, confused.

'Well, she's found you now, hasn't she?'

The maiden felt foolish for coming and declared the woman mad.

'Please! You gave my husband this trinket. Can you tell me more about it?'

The old woman laughed. 'Only one may tell you what you desire to know, my dear' she said. 'Hold tight to the trinket and reveal your heart's desire.' The maiden eyed the woman skeptically.

She laid in bed that night feeling irritated and foolish. So much so that she removed the trinket from her finger, put it on the table beside her bed and turned her back to it, ready to be rid of it. But the longer she laid there without the comfort of her trinket, the more restless and hopeless she felt.

Giving in to its unexplainable power over her, she reached once more for her ring. She gripped it in her hands and said a small prayer, then swiftly drifted to sleep, only to awake in a dream world. A world where her warrior had never left her side.

The maiden's heart was full as he held her in his arms and whispered in her ear. He told her how much he loved her, whispered all that he hoped for her, and promised he would always be with her. He spoke so softly and lovingly that the maiden didn't dare interrupt. When the warrior had finally finished saying everything he needed to say, he kissed her.

The next morning, when the maiden awoke, she couldn't believe how real her dream had been and was bitterly disappointed that she had woken at all. As she reluctantly prepared for the new day, it surprised her to find the old woman waiting just outside her door.

Before she could say anything, the woman announced she had one last message to share.

'I am sorry to say you will not see your warrior again for a very long time, but as long as you keep your trinket close, he will always be a part of you.'

The woman left without another word, but the maiden seemed to understand her meaning. From that day on, anytime things became difficult, or she was feeling helpless, she'd hold her trinket close and say a small prayer and she knew her warrior was standing right beside her." Daniel said, ending the story.

"You're a better storyteller than you give yourself credit for," she said after a small pause.

Daniel blushed. "After my mother told me that story, she taught me to believe in the power that ordinary objects can possess, especially when endowed with love." he paused. "That's why I always have this."

Daniel pulled up his sleeve to reveal a tattered looking braided bracelet Kat had somehow never seen, or just never took the time to notice. She leaned in a little to inspect the mysterious object.

"The leather was from the hilt of my father's sword."

"Just like the story?"

Daniel nodded shyly.

"And the lace?"

Daniel cleared his throat hesitantly. "It was from my sister's favorite dress," he explained. "My mother told me as long as I wear it, they'll always be with me."

Kat smiled sweetly at Daniel, but moments later seemed a bit perplexed.

"What is it?" Daniel asked.

Kat stood with a frown and reached once more for her pendant. "Do you think it still works if it's not from them?" she asked.

"What do you mean?"

Kat rubbed the pendant between her fingers. "I'm not sure where, or who, this came from. Someone slid it under my door, along with a note. What if he had nothing to do with it?"

Daniel stood and gave her a reassuring look. "Does it matter?"

Kat looked up, confused.

"What matters is what it means to you and," he paused and tucked a stray hair behind her ear, making her blush. "I'd be willing to bet *whoever* gave it to you cares a lot about you and just wants to see you happy."

Daniel smiled warmly at Kat, and she answered him with a tender embrace.

"Thank you," she breathed into his neck.

"What for, Princess?" he asked, slightly concerned she may have solved the mystery.

Kat shrugged. "The song, the story, being here... everything."

Daniel sighed and gave her a warm squeeze. "I'll always be here for you, Kitty Kat."

Kat held tighter. "I know."

The sound of someone clearing their throat behind them made the pair jump.

"I guess you didn't need me here after all," Jerren said, raising an eyebrow. Daniel shook his head at him. "Shall I make my leave?" Jerren teased further.

Daniel turned back to Kat and lightly kissed her cheek. "Good night, Princess," he said. He turned and walked towards the door, shoving Jerren as he passed.

The Prince chuckled, but made no retaliation. Daniel took one last look at Kat and smiled. A warmth spread through her and her heart felt a little lighter. "Good night, Daniel."

Birthday Surprise

Kat stood on her balcony and watched as a soft winter shower fell from the sky. The air was crisp; she pulled the purple and gold blanket Daniel had given her a little tighter around her shoulder as she absent-mindedly twisted the pendant that hung from her neck.

It had been months since Sir William's passing, but the pain she felt was still new, still fresh. Since then, the only thing that seemed to bring her any true comfort was her pendant. On the particularly heartbreaking days when she was missing her uncle, or her mother, or she just couldn't find the light, she knew just how to cure it. She would close her eyes, hold the pendant tight, and recite the poem that came with it. She wasn't sure how, or why, but doing it just made things better; and each day she put it on, it brought her a little more warmth and a little less sorrow, making her question whether the pendant really held some sort of ancient magic, or if Daniel's story had just gone to her head. Regardless of the answer, the power she felt from the little ritual was genuine enough for her. The pendant was her beacon in the dark; the talisman that guided her way, and she knew as long as she held it close, she could make it through... *almost* anything.

It was the eve of her birthday, and even though she should've been excited, all she felt was hollow. Her birthday used to be her favorite day of the year. A day filled with all of her favorite foods and activities; without rules or expectations; a carefree day spent with the people she loved.

The very first memory Kat had formed was sitting in the castle gardens, and watching the sunrise with her mother on her 2nd birthday. It was something her mother had done with her since the day she was born; a mother/daughter tradition that had been passed down through the generations. It wasn't a grand tradition, but one that was dear to Kat's heart.

After her mother passed, her father attempted to continue the tradition, but it hadn't gone as planned. She couldn't quite remember who had cried more that day, her, or her father. She figured it was just as painful of a reminder to him as it was to her, and so after just one attempt, Kat suggested they end the tradition. The very next year, though, she woke to a gentle knock just before sunrise.

Her uncle snuck in with a smile and told her to dress as quickly as she could. She remembered being reluctant to do so, but the warm expression on her uncle's face had changed her mind. She obeyed his directions and then just the two of them rode together to Thyrion's Cliff, which overlooked the Shimmering Valley. They had a picnic with all her favorite treats and watched the sunrise together while he told her stories. Stories about her mother, about her father, even some of his own adventures. That year a new tradition was born, one that meant just as much to Kat as the one she shared with her mother; knowing this year it would all finally end, brought on a sadness even her pendant couldn't cure.

Kat felt like the small, sad child who was painfully aware that her mother wouldn't be there to wake her in the morning; the thought of waking to anything other than a gentle knock at her door before dawn made Kat want to skip the day altogether; though, that would be impossible.

The fact of the matter was, it wasn't just her birthday anymore, it was the day of her very first suitors' feast. She had been looking forward to this day for years, but since the loss of her uncle an unshakeable bitterness had set in concerning the feast. The celebration was to be her coming out, a day that marked her as an "eligible" young woman; one that most girls spent years dreaming of. But, somewhere in the last few months, Kat had finally realized that the suitors' feast was more of a beastly competition than a "noble tradition."

Noble families, foreign dignitaries, and young men from all across the kingdom were invited to attend; all hoping they would gain her favor. They would parade her around the room like a slab of meat held before ravenous dogs, each one ready and more than willing to take a bite; and then she would be forced to dance with *whomever* chose to ask her. The idea of the whole so-called tradition was terrifying, and she was less than enthused at the prospect of being carted around the dance floor by a bunch of intolerable snobs.

She used to think people throwing themselves at her feet and doing anything imaginable to impress her was somehow romantic; After Sir William's passing, she realized the feast was never about love, just a chance for some young man to boost their status; and Kat had no interest in being a pawn in someone else's game... she wanted to be loved, not won.

Her whole life she had been told the story of the three sisters and to her, it was a story of true love: one that she had hoped to experience herself. She blamed her once high expectations for the gathering on the stories Mara had told her as a child of beautiful gowns, and handsome men. But, in reality what really skewed her expectations was the people around her that constantly built up her confidence, making her believe she could truly have the fairytale life she always dreamt of; *i.e. her father, brother, and best friend.* Her loyal band of men, who at present, were conveniently absent.

Her father spent his days in council meetings and court gatherings, discussing the prospect of granting Rollin Breken lordship over the eastern territories, effectively replacing his father, whose health had rapidly declined. The issue was controversial for several reasons, though Kat was oblivious as to why, and wished they would conclude the matter sooner rather than later.

Her brother had been less involved in matters of politics and much too occupied with 'sowing his wild oats' throughout the village taverns, while occasionally assisting their father when the mood struck him to do so. He seemed to want nothing to do with the Breken situation, a point which seemed to confuse Kat even more because of his once adamant attachment to a certain young lady.

And then there was Daniel, who since becoming a full-fledged knight, and presented as Sir William's proxy, had done nothing but travel to and from different hold fasts as an emissary to the crown. It seemed like he was gone much more than he was home, and the distance from him grated on her.

With her support system crippled and non-existent, Kat felt more alone now than ever before, and maybe that was the real reason the day seemed so bleak. *How could she celebrate her birthday when she felt so empty?*

The sun finally set and a cold winter wind chilled her to the bone. Kat retreated to her room and sat herself in front of the fireplace. The light and warmth of which only seemed to deepen her despondent mood; there was nothing *warm* about the way she felt. Her pendant, poem and even the comfort of her favorite blanket couldn't soothe her. After sitting for some time staring into the void of the fire, desperate to grasp its heat, she gave up and put herself to bed, only to realize sleep would not come. She laid there for minutes, then hours, staring blankly at the ever shrinking flames, thinking about nothing... and everything.

The flames turned to embers, and as Kat rolled over; she knew dawn was soon approaching. A solitary tear trickled down her cheek, and she buried her face into her pillow, readying herself for the flood of tears that were sure to fall, when suddenly there was a gentle knock at the door.

Kat gasped and sat up straight. Her heart raced as the door slowly opened, but when Jerren appeared in the frame, the hope that bubbled within, shattered like glass.

"Happy Birthday, sis!" he whispered, wearing a large grin.

"What do you want?" she half spat at him; Jerren's face fell. Kat knew her brother was only being kind, but any attempt he had made to carry out the tradition would be futile. She laid back on her side, feeling rather helpless, then pulled the blanket up to her chin.

Jerren sighed. His heart ached for his sister, and he desperately hoped he could convince her to play along. "I have a surprise for you!"

The hopeful tone in her brother's voice intrigued her, but not nearly enough. "I know what you're doing, Jer, and I'm sorry. Honestly, I am... But please, just go away."

Kat heard the door shut and thought the interaction had ended, until she felt the weight of her brother sitting at the end of her bed.

"What are you-"

"Just hear me out, okay?"

Kat sighed.

"I know today will be difficult for you, for several reasons, and I know nothing *I* could do would compare to what *he* did, but I promise if you just come with me, it will be well worth it."

Jerren offered a warm smile, and tears brimmed in Kat's eyes. She had spent the entire night dreading the fact that there would be no knock, she hadn't stopped to consider how she'd feel if one came.

"What do you say, Kat?"

The Princess wiped away the bit of water from her eyes and nodded in agreement.

"Perfect! Dress warm as you can and meet me just outside the orchard!" Jerren said. "Oh, and Kat…"

She turned to acknowledge him, and he smiled. "Try not to take a million years."

Kat rolled her eyes as Jerren winked and shut the door behind him. Jerren had always been there for her during the most difficult moments of her life, so playing along for one morning seemed the least she could do. She dressed, then quietly made her way through the still sleeping castle, out the kitchen doors, and to the orchard. When she found her brother, he looked increasingly mischievous. It was still fairly dark, but the playful look on his face was plain, and Kat couldn't help but smile along.

"Well, it's about time! It's freezing out here!"

Before Kat could make a reply, Jerren shoved a bit of cloth into her hands.

"Put this on," he demanded.

The cloth was light, but thick, the perfect blindfold. She responded with a queer look, to which he replied, "Just trust me!"

"I feel as though I'm going to regret this..."

Jerren scoffed and helped to secure the blindfold around her eyes, then looped one arm through Kat's and led her forward.

"Jer, I can't see a thing."

"That's kind of the point."

Kat clung tightly to her brother. "I swear if you walk me into a tree or cart or something..." she threatened.

"We couldn't do that to the birthday girl!" another voice chimed. Kat perked up at the familiar sound.

"But we will keep the idea in mind for another day."

Kat reached up excitedly to take off the blindfold.

"Uh- no peeking Kitty Kat!"

Excitement overcame her, and she leapt blindly toward the voice wearing a face splitting grin. Daniel caught her and hugged her tightly.

"Happy Birthday, Princess," he said. The warmth of his voice instantly thawed Kat's despondent mood.

"You're back! I've missed you!"

"I've missed you too..."

Jerren cleared his throat, interrupting the somewhat tender moment. "Can we get to the surprise now, or should I just come back later?" he half teased.

Kat released Daniel quickly. "That wasn't it?" she asked before she could stop herself. Daniel smiled and Jerren let out a hearty, "HA!"

"We've got something much better planned, Princess," Daniel said, leading Kat to a horse.

"Though if you'd rather just-" Jerren said in a low, suggestive voice. Daniel shot him a warning look, making him chuckle.

"What are you talking about? What's funny?" Kat asked, feeling as though she was being laughed at.

Daniel carefully raised himself onto the same horse as Kat and sat in front of her. "Don't mind him, Kat. He's just jealous you're never as excited to see him as you are to see me."

Jerren rolled his eyes. "I wonder why that is..." he muttered.

"Or maybe just because he knows I'm so much better than him at... well, everything."

Daniel smiled snidely at the prince as he brought their horse around to meet Jerren on his.

"For instance, there is no way he could beat us in a race..."

Jerren scoffed, then took off on his horse.

"Hang on tight, Kitty Kat."

Daniel clicked his teeth and off they went. Kat held on tight to Daniel as the pace quickened. There was something exhilarating about riding that fast while blindfolded. A sudden burst of excitement filled the pit of her stomach and she couldn't help but laugh. Daniel smiled at her reaction and pushed the horse a little harder. Kat squealed with delight. She didn't know where they were going, but she was already having more fun than she'd had in quite a while.

"Is that all you've got, your Highness?" Daniel hollered to Jerren, who glared as Daniel and Kat passed him. Kat only knew they had pulled ahead because of the shouts coming from behind them. She laughed and cheered Daniel on further.

The cold winter air filled her lungs and stung her cheeks. She buried her face in the fur-lined cloak on Daniel's shoulders and held on tighter. A warmth spread through her; though she wasn't completely sure if it was from the thick fur of his cloak, or the blush that seemed to consume her as she felt the muscles below Daniel's shirt. All too soon, Daniel slowed the horse to a trot, and Kat reluctantly loosened her hold and unburied her face.

"So, where are we going?"

Daniel chuckled, realizing she was trying to peek through the gaps in her blindfold. "Don't worry Princess, we're close."

Kat heard hoofs slow beside them. "It's about time you caught up," she quipped. Jerren gave a sarcastic laugh. "See if I ever do anything nice for you again."

Suddenly, Daniel stopped and dismounted. Anxiety bloomed in Kat's chest. So far, her brother had kept his word about it being worth her while, but she had no clue what could come next. She clumsily swung her leg around to the same side she had felt Daniel dismount.

"Here, let me help you."

He reached up and grabbed her waist, sending a tingle up her spine. "Can I take this thing off now?" she asked as Daniel lowered her down. Kat could feel the snow was at least ankle deep. She stumbled, but Daniel steadied her before she could fall. His arms were snug around her and she could feel his breath against her cheek. She was sure that had she leaned in just a little, the tips of their noses would touch. A fleeting thought of Daniel leaning in to kiss her filled her stomach with butterflies.

"No! You can't take it off yet!" Jerren called as he dismounted.

Daniel straightened her and backed away. "Careful Kitty Kat."

Kat couldn't help but notice the slightest bit of husk in his voice, and it made her heart race. "Thank you," she muttered.

Daniel stepped away, leaving her standing beside the horse, unsure what to do or say, hoping he would return at any moment. Her mind flooded with thoughts of him until the muffled sound of her brother's voice brought her back to earth. "I'm sorry... what?"

"You alright?" Jerren asked.

"Yes!" she all but yelled. "I didn't sleep very well last night, is all..."

Jerren studied her for a minute, trying to determine what had her so anxious. Ignoring a fleeting thought, he looped his arm through hers and led her a couple of yards to the left, then up a small slope.

"Come on Jer, where are we?"

The gaps in her blindfold filled in with light and she was growing impatient, though equally excited. Jerren led her a few more steps, then positioned her just so.

"Ready?"

"Yes!"

"Are you sure?"

Kat giggled. "Jerren!"

Her brother unticd the blindfold and pulled the fabric away. "One... two... and TA-DA!"

Kat had to blink rapidly to filter the bright light of daybreak, but when the view came into focus, she gasped in wonderment. The hill they stood on overlooked a small valley. In the lowest part of the valley was a small lake that sat at the base of a trickling waterfall. The whole of the lake, the waterfall, and each surrounding tree glistened encased in ice, and a fresh layer of soft powdery snow made the glade sparkle in the sunrise. It was the most beautiful thing Kat had ever seen.

"What do you think?" Jerren asked, his hands on either of Kat's shoulders.

Kat reached up, grasped her brother's hand, and squeezed. "Jer, this place is incredible!"

She smiled up at him, and he smiled back, pride clear on his face. "Now then! Are you ready for some fun?"

Kat gave her brother a confused look.

"Well, we're not just here to look at it!" Jerren exclaimed.

"Oh? We're not?"

Daniel marched up the hill behind them with a satchel on his shoulder and a grin on his face. "No, Princess. We're not."

From the satchel, Daniel pulled an odd sandal like contraption with a blade attached to the bottom. She'd seen nothing like it before, and a nervous bubble rose in the pits of her stomach. "What is that?"

"Come and find out!" Jerren yelled, as he threw a ball of snow at Kat, then ran down the hill. Kat yelped at the sudden cold impact, and the boys laughed. She reached down to gather a ball of her own to throw at Jerren, who taunted her from below. Then reared her arm back, and flung the ball into the face of an unsuspecting Daniel. Kat and Jerren burst into laughter, as a very surprised Daniel turned his snow-covered face toward Kat, who could suddenly see she had made a horrible mistake.

"I'm sorry, I couldn't help it," she blurted, trying not to laugh. Daniel set the satchel down and brushed the remaining snow from his face. His eyes bore into Kat's, and she knew what was coming. She retreated slowly down the slope.

"Daniel-" she said as sternly as she could through a smile. She giggled and backed away a bit more. "Please-" Daniel stalked towards her, waiting for the right moment to strike. "But It's my birthday!" she squealed as Daniel leapt towards her, pulling her down into the snow beside him.

"Ow!" Kat cried out.

Daniel hopped to his knees, alarmed. "What's wrong? Are you okay? I didn't mean to hurt you!"

Kat winced and grabbed the left side of her back. Daniel bent to inspect the injury, and as he did, Kat gradually filled her right hand with a mound of snow.

"Does this hurt?" Daniel pressed his hand near where she had placed hers and looked up to catch her reaction. Kat smiled, and Daniel's confused face received a handful of fresh snow. Kat jumped up and sprinted down the hill, and her laugh echoed through the valley; the sound was so gratifying that Daniel didn't seem to mind the snow that clung to his cheeks. He brushed the flakes from his face once more, grabbed his satchel and raced after her.

Jerren and Kat had begun a miniature war near the bank of the lake, and just as Daniel was about to join in and exact his revenge, Kat put her arms up in surrender.

"So, what are those things? How do they work? What are we doing? Will you show me?"

She flashed her long eyelashes at Daniel, who could only laugh and shake his head. "You win this round, Princess."

Daniel winked, then threw the large ball of snow he had in his hand at Jerren.

"Ha, ha.. Very amusing," Jerren said dryly, as Daniel and Kat cackled. Daniel opened the satchel and pulled out three sets of the sandal-like contraptions. He handed one set to a still bitter looking Jerren, then led Kat to a large boulder and told her to sit. He knelt down and fastened the blades to Kat's boots. It didn't seem like a special moment, but the same butterflies from before rose in Kat's stomach at his touch.

"Is that too tight?" Daniel asked, stopping to look up at her. She shook her head. "Good," he smiled and all too soon bent back down to attach the next blade.

"Hey! Are you guys coming or what?" Jerren called out.

Kat looked up and saw that Jerren was standing in the middle of the lake. Daniel chuckled, but fear rippled through Kat.

"We won't fall through, will we?"

"I tested it late last night when I first arrived. I promise you won't fall through," Daniel said, sitting beside her to fasten his own blades. He stood and offered Kat his hand. She eyed him with skepticism, but his reassuring smile won her over. "I won't let anything happen to you, Kitty Kat."

Kat took a deep breath and then Daniel's hand. He smiled and swiftly pulled her to her feet. The sudden jolt surprised her, and she giggled. Her legs wobbled as she tried and somewhat failed to find her balance on the thin blades. Daniel chuckled and steadied her.

"Easy now, just one step at a time."

"Daniel. I can't even stand. How in the world am I going to do that?"

She directed his attention to Jerren, who was gliding across the ice. "You'll get there. Besides, he's not really that good."

As he finished his sentence, Jerren slipped and fell down, proving Daniel's point. Kat let out a burst of laughter that threw her off balance. Daniel chuckled and steadied her once more. One step at a time, they made their way towards the lake, until finally meeting its edge. Daniel took the first steps out onto the ice, then urged her to follow.

"Alright, your turn," he said, with arms out ready to catch her. Kat took a very hesitant step forward, but slipped. Daniel caught her just in time and chuckled.

"It's not funny!" Kat snapped.

Daniel bit his lip and tried to hide his amusement, which made her laugh a little at herself.

"I'm sorry..."

Daniel smiled, shook his head, and urged her to try again. She took a deep breath and stepped out onto the ice. "Good! Now find your balance."

"I'm trying..." Kat spluttered, as she clung to Daniel for dear life. She wobbled back and forth, until finally she found her center.

"Great! You did it!"

He smiled proudly at her, and she grinned. "Now, try to keep your legs even with your hips, okay?"

Daniel glided slowly backwards, pulling Kat along with him. She protested and panicked, but he only smiled and continued. She closed her eyes tight and made an anxious sort of squeal.

Daniel laughed, "Open your eyes Kat, I've got you."

Reluctantly, she opened one eye, then the other, then giggled, and Daniel gave her a mischievous smile. "Let's go a little faster."

Kat protested once more, but it was too late. Daniel pushed hard against the ice and increased their speed. It was unlike anything she'd ever felt before. It was almost as if she was flying. Unbridled joy erupted within her. Daniel took a sharp turn that tickled her insides, but then came to a rather abrupt stop, causing Kat to fall into him. He tried to steady them both, but the collision cost him his own balance. He fell back onto the ice, unintentionally pulling Kat down with him, and the shock of it sent them into a fit of laughter.

Jerren glided to a stop next to them. "Having fun yet?"

"Something like that," Kat chuckled.

Daniel stood, and with Jerren's help, they got Kat back on her feet. Together, the three of them glided across the ice. Each of the boys offered Kat different bits of advice; how to stand, which way to position her foot, etc. Eventually Jerren let go, knowing she could handle it on her own; Kat was less sure and gave Daniel a pleading look not to leave her side. He laughed, but agreed not to leave her until she felt ready to try on her own. Several laps around the lake later, Kat finally found her confidence.

She couldn't remember the last time she had felt this happy and her cheeks hurt a little from smiling so much. She had been so unsure at first, but was undeniably grateful that her brother had knocked on her door that morning. As she and Daniel, hand in hand, took one last lap around the lake, she couldn't help but think it had been the perfect outing.

It was midmorning by the time they arrived back at the castle. Kat was famished, and somewhat frozen, but her spirits were high. As they dismounted at the stables, Kat leapt towards her brother, throwing her arms around his neck.

"Thank you!" she whispered.

Jerren was so surprised he had barely caught her. He looked up at Daniel and opened his mouth to say something, but stopped when Daniel shook his head. Jerren sighed and hugged his sister.

"Happy Birthday."

Kat smiled and released her brother, fluttered over to Daniel, and gave him one more quick hug. "I'm so glad you're home!"
she smiled, released him, and then ran off towards the castle without a second thought.

Sweet Dreams

Daniel and Jerren stood at the entrance of the stables and watched as Kat skipped happily away.

"I should've told her," Jerren said to Daniel.

"It doesn't matter," Daniel shrugged.

Jerren groaned. "Of course it matters! She should know this whole thing was your idea!"

Daniel rolled his eyes, unbothered by the Prince's dramatics. "What matters is that she had a brilliant morning, and it took her mind off of everything else."

"Why don't you just tell her how you feel? You know she feels the same way... stop sneaking around performing all these grand gestures and try taking the credit for them!" Jerren insisted.

"I'd better go check in on Aunt Ada," Daniel replied, ignoring the prince's suggestion. Jerren groaned as Daniel mounted his horse once more and rode off towards the village. "You know I'm right!" He called after him in vain.

As Jerren entered the small hall for breakfast, he heard Kat telling their father about the events of the morning. The excitement in her voice made him smile; It had been months since he had seen his sister this happy, and just for a moment he thought maybe Daniel had a point; at least she was smiling.

"Where's Daniel?" Kat asked, interrupting Jerren's train of thought. The perplexed and somewhat disappointed look on her face was just enough to renew Jerren's frustration.

"He left to check on Ada," he said, trying to hide his annoyance with his friend's lack of common sense.

"How is she doing?" the King asked, surprising both his children. Jerren gave him a bittersweet smile. "She's due any day now."

His father gave him a melancholy sort of nod, but smiled.

"I still can't believe she's having a baby! I can not wait to meet her!"

Jerren gave Kat a strange look. "What makes you so sure she's having a girl?"

Kat shrugged. "Just a hunch."

Kat ate more food than she should have, and between the sugar she had consumed, her active morning, and the lack of sleep from the previous evening, her body was screaming for rest. She slumped her way up the stairwell that led to her bedroom, hoping she could close her eyes for just a short while.

As she lazily swung her door open, she found a large parcel sitting on her bed. Curiosity overpowered her exhaustion as she crossed the room to investigate. The wrapping was nothing special, but the calligraphy on the note that laid on top, she would recognize anywhere.

To my darling girl on a very special birthday.
I'm so proud of you.
I love you always.
X Your Father.

Kat's heart swelled. She tore into the parcel, then gasped. From a shallow box, she pulled the most beautiful gown she thought she'd ever seen.

White silk rippled down as she gently freed the dress from its wrapping. She held it up in front of her, completely in awe of its beauty. A large, dark green ribbon separated the soft silk skirt from the intricately beaded bodice. The neckline cut straight across so that both shoulders were visible, and the sleeves were pure white lace that extended and fastened around the wrist.

"What do you think?" her father asked from the doorway. Kat laid the dress back into its box with care. "It's beautiful!"

Her father's face beamed with pride. "I'm glad you like it."

He smiled, though Kat noticed a sad tone in his voice.

"What is it?" she asked, concerned. Her father gave her a half smile. "I was just thinking about your mother and how much she would've wanted to be here today."

Kat's shoulders fell.

"I'm sorry, Katiana. I didn't mean to upset you..."

"No... It's okay. I wish she was here, too."

Her father pulled her into a warm embrace and left a soft kiss on her temple. "She would've been so proud of you."

Kat gave him a half - unsure smile.

"She would've," he insisted. "You remind me so much of her. You're bold, loving, creative, thoughtful, and full of warmth, just like her... And I know you'd rather be anywhere else than at that ball tonight, which is also a trait you inherited from her."

Her father smiled, and Kat chuckled, agreeing with him. "In fact, if she were here, I'm sure she would've devised some grand scheme to get you out of it completely."

"If only!" Kat giggled. She thought back on all the stories she had heard about her mother and wondered what her first feast had been like. "Can I ask you something?"

"Of course, my darling."

She chewed her lip anxiously, pondering whether to ask the loaded question she had prepared.

"Do you think it's possible for someone to love me as much as you loved her?"

Her father sighed. She could see every emotion that mixed in his mind, and almost regretted asking. "I know it is..." he said finally, contemplating how much his little girl had grown in such a short time. "And I dread the day I see it come true!"

Kat giggled at the dramatic way her father spoke, but knew he was making light of a situation that he honestly and truly dreaded.

"Don't put too much pressure on yourself, or on tonight... It's just another party. Hm? Love will come in its own time. Often when we least expect it... and I promise, as long as you follow your heart, it will be well worth it."

Kat wrapped her arms around her father and thanked him for his words and the beautiful gift he had given her.

"Happy Birthday my Katiana."

He kissed the top of her head, then left her with her thoughts. Between the time spent with Jerren and Daniel, and the moment she had just shared with her father, Kat's heart warmed with the idea that her band of loyal men was once again rallied around her.

A large yawn from deep within seemed to transfer her warm thoughts to those of a warm bed. She moved her fingertips across the gown, once more admiring it, then with the greatest care, lifted the gown from the bed, and hung it safely on the back of her wardrobe. She would surely shine in such a lovely dress, but she was still anxious about what the evening may bring. The fleeting thought of her mother devising an escape plan for her filled her heart with a bittersweet melancholy.

She fell back on her bed, utterly spent, in every way imaginable. She closed her eyes and fresh hopes, dreams, and wishes seemed to swim around her head. Wishes that allowed her more time with her mother and uncle. Hopes that the evening would prove as wonderful as everyone insisted, and that her nerves would vanish. Dreams of finding love or maybe even having her first kiss. The thought sent a nervous excitement straight into her heart. She grasped for her pendant, recited her poem, then peacefully drifted to sleep.

As she drifted, she entered a dream world. It was the Grand hall, only it wasn't. The surrounding stone wasn't cold and gray, but warm and seemed to glow with an iridescent haze. She looked down and realized she was wearing the dress her father had given her; she smiled, and lightly twirled the beautiful silken skirt. When she looked up she found the people she cared for the most suddenly surrounded her. Her father, her brother, Ada and Tom, each member of the Enid family and, to her great surprise, her mother and uncle.

Before Kat could utter a single word, Daniel took a step forward from the group. He smiled warmly, and bowed his head, then extended his hand for her to take. Pulled by the narrative of the dreamscape, she graciously accepted, and the moment their hands met, a soft melody seemed to radiate from the walls around them. Kat smiled as Daniel pulled her into his arms, then slowly began to waltz her around the room. The stone floor suddenly turned to clouds that whirled around their feet, lifting them straight into the air; it was just the two of them. Slowly the clouds began to dissipate, lowering them back to earth, and when the music finally stopped, her small circle of cherished loved ones began to applaud and cheer.

Daniel spun her from his arms, keeping hold of just one hand, and bowed once more to her. He brought her hand to his lips, left a sweet kiss, and stepped back into the circle her family had made. Then, one by one, each member of the small party came forward to speak to her.

Her father and brother told her how wonderful she looked. Leanna, Ada, and Tom told her how graceful she was, and Declan and Archer asked for a dance of their own. She turned to her uncle, who wrapped his arms around her and kissed her head; he told her how much he missed her and that he was never too far away. She turned to her mother, who kissed her cheek and cupped her hands around Kat's face; she told her how much she loved her and how grateful she was to have such an amazing daughter.

Tears of joy welled in Kat's eyes, and her heart swelled with each tender word spoken; for they were words she longed to hear. She turned to Daniel, who had yet to speak, and waited expectantly, but he remained silent. "Why aren't you saying anything?" she asked, confused.

He smiled a smile so bright, that even in her semiconscious state she could feel her heart flutter. He took each of her hands in his, and took a step closer, closing the distance between them. He leaned in, letting his nose brush along hers. "It's not my turn, princess," he whispered.

They sat for just a moment in pure silence, lost in one another's gaze. His sparkling sapphire eyes were full of joy and adoration, and before she knew what was happening, Daniel leaned in, and left a precious kiss against her lips.

Kat suddenly jolted awake. Her head was swimming, and her heart racing with excitement. A light sigh escaped her, and she wasn't sure if it was in awe of such a lovely dream, or in disappointment that it had ended so soon. She sunk back into her bed with a smile on her face, hoping the warmth she felt in her heart would linger just a while longer. Reaching for her pendant, she whispered a grateful prayer; Knowing only the power it processed, or the Gods themselves, could have brought her such a beautiful and unforgettable dream.

The dream had been nothing more than a figment of her own imagination, regardless of that knowledge though, Kat vowed to cherish it always. She closed her eyes, etching every tiny detail of the fantasy into her memory. It had all felt so real, so genuine, and she was not eager to forget it. She brought the tips of her fingers to her lips and swore she could still feel Daniel's kiss, causing a deep blush to spread across her face, and her heart flutter once more. There was something about the way he had looked at her, something about what he had said; she couldn't shake the feeling that maybe there was more to it.

For months, *years, if she were being honest with herself,* her feelings for Daniel had shifted and grown. It was hard to put a name to them because they ran so deep in so many ways.

He was everything to her: her confidant, her bodyguard, her calm in a storm; he was her best friend. The thought of losing him for any reason sent a chill down her spine, and she absolutely refused to tempt fate in that regard.

She replayed the moment of their dream kiss once more in her mind, and the sudden flash of being so close to him earlier that morning sent a sort of thrill through her. "Oh, get a grip! It was only a dream," she sighed, suddenly annoyed with herself. *Why now?*

She didn't understand what had brought on this sudden affinity and concern for how Daniel saw her. She had no intention of changing the way things were between them… no matter how badly she wanted to. In her heart, she knew it was impossible for Daniel to feel the same; to him, she would always be the reminder of the sister he lost, a dear friend, and nothing more.

The dream had been just that, *a dream.* Kat immediately dismissed any notion of being more to Daniel than what she was; insisting to herself that there were more important things to think about. *Like the impending suitors feast.*

Reality abruptly reeled her back in, and a terrifying thought seemed to burst the blissful bubble of the magical dream once and for all. A thought she hadn't even considered until that very moment. Her choice in the dream was so blatantly obvious, but the dream was gone. Aggravation, and annoyance concerning the suitor's feast that took hold of her the night before, was quickly replaced with unbridled fear and overwhelming anxiety...

Who in the hell was she going to choose to share her first dance with?

Unanswered Questions

On every birthday Kat could remember, she'd gone shopping in the village; and in the last few years, the eventual stop was always at the Spear and Thistle Inn. As she walked through the door to the inn, expecting nothing more than her usual dose of Aunt Ada, it surprised her, in the best possible way, to find Lady Leanna, Declan, and Archer.

"Kat!" The young boys cried in unison, as they ran to hug her. She welcomed their affection gladly, and made a point to acknowledge how much they had grown. The younger Enid brothers were growing as quickly as Daniel had. Archer was now a head taller than half the door frame and Declan stood just below eye level.

The boys, especially Archer, blushed at her loving compliments, but before they could reciprocate any sort of reply, their mother ushered them aside and stood with open arms for the princess. "Happy Birthday, beautiful girl!" Leanna smiled. Kat grinned from ear to ear and gladly stepped into her loving embrace.

Over the years, Kat and Lady Leanna had become very close. After the events of the river, Kat had taken her up on her offer to come to her whenever she needed, and spent as much time with her as she could when they were in Eraduun. While Leanna was away, they wrote to one another as often as possible, sharing all of life's woes and magical moments. Kat was truly grateful for the bond they had formed, *and that it made her miss her mother just a little less.*

Kat looked around the inn, expecting to be swarmed by Aunt Ada, but saw no sign of the soon-to-be mother. When she asked after her, Leanna informed her that the local healer had put Ada on bed rest, *quite against her will.* They both giggled at the thought, knowing Ada was not one to be idle, nor was she one to tolerate being doted; doting was *her* job.

"Gods help poor Tom," Kat said with a smile.

Together, Kat and Leanna sat down at a nearby table and caught up on everything the other had missed, as if they were old friends reunited at last. The very first thing Kat told her, of course, was about that morning's adventure.

"Oh, that is such a special place," Leanna sighed. "I have so many wonderful memories there."

Kat was surprised at her knowledge of the place, and raised a questioning brow.

"Rumor has it, it's an old 'Enid family secret'" Leanna smiled. "Daniel's father took me there for the first time, many, *many* years ago."

Her friend quickly became transfixed on a memory, leaving Kat to contemplate a few newly burning questions. If it was so special, *why had Jerren and Daniel even taken her there?* She suddenly felt guilty, as though she had intruded on a very important tradition.

"Are you excited about this evening?" Leanna asked, pulling Kat out of her thoughts. She wanted to tell Leanna she was far from excited, but thought it best to keep that to herself. So instead of divulging her anxiety about it all, she smiled as brightly as she could and nodded a little frantically. A wave of relief consumed the princess when Leanna began to riminess instead of investigate.

"I remember my first suitors' feast…" she began. "*I was so nervous…* So nervous, in fact, that I contemplated running away."

"Lena!" Kat said, stunned by the admission.

Leanna chuckled. "I would have too, had your uncle not stopped me."

A sad smile seemed to inch across Leanna's face. Kat had never seen Lady Enid so melancholy. Everyone knew how close She and William had been, but Kat wondered if their friendship had been more than what it appeared.

"He told me that running away from my fears wouldn't solve anything, and he promised that if I stayed and went through with it… he'd make sure the evening would be *magical*… and, of course, it was."

Kat smiled, but it felt hollow. The story oozed every ounce of selfless love she had known her uncle to possess, and it made her miss him all the more.

"I shared my first dance with him," Leanna continued, hoping to distract Kat from her looming grief.

"I never knew!"

"I remember being so flustered. My heart pounded, my hands were sweating, and I swear I almost fainted."

Leanna chuckled at the memory, as if it had been such a ridiculous notion, not knowing the fear Kat had of the very situation she had just described.

"And then it was like the crowd parted and there was William, smiling right at me. He made the pressure of it all disappear with a single look... I was so grateful to him for that first dance because everything after that was... effortless."

Leanna paused, and Kat couldn't help but notice a fleeting look in her eyes. She was just about to ask her about it when Leanna said something that seemed to throw her off track once again.

"And just between us girls," she said in a hushed tone. "I had my first kiss that night, too."

The two of them giggled together, and Kat wondered if her uncle had been the one Leanna had kissed, but was far too shy to ask.

"Ka - I mean, Princess, what are you doing here?" Daniel said, entering through the back door with an arm full of firewood.

"She came to seek a wise woman's advice, but your aunt is taking a well-deserved nap, so she's been stuck listening to me riminess about days past," Leanna said, giving Kat a small wink. Daniel looked at the two of them, a little confused, but with a certain sparkle in his eyes.

"I heard you took our Princess to a very special place this morning," Leanna said to her son with a peaked brow.

Kat looked back up at Daniel and saw the color simultaneously drain, then overfill his face.

"Well *Jerren* and I did... I should get these to the kitchen."

"I can help!" Kat said, jumping up to meet him.

"Oh, that's okay... I've got-"

Kat rolled her eyes at his obligatory response, making him chuckle, and shake his head, clearing forgetting whatever anxiety had formed within him. She gave him a playful nod, took a couple of logs from the top of the bundle, then followed him into the kitchen.

"You don't have to do things like this, you know, Princess," Daniel said, discarding his armful near the stove.

"I am not the Princess when I'm here, Daniel. I'm just Kat, and *Kat* is more than capable of helping if she'd like to."

The look on Kat's face was definitive, and Daniel couldn't help but chuckle once more. "As you say, Kitty Kat."

He winked, and Kat answered with a shy smile. "Besides..." she began. "I was hoping to talk to you about something."

Daniel gave her an intrigued sort of grin, as he took the logs from her arms to place with the others.

"Just an idea I had."

Daniel turned to face her, clearly amused by her bashful demeanor, then leaned against a nearby counter, using his hands to prop him up. "Well, don't leave me in suspense... What can I do for the birthday girl?" he asked with a smile.

"Well, before I get into all that," Kat began, eager to repay his taunting smirk. "I'm curious to know why you seemed so embarrassed when your mother brought up where we went this morning?"

A bit of color rose in Daniel's cheek at the mention, and Kat knew justice was served. "I wasn't embarrassed," he insisted, hastily.

"Daniel, you're blushing!"

"I am not!"

Daniel's mental slip manifested physically with the slip of one of his hands against the counter. He caught himself, hoping Kat hadn't noticed, but it was too late. She bit her lips to conceal a laugh, but to no avail.

"Something funny, princess?" he asked with a slightly raised brow. Kat scrunched her nose and held her forefinger and thumb a tiny distance apart. Daniel grabbed Kat unexpectedly, threw her over his shoulder, and spun her around. She squealed and giggled, then lightheartedly demanded to be put down. Daniel chuckled, obviously pleased with himself, then carefully lowered her back to the ground, not quite breaking their connection.

As he lowered her, Kat hooked her fingers at the base of his neck so that her arms were resting on his shoulders.

Their playful giggles slowly subsided, and something in the air between them seemed to change.

Kat looked deep into Daniel's eyes and felt a pull to them. Her heart raced, and butterflies filled her insides, as she was momentarily transported back into her dream. Her heart was pounding so hard she was a little afraid he could hear it. Whatever was happening, she was sure he felt it too. *He had to.*

Daniel tucked a loose bit of hair behind her ear, then swallowed hard. He leaned in slightly, and Kat mirrored his movement.

"Eh-hem!" a small angry voice exclaimed, making the pair jump. They turned their heads towards the kitchen door to find Archer with his arms crossed, his foot stamping, and scowl on his face that was aimed at his brother. At the same moment, Daniel and Kat released one another. Daniel cleared his throat nervously, and Kat tried to hide the blush that crept across her face.

Curious as to what had made him so bitter, and eager to erase the embarrassment she felt, Kat kept her eyes on Archer as he grabbed a plate of cheese and bread, then placed it forcefully on the counter in front of them. The small boy's eyes, which seemed to drill into his brother, burned with fury. He ripped a small piece of the bread angrily from the loaf, then all but threw it in his mouth. The scowl on Archer's face made it clear he had no intention of leaving his brother and the princess alone again.

"Archer!" Leanna called from the other room. The young boy groaned slightly, then at the pace of a tortoise, he backed away towards the door, his eyes never leaving his brother's. At the very last moment, just before he turned away, he looked over at Kat, and his scowl turned into a bright smile as he waved his fingers at her. She giggled, then returned the sweet smile and cute wave.

"He's still convinced you're going to marry him some day," Daniel said as his baby brother left the room.

Kat chuckled, and a coquettish grin spread across her lips. "Well... If he grows up half as good looking as his *brother*, maybe I will."

Kat took a flirtatious step forward, and Daniel stood a little taller. "*Declan is just ever so handsome!*"

Kat batted her eyelashes at him, and Daniel frowned, then rolled his eyes in agreement. "I guess he is pretty sharp," he admitted, and the pair chuckled once more.

They hadn't chanced a true gaze at one another since Archer had entered the room, and an awkward feeling seemed to consume them.

"So... your idea?" Daniel asked, hoping to move the subject along. Kat was momentarily caught off guard by the whole situation, and had nearly forgotten what had inspired her need to speak to him.

"Oh, right!" she blushed. "Well, I guess it's less of an idea and more of a... question," she said as she knotted her fingers. After whatever moment they had shared, the idea of asking him for a favor seemed unimaginable — especially one as big as this. The nerve she had built up before arriving at the inn had failed her completely as she rambled.

"This is probably going to sound a little silly... And I'm sure this isn't how things are done... And please don't feel obligated to answer one way or another... right this minute, at least... I mean, it's not like it's this *enormous* deal or anything-"

"Kat!" Daniel took one of her hands, hoping it might calm her enough to make sense. "What is it?" He chuckled, and his winsome smile only fueled Kat's anxiety.

"I was wondering, well, hoping," she corrected. Before continuing, Kat looked up at Daniel's confused and obviously amused face. She took a deep breath in, knowing she would have to hold it until he answered her unasked question. "Would you be my first dance at the feast tonight?"

"Oh." Daniel answered, amused that it had seemed like such a troublesome question. Then, a realization hit him like a boulder. "*Ooh!*"

"Please?" Kat asked with a nervous smile. Daniel instantly released her hand, then shrugged against the counter, as he rubbed the back of his neck. Kat's heart dropped at his reaction; it was all the answer she needed. "You know what... nevermind!"

Kat's forced smile was painfully obvious, but she continued anyway. "I just thought it would be fun... But, now that I say it out loud it seems silly."

She made a move to leave and Daniel grabbed her hand. "Wait Kat, I didn't mean- I mean, you really want *me*?" he asked in disbelief. "To dance with you…" he added, shaking his head.

Kat anxiously leaned against the counter next to him. "Well, I thought it might take some of the pressure off," she said, thinking back to what Leanna had told her.

"Oh…" Daniel replied, a little deflated.

"What I mean is… You're my best friend," she said, looking up at him with hopeful eyes. Daniel's eyes bore into hers, and she felt the slight pull in the surrounding air. This time, though, she put it aside and glanced down at her feet. It was more obvious, now than it ever had been before, that he did not see her in the same way she saw him, but she couldn't risk letting whatever she had been feeling impede their friendship now.

"You're like a second big brother to me, and if I could, I would've asked Jerren, but I can't, so…"

"I see," Daniel said, casting his eyes to the floor.

They sat in an awkward silence for a moment. The idea had rendered Daniel speechless. Kat, however, felt like an utter fool. *Why had she thought this was a good idea?*

"Forget I asked… It's not a big deal. I mean, there's going to be so many people there. I don't know what I was feeling so anxious about."

"Kat…" Daniel sighed, knowing he had hurt her feelings.

"Honestly! It's okay!"

Kat smiled as bright as she could, stifling her feelings of rejection, and put a reassuring hand on his arm. Daniel opened his mouth to speak, but stopped and lowered his head.

"Was that all, princess?"

Kat dropped her hand instantly. "Yes," she chirped. "That was it."

She turned to leave, but didn't quite make it to the door. This was the awkward moment she had hoped to avoid. It was everything she imagined it would be; heart wrenching and humiliating, but she refused to let it ruin what they had. She raced back to Daniel, threw her arms around his neck, and hugged him as tightly as she could. "I really am glad you're home," she whispered.

Daniel was so stunned by the display, he could hardly move. He just stood with his arms out, wondering what his next move should be. Kat tightened her embrace, and his arms melted around her. "Me too, Kitty Kat."

Kat pulled back just enough to meet his gaze, but did not release her hold. "Having you home is one of the best birthday presents I could have gotten…"

Daniel's heart swelled and ached all at the same time. "I wouldn't have missed this day for the world!"

Kat hugged him once more, then pulled away to leave. She'd only made it a step or two before Daniel caught her hand once more. "I really hope you've had a great day… I know this evening will be even better."

Kat gave him a half smile. "You're going to be there?"

Daniel's thumb grazed her knuckles, and a mess of goosebumps ran up her arm. Before she knew what was happening, Daniel brought her hand to his lips and kissed it. "The Gods couldn't stop me."

Kat's heart fluttered. The look on Daniel's face told her he was battling some internal struggle, but there was no way she could ask him about it now. He opened his mouth to say something, but she cut him off, hoping she was rescuing him, *or herself,* from something irreversible.

"I should get going," she smiled. "I've got lots to do to get ready."

She left the kitchen, and Daniel followed behind. "Kat, wait."

"I'll see you tonight, okay?" She replied, ignoring his request. Kat said a frantic goodbye to the rest of the Enid family and quickly made her leave. Daniel followed her all the way to the exit, but stopped in the doorway. He leaned helplessly against the door frame and watched as she disappeared up the lane.

She turned back for just a second and gave him a half-hearted smile. He waved, but when she turned away once more he groaned internally, angry at himself for not being able to give her some peace of mind. *Why couldn't he just tell her how he felt?* He hung his head in frustration. "It'd be pointless anyway..."

Daniel let out a low, disappointed sigh, and shut the door behind him.

The Suitors Feast

"You're quiet this evening, princess," Mara said as she pulled a brush through Kat's hair.

Kat stared blankly past her reflection; she was in a world of her own and hadn't heard the nanny speak. Mara paused slightly. "Princess?"

"Hm?"

"I said you're quiet this evening. Have you not had a pleasant day?"

Kat shook her head. "I mean! Yes! I've had a splendid day."

The old nanny raised a questioning eyebrow, and Kat chuckled. "I guess I'm just a little nervous."

"Don't you fret one bit! It's just another feast. Understand?"

Kat gave a small smile and nod to placate the au pair, but that didn't keep her nerves from running rampant. The remainder of the time Mara spent helping Kat prepare herself was peppered with small talk and idle chit chat; anything that would keep the nanny occupied enough to not question, or lecture, the princess further. Mara had just laced the back of Kat's dress when there was a knock at the door.

"Come in!" Kat called. Her father entered, and Mara excused herself with a curtsy. Before turning to face her father, Kat plastered a smile on her face, hoping the same charade she had used with Mara would carry over with her father.

"What do you think?" she asked, as she twirled her skirt. Her Father smiled lovingly, taking in the sight as much as he could. "Absolutely gorgeous! There's just one thing missing," he suggested with a slight glint in his eyes. Kat eyed him carefully as his smile broadened, and he pulled a wooden box out from behind his back. "I've been saving this for you."

Kat gratefully accepted the box with the sincerest of smiles. "But you've already given me a gift."

"And since when is a father limited to the number of gifts to doute his daughter with?"

Her father's eyes shone with love and pride, and Kat could no longer contain her excitement. She opened the box, and gasped. Inside the velvet lined case was, quite possibly, the most beautiful crown she had ever seen. The band was made of intricately crafted rods of gold loosely intertwined to look like vines or twisted branches, with delicate golden wildflowers splayed throughout. At the center of the tiara was a small replica of the royal crest; golden sun rays encircled a jeweled centerpiece with a diamond representing the sun, and a crescent cut sapphire the moon.

"It was your mother's very first crown," her father explained as Kat admired the magnificent tiara. "She designed it herself, and I thought you might like to wear it tonight."

Kat's eyes shot up to meet her father's. He smiled, but his eyes shimmered with tears.

"It'd be an honor," she breathed, obviously in awe of the gift. The king pulled the crown carefully from its resting place, gently nestled it on top of her head, then stood back and smiled with wonderment.

"Oh! And I almost forgot... just *one* more thing!"

Her father reached into the pocket of his tunic, then presented another, smaller, wooden box. Kat gave her father a stern look, silently reprimanding his actions; her father smirked, and lightheartedly waved off her disapproval. He opened the box this time, and pulled a piece of jewelry out, then put the box aside.

"*This ... I* had made for *you.*"

The king held up an elegant choker. The necklace had several small golden replicas of the royal crest lined across it, the center most encrusted with solitaire diamonds; thin chains hung in semi-circles connecting a few of the crests, and a line of diamonds hung from the center. It was beautiful, but as he lifted it towards Kat, she seemed to realize something else was in the way. She reached instantly for the sacred pendant that hung around her neck. The thought of facing the night without the power of it petrified her, but *how could she refuse her father's gift?*

Her hands trembled as she disconnected the clasp and carefully placed the necklace on her vanity; then stepped anxiously in front of her father, allowing him to secure his gift.

"There now!"

Kat took a deep breath, and turned to admire the finishing touch in the mirror. The image before her was almost unrecognizable. From her gown, to her mother's tiara, to her father's wonderful gift, she looked every bit the regal princess she was supposed to be; *everything was absolutely perfect.*

"Ready?" her father asked, breaking her from her trance, and presenting his arm to her. Kat said a silent prayer that, with the absence of her trusty pendant, her mother's crown would give her all the strength she needed to make it through the evening. She took one last steadying breath, then beamed at her father. "Yes."

When Kat took his arm, her nerves calmed and were, at least momentarily, forgotten. Her father kissed the top of her head, then escorted her to the grand hall. As they entered, the gathered crowd erupted in applause. Kat smiled brightly as she scanned the audience before her, taking in a few familiar faces and several unknown ones. Her father presented her with the seat of honor, and the feast began.

With each passing moment, Kat's nerves built more and more. Everything seemed much more grand and important than she was used to, even as the princess. She carefully scanned the room and her eyes met Daniel's.

"*Wow!*" he mouthed with a bright smile. He lifted a glass to her, and her heart fluttered. She smiled shyly and tilted her glass to him. He mimicked taking a deep breath, then stood a little taller, every pore exuding confidence. Kat answered with a nod, then mirrored his actions, and to her surprise, her confidence seemed to grow. *"Thank you,"* she mouthed back. He answered with a wink, then far too soon turned to speak to the guest next to him.

The evening seemed to pass with ease after Daniel's silent lesson. Kat ate her favorite foods, talked and laughed with those who were sitting near her, and cheered loudly for the entertainment her father had arranged. She thought perhaps her father and Mara had been right... *this was nothing more than another feast*... That is... until they cleared the tables from the dance floor and called all eligible young men forward. Her mouth went dry, and she took a large drink of wine, hoping to steal her nerves. *It was time to choose her first dance partner.*

The very first dance of a suitors' feast was a tradition that dated back to the kingdom's inception. It was the most significant dance of the evening, performed only by the woman of honor and the partner of her choosing. The tradition originated with the story of the three sisters, who used their dance to create and solidify the alliances that formed the kingdom. Over the centuries, though, it became less of a means of unity... and much more like a pageant show.

The first dance showed off the young woman's elegance, poise, and beauty; and was as much a chance to rise above their station as anything else. Who a woman chose as her first dance spoke volumes about who she was, and more importantly who she had the potential to be. For most girls, choosing a partner was simple. They would find the highest ranking young man in the room and follow his lead. Jerren was the highest ranking boy there, but as much as the first dance was to show off the young woman, it was also to encourage a potential match, so picking him was out of the question.

Kat stepped cautiously into the middle of the dance floor, and young men by the scores made layered rings around her. Young knights, noblemen, lords, and even a couple of foreign princes surrounded her, but she had no interest in being like the other girls and choosing a partner because of his status, or for some sort of political gain. She wanted her choice to mean something to her, and to her alone.

Slowly, she walked the perimeter of the inner ring, taking stock of her options, hoping she'd know the right partner when she saw him. She made it halfway around the circle, and had yet to discover a suitable partner. Kat's nerves rose, feeling the hundreds of eyes that burned into her, waiting in anticipation to see who she would choose. *This was taking too long.* Her mind raced, and her anxiety grew with each step she took. She had nearly made a hasty decision out of growing necessity when a movement in the corner of her eye caught her attention.

A slight murmur echoed across the crowd as Daniel made a path to the inner circle. He stopped in line with the other young men and stood with an unwavering air of confidence. When Kat's eyes met his, he smiled and gave her a small wink; relief flooded her system. He had always been there when she needed him, and tonight was no exception.

She took a few more steps around the circle, then presented her hand to Daniel, which he proudly and humbly accepted. When he took her hand, every ounce of anxiety she had melted away. Side by side, they made their way towards the King, who must approve the selection. Her father smiled warmly at her, gave his blessing, then cued the musicians. As Kat and Daniel stepped to the middle of the dance floor, Daniel leaned in and whispered to her.

"You look stunning, Princess."

Kat smiled, and they took their positions.

"Ready?" he mouthed. She gave him a confident nod, and suddenly the music began. In Daniel's arms, dancing was *effortless*. He made her feel calm and confident, as he waltzed her around the floor with ease, and for a moment, the world around them seemed to melt away. A tinge of pink crossed Kat's cheeks as memories of her dream that afternoon came flooding in. Daniel gave her a questioning look, but she only shook her head. When she woke from the dream, she thought she could never experience something as wonderful as it had been; but this, being in Daniel's arms as they glided around the room, this moment was so much better than her dream had been. It was no longer a figment of her imagination; *it was real*.

She and Daniel hit a final pose as the music ended, and the whole of the room boomed with cheers and applause. Daniel swung Kat outwards, presenting her to the roaring crowd, then kissed her hand, and joined the others in the celebration. Kat's elation was clear; she could not have asked for a better partner to share her first dance with. It had given her the confidence she needed, and from that point on, she danced every dance with a new partner. Some were more agreeable than others, but overall, she couldn't complain.

The whole of the kingdom, it seemed, was throwing themselves at her feet, and though the very thought had terrified, and slightly disgusted, her hours ago, she'd be lying if she were to say she wasn't enjoying it *just a little*.

She had danced so much, and sat so little that at one point, she had to sneak away, just to take a breath. With so many people in attendance, and all the dancing, the hall was uncomfortably warm, and she could no longer stand it. She slipped out a side door and onto a balcony that overlooked the courtyard, narrowly escaping a gaggle of young men. The cool winter air felt nice on her hot skin, and she felt as though she could finally breathe. She leaned over on the stone rail and sighed heavily, feeling relieved and somewhat elated.

"You alright, Princess?" a voice chuckled behind her. Kat jumped, and Daniel chuckled once more. He stepped beside her, and leaned his back against the balcony wall. Kat smiled. "I'm exhausted."

"It must be hard work making all those fancy chaps fall in love with you," he teased, giving her a nudge with his arm. Kat sucked her teeth and nudged him back. "Oh, shut up."

"I noticed a particular few seemed *very* intent on grabbing your attention." The thought of which made him ill.

"I don't know what you're talking about."

Daniel smirked at her feigned innocence, but gave a lighthearted chuckle. "I'm sure you don't."

Unable to meet Daniel's gaze, Kat cast her attention to the courtyard below, where she spotted a young couple sneaking away, only to huddle into a corner behind a statue. A pang of jealousy shot through her, and she couldn't help but wish someone would whisk her away, too.

"Is it better than you thought it would be?"

Kat had fixated so much on the young couple holding each other, she wasn't sure what Daniel meant. "Is what better?"

Daniel gave her a perplexed look, then turned to see what had caught her attention. When he spotted the couple, an amused grin crossed his lips.

"Your party…" he expanded. Kat blushed. "I suppose so."

The young couple she had been watching shared a sweet kiss that quickly turned passionate, and Kat turned sharply away, feeling as though she was now intruding on a very private moment.

"*They're* certainly enjoying themselves."

Kat rolled her eyes and shook her head. "Don't be so crude," she admonished. Daniel chuckled again, but the moment she spoke, Kat had honestly stopped paying him any attention. A sudden frightening thought crossed her mind, and before she could stop herself, words she had never intended on speaking aloud came pouring out.

"Do you think anyone will ever kiss me like that?"

Daniel's eyes widened, and he stumbled a little over his response. "Of course I will- SOMEONE will... Of course *I think, someone* will," he corrected, hoping she hadn't caught his mistake. "Why would you ask a question like that?"

Kat shrugged. *Why had she asked him that?*

She suddenly found herself fantasizing what it would be like to sneak around the castle grounds hand in hand with a handsome young man; what he might say to her to make her insides flip, and her cheeks blush; what it would feel like to be wrapped in his arms, and have his lips pressed against her own. Her gaze wandered up towards Daniel, and she couldn't stop herself from wondering what it would be like if that handsome young man were *him. What would it be like to kiss him?* Not a sweet timid kiss like in her dream, but a genuine, heart-stopping, soul-melting, kind of kiss. A warm blush spread across her cheeks at the thought, and she glanced down at her feet.

"I've never had a *real* first kiss," she admitted shyly. Her voice was quiet, bordering on pathetic, and she felt foolish admitting something so personal, but even more foolish that at her age she had yet to experience a proper kiss. While Kat felt disgusted by the thought, something about her admission made Daniel feel relieved.

"You say that like it's a bad thing."

Kat gave him a sideways look that told him exactly how bad she thought it was.

"It's not," he shrugged. "It just means you haven't found the right person to share that moment with."

Kat rolled her eyes. "And what if I never do?"

Daniel squirmed a little at the idea of Kat kissing anyone, but knew she was searching for reassurance. "You will, I'm sure of it... *and when you do*, you'll be glad you saved your first kiss for someone special, someone you care for."

"Is that what *your* first kiss was like?"

Daniel's face turned a light shade of pink. "What'd you mean?"

"Was your first kiss with someone special that you cared for?"

Daniel knew exactly what she was asking, but didn't want to give her the answer.

"*Well?*"

He sighed. "I wish it had been... I mean, she was a gorgeous girl, and it was a pleasant kiss, but it didn't *really* mean anything. You know?"

Kat cast her eyes to her feet once more. The thought of Daniel having a *'pleasant kiss'* with a *'gorgeous girl'* irritated her, though she knew it shouldn't. "No... I wouldn't know."

The more she thought about Daniel's first kiss, the more irritated she became. The pair stood next to each other in silence; Kat, too annoyed to speak, Daniel, unsure of what to even say.

"Maybe we should go back in," he finally suggested. "They'll miss you in there."

He reached up to tuck a stray trundle of hair behind her ear, but stopped himself. Kat, who was infuriatingly ignorant of the situation, didn't seem to care whether *anyone* missed her. At the moment, she found herself out of sorts and she couldn't figure out what was bothering her more: that she'd never had a kiss, or that Daniel seemed to have ample experience in the matter.

"Who was it?" she asked without warning. Daniel's face froze with a stupid expression, hoping to the Gods she wasn't asking what he thought she was asking.

"Who was your first kiss?"

Daniel rubbed the back of his neck, realizing he had guessed her query correctly. "It's a little cold out here, don't you think?"

Kat narrowed her eyes at him, not giving his attempted diversion a second thought. When there was still no response, she settled back on her heels, and crossed her arms. She was getting her answer, and she didn't care how long it took to get it.

"Oh, come on, Kat!"

"Well, excuse me for being curious. I thought it meant nothing to you, so I don't know why you're being so secretive about it."

Daniel chewed his lower lip, thinking hard about whether he should answer, knowing it was a delicate matter. He glanced down to meet Kat's gaze, only to find her glaring up at him. He half groaned, letting his head hang dramatically.

"Seydi."

Kat rolled her eyes. His answer didn't make her feel any better, if anything, it fueled her annoyance further. "Figures..." she said flatly. "Who else?"

"Kat!" Daniel scolded her boldness, but she only shrugged. "Well, she may have been the first, but I know she wasn't the last. How many others have there been?"

Daniel scoffed and walked to the other side of the balcony. "I'm *not* having this conversation with you."

Kat followed close behind, unwilling to drop the subject. "And I assume they didn't *all* hold some *special* meaning to you."

"What's your point?"

Daniel felt as though he was being put on trial, and the more she pushed, the more his defenses rose. But what she said to him next would smash every barrier he had tried to put up.

"Kiss me."

"What?!"

"I mean, it's not like you've never kissed me before…"

Her suggestion had been so outrageously out of character, and surprising that Daniel's typical confidence disintegrated, and he grew increasingly flustered. "On the hand or- or the cheek, yeah but-"

"It can't really be *that* different…"

Kat took a flirtatious step forward, but Daniel side stepped her advance and gave her a hard look.

"It is different. *Very different*! I mean you're-"

"The princess," she said, finishing his sentence for him.

"Right. But mostly, your first kiss should be-"

"With someone special? You said that already."

Daniel sighed, dragging his hand through his hair. His nerves crashed through his body at the thought of it all, and he suddenly wished he had been anywhere else, while also knowing there was nowhere else he'd rather be. "And I meant it! Gods! I wish my first kiss would've been with -" he glanced up at her, and suddenly stopped himself from divulging anything else.

"With who?" Kat asked, thoroughly intrigued.

Their eyes locked, and Daniel knew there was no escape. A thousand responses flashed through his mind, but no words would come out. He was lost, silently transfixed on her deep emerald eyes, and he knew the only way out of it was to tell her the truth... *but maybe not the whole truth.*

Daniel took a calming breath, and a step forward, finding what little courage remained in him. "I wish, *more than anything in this world,* that my *first kiss* had been with someone I truly care about... someone that makes me feel happy and warm. Someone that means the world to me and that I trust with every beat of my heart."

Daniel's eyes sparkled with sincerity, and it completely melted Kat. Something in his stare made her hope that maybe the *someone* he wished for, was *her.* Daniel took her hand, and gently grazed his thumb across her knuckles. The air around them seemed to still, and Kat became rooted to the cold stone beneath her feet; she couldn't have moved, even if she wanted to. Daniel moved his free hand like he was going to reach for her, but quickly dropped it.

"Don't cheat such a special moment the way I did..." he pleaded. "Wait for the person that makes you feel... *magical.*"

Kat quickly contemplated each suggestion he had made, but the further down the list she traveled, the clearer the answer became.

Someone you truly care about.
Someone that makes you feel happy and warm.
Someone that means the world to you and you trust with every beat of your heart.

Someone that makes you feel magical.

Staring deep into Daniel's eyes, Kat suddenly realized something that seemed so obvious. She blushed and turned away from him, not sure she could face him while speaking *her* truth.

"*You* are all those things to me..."

Daniel's heart swelled, but he knew she had no way of knowing what her words truly meant, not to him at least. "Kat..." he sighed

She turned back to face him, not knowing he had stepped closer. They stood nearly face to face, eyes pouring into one another. The surrounding air shifted, and she felt it, the pull to him. It was the same feeling she'd had all day being this close to him. Her heart raced, and her stomach flipped, but she didn't dare turn away.

"Please, don't look at me like that..." Daniel said, sliding his hand against her cheek and brushing the pad of his thumb against her skin.

"Like what?" she breathed.

Kat was completely ignorant of his meaning, though she had the strangest feeling that her world would suddenly end without him in it. She took a step closer and placed her hand just over his, holding it in place against her cheek.

"Kat."

She ignored the warning tone of his voice and placed her other hand on his chest. "Daniel... please."

Her voice was soft and pleading, and the look in her eyes made Daniel's heart pound. He had to fight every urge in his body just to keep from pulling her to him. He wanted to give in, to pull her lips to his and lose himself in her kiss, knowing it would be everything he had dreamt it to be, but how could he let her waste something so special on him? *Could he be that selfish?* He leaned in, just a little, tempting whatever fate had in store.

Kat's heart was pounding. She closed her eyes and felt the tip of Daniel's nose brush against hers causing butterflies to erupt in her stomach. She wanted to lean in closer, but didn't dare move.

"Kat..." he half whispered. His warning tone had dissipated and left a reverent prayer in its wake. He stepped even closer still, releasing her hand, and curling his arm around the small of her back. His lips hovered just in front of hers, and the moment they had both dreamed about for so long was finally within their reach. Kat could feel his breath on her lips, and it sent a ripple up her spine. "Daniel," she breathed.

"*I... I can't,*" he sighed.

The butterflies in Kat's stomach turned to stone and dropped hard; and when she opened her eyes, Daniel could see the hurt in them. A wave of shame and guilt suddenly coursed through him, and he pulled away from her. He truly hated himself for it, but knew he was doing the 'right' thing.

"I'm sorry..." he said, though his apology did little to ease her anguish or embarrassment. "Please, try to understand..."

He took a step toward her to explain, to comfort her, but she backed angrily out of his reach. Her recoil shot through him; had she stabbed him in the heart with a dull knife, it would have hurt less. All he could do was hang his head and apologize again.

Kat felt like the biggest fool in the universe, *yet again*. Tears welled in her eyes, though she desperately tried to fight them back. *What could she have possibly been thinking? What could have possessed her to try such a stupid, stupid thing?*

"There you two are! I've been looking for you everywhere!" Jerren called out, bursting through the doors. "You're missing all the fun!"

Kat glanced over at Daniel; the look in her eyes was a mixture of regret, pain, and shame. He opened his mouth to speak, to apologize again, but Kat wouldn't grant him the opportunity. She left the balcony as quickly as she could, bumping into her brother as she passed him.

"Kat, wait..." Daniel called to her, but she didn't stop. Either she hadn't heard him, or, more likely, had just blatantly ignored him.

"What's wrong with her?" Jerren slurred, and Daniel knew he had already indulged a little too much. *Though maybe the prince had the right idea.* Unable to bear the thought of *what could have been* any longer, Daniel grabbed the almost full goblet of wine from Jerren's hand and downed it in a single breath.

"That's the spirit!"

The prince put a friendly arm around Daniel's shoulder and ushered him back inside. As they passed through the door, Daniel nabbed yet another full goblet of wine from a surprised serving girl.

"Bottom's up!" He toasted Jerren, finished the cup in seconds, then reached for another. Daniel returned the empty goblets to the girl with a wink and wolfish grin that made her blush. Jerren cheered, and the pair went in search of more refreshments, *and then some.*

Daniel felt like a fool. He replayed the moment over and over in his mind. The way she looked at him, the way he yearned for her; he was so close and had blown the only chance he would have ever had to kiss her. But he knew he could never be enough for her. *Couldn't she see he was only trying to do what was best for her?*

Flashes of her pained expression wouldn't leave his mind, and he desperately wanted to forget the whole thing. Across the room, he watched as Kat danced and flirted with all the bastards he knew he could never be. The thought was maddening, and the more he thought about it, the more he drank.

It wasn't long before he finished a full pitcher of wine by himself. For he found the more he drank, the easier it was to forget what an idiot he was. Ironically, though, the more he drank, the more of an idiot he became.

Confrontation in the Garden

As Kat re-entered the feast, she did her best to put the humiliating situation with Daniel out of her mind. She didn't want to spend a single moment thinking about what could've been or what had almost happened. Instead, she surrounded herself with a crowd of people. She danced and flirted and even allowed herself a little more wine than she typically would.

Amid her quest to forget, the occasional uproar coming from across the room would distract her. In the center of the action, she always found Jerren and Daniel; laughing, singing, or pulling some stunt. Seeing Daniel was wholly unaffected by the situation only made his rejection cut that much deeper, while somehow also strengthening Kat's resolve to forget about it.

The evening had grown late, and Kat realized she had indulged a bit more than she intended to. Her head felt fuzzy, and the room tilted around her. She made her way toward the courtyard in hopes the cool air might help clear her head. As she reached the outer doors, she came across a small group of people, obviously drunk, but having a great time. Their general merriment amused her at first, but upon further inspection, she thought maybe it was possible to have too much of a great thing.

Her eyes went almost instantly to a couple in the corner, enthralled by a passionate kiss. They seemed a little older than herself, and a bitter thought passed through her mind. She knew she should look away, but she couldn't. The young woman positioned herself snugly on her partner's lap, as his hands seemed to travel the length of her body. Kat's heart raced at the sight. She wanted to feel whatever the young woman was feeling; she wanted it so much it ached. But the moment she realized who the young woman's partner had been her feelings flashed from great envy, to monstrous jealousy.

The whole of Kat's being froze. She was a statue, immovable, and cold. One of the drunken men in the group bumped into her by accident, snapping her out of her trance. He quickly and loudly apologized, then wished her 'the happiest of birthdays.' When Kat looked back, the woman sitting on Daniel's lap had shifted her attentive lips to his neck, and somehow his eyes found hers.

Daniel paled in an instant; he looked as though he had seen a ghost, and his expression swiftly faded from shock to panic. Kat, however, felt nothing but ill. How was it he could kiss this random girl, but not her? *'What's wrong with me?'* she thought, feeling undeniably worthless. She broke eye contact for just a moment, but couldn't stop herself from looking back.

As politely as he could, Daniel pushed the girl away from him and moved towards Kat. She looked up at him in disgust, realizing there was nothing wrong with *her*, but everything wrong with *him*. She wanted to scream and yell, but there were too many people around.

Daniel was doing his best to fight through the huddle of people and tables and chairs to get to her, but she didn't want to be anywhere near him. Kat quickly escaped through a side door, hoping to rid herself of him and the entire situation.

The bitter night air cut through her lungs, and for a moment she struggled to breathe. She dashed down the hall, knowing Daniel was not far behind, but she couldn't force herself to go any further. She leaned one hand against the wall and clutched at her tightening chest. Her head was spinning, and her lungs refused to fill with air. She grabbed at the golden choker around her neck and pulled frantically until the clasp broke apart.

At last, the air she had so desperately craved filled her lungs. She leaned her forehead against the cool stone wall and took several deep breaths. The panic subsided, but overwhelming heartbreak swiftly took its place. Hot tears full of rage, sorrow, and jealousy slipped down her cheeks, and she wished she had been anywhere else in the world.

The sound of a door bursting open down the hall made her jump. It was Daniel. He looked flustered and unsure of himself, or anything else. Kat turned her head to wipe her eyes, not wanting to give him the satisfaction of seeing her hurt. She straightened herself, then hurried away. When he finally spotted her, he called out, then jogged to catch up.

"Kat," he called again. She ignored him once more and quickened her pace. "Kat, *please*... Just let me explain."

"Explain what? You have nothing you need to explain to me Daniel," she said as easily as she could, though her tone betrayed her message. He cut in front of her. "Kat, please."

His expression seemed pained and sincere, but Kat was currently low on sympathy for any explanation he might have. She moved to sidestep him, but he blocked her.

"Move out of the way, Daniel."

"No... please just listen to me, what you saw-"

Kat rolled her eyes and made a move to go around him once more, but he was too quick. She pushed him back hard, then turned and marched into the southern gardens.

"Kat!"

Daniel grabbed her arm to stop her, which had apparently been the wrong thing to do. She whirled around and slapped him hard across the face. He'd had too much to drink, and, without thinking, he grabbed her hand harder than he meant to. She let out a small yelp and fear flooded her face. Daniel went deathly pale, released her immediately, and took a step back.

"I'm- I'm sorry Kat. I didn't mean... *I would never!*"

"How dare you!" Kat screeched. Where she had felt sorrow and fear seconds before, she now felt nothing but white-hot rage. Daniel stumbled back at the recognition.

"Kat, please, you know I never meant-"

"Stop calling me that! You no longer have the right!"

"K- Princess... I'm sorry. I'm so sorry."

She turned to walk away, and he reached out again, though this time when she whirled around he had sense enough to jump back.

"Don't touch me!" she hissed.

"Kat, please... *it's me...*"

"I told you. Don't call me that! I am your princess and you will address me accordingly!"

Her face burned, and the more Daniel shrank, the more power mad she became. "You say 'it's me' like that's supposed to mean something! I think you've made yourself a little too comfortable around here. For years you've walked around as if you were someone equal to my brother and I, just because our uncle took pity on you."

Kat's rage and level of intoxication pushed her further and further, fuelling her tirade. She reverted to an old habit, making sure that whoever had crossed her felt just as low as she did; though this time she felt Daniel may have actually deserved it.

"The fact of the matter is, now that Uncle Will is gone, you have no business here... as anything. You did nothing to earn the small title you hold, and if it were up to me, I'd send you packing back to where you came from, never to be seen again! Nobody wants you here! You're cruel and worthless and much too low to be associated with me or my family, for any reason! You are *NOTHING*!"

"*Katiana!*" a voice off to the side called out angrily. Kat turned her fiery eyes towards her brother. "This is *none* of your business, Jerren! So back off!"

She glared once more at Daniel, who was now completely sober. He opened his mouth to say something, but only seemed to wilt under her stoney gaze. Satisfied with his reaction, she marched towards the tall shrubs and away from them both, deliberately staying out of reach of her brother.

"What the hell was that all about?" Jerren probed once Kat disappeared.

Daniel shook his head, waved the prince off, then walked away. But Jerren was not one to let things like this go. He caught up and cut him off. "Hey! She had no right-"

"She had *every* right! At least she finally knows where I rank in the world."

"What's that supposed to mean?" Jerren shot back, angry that his friend had such a low opinion of himself. Daniel rolled his eyes, bitterness and self-loathing seeping from each retina.

"Oh, cut the crap Jer! We both know what it means... I know you saw the faces and heard the whispers when she chose me to dance with over all those other assholes... I never should have been in that crowd."

Jerren rolled his eyes. "Then why were you?"

"Because she asked me to!" Daniel yelled, frustrated. "She deserved better than a bunch of snobs whispering behind her back because she chose me as her dance partner and I wasn't about to let her make the same mistake twice…"

Jerren gave him a confused look.

"And then I had to go and…" Daniel groaned in frustration. "Just forget it, it doesn't matter," Daniel mumbled, walking away.

"Daniel!"

"I said forget it!" Daniel shouted.

Just then, a small group of people walked by and stared in horror at his outburst. He took a calming breath and bowed deeply to Jerren. "My apologies, your Majesty, I have clearly had a bit too much wine this evening. Good night."

"Daniel!" Jerren called out again, but there was no use. There was no talking to him now.

Daniel turned a sharp corner and came face to face with Rollin Breken. "Watch where you're going, mutt," Breken said, pushing Daniel back. Daniel's fists clenched. He had waited months to tear into Breken, but he knew it wasn't the time or the place. Instead, he took a deep breath and continued his path, or at least he tried.

"What's the matter, mutt? Trouble in paradise?" Breken taunted.

Daniel was already so far past his breaking point, he couldn't control himself. He exploded. "Don't you ever just shut the fuck up, you stupid, entitled prick?!"

In one swift movement, Breken had Daniel pinned against the wall. "What did you just say to me?!"

Daniel broke free of Breken's grip and pushed him back hard. "You heard me, *asshole*! You have no right to even be here after the stunt you pulled after the festival!"

Breken reached towards his belt, and just as he was about to charge at Daniel, with what he assumed was a dagger, the door next to them burst open and a flood of party goers spilt through. Daniel seized his opportunity to escape and slipped through the crowd until he knew he was free of Breken.

❖   ❖   ❖

Kat, who had concealed herself in the garden waiting for Jerren and Daniel to disperse, emerged from her hiding place. She had so many questions and felt so confused about… everything; and overhearing the conversation between Jerren and Daniel did little to soothe her confusion, though it explained some things.

Everything leading up to that first dance was hazy, and though she didn't see or hear any objections to her choice of dance partner, she supposed it wasn't out of the question. *Had choosing Daniel been a mistake?*

Daniel was a knight after all, as well as Sir William's proxy, but maybe there were some people who didn't think that meant much. She felt a little guilty about putting him in such an awkward position, but maintained it was a poor excuse for the way he had behaved.

She thought about how he had misled her, then blatantly rejected her. But maybe she had pushed him more than he had misled her... She could almost forgive him for that crime, but the way he was with *that girl*. A chill ran down her spine at the thought, and she knew the surrounding cold played no part in her body's reaction.

Kat peered around the thicket of shrubs she had been hiding behind and found an empty courtyard. She strolled thoughtfully through the courtyard and happened upon a solitary figure sitting on a bench. As she drew nearer, she saw the figure was Rollin Breken.

She paused for a moment and considered finding an alternate route; she wasn't sure she was prepared to face anyone, let alone *him*. But, in true princess fashion, she put her own troubles aside and marched forward with confidence. That, unfortunately, did not last long.

The snow from the garden had dampened her boots, making them slick; the moment they met the stone pavers, she slipped and fell. This was just her luck, and just like that, every emotion she had previously held in came spilling out in a cascade of tears. Rollin Breken rushed to her side to assist her.

"Are you alright, Princess?" He asked, kneeling down beside her. Kat could do nothing but cry. "Are you hurt?"

"I'm sorry. I'm okay..." she answered, wiping her face. Breken pulled a handkerchief from his doublet and wiped her tears away, first with the cloth, then with his thumb. Kat was so stunned when his skin met hers that she had nearly stopped breathing.

"There now. All is well," he smiled. Kat was at a loss. She felt as though the ice on the ground had spread through her veins, leaving her motionless and mute.

"Can you stand?" he asked. Kat's eyes grew large. She tried to speak, but nothing came out. Breken chuckled, then put his arms around her and lifted her from the ground. Kat blushed a deep pink. He walked her towards the door, then gently lowered her down.

"Thank-" a bubble had formed in Kat's throat and she had to clear it before she could speak again. "Thank you, my lord. I'm sorry you had to witness all that..."

"I'm not. It's nice to see that the royal family is just as human as the rest of us," Breken said, as he tucked a stray trundle of hair behind Kat's ear. The small gesture sent her mind instantly to Daniel and everything that had happened.

"Are you sure you're alright, Princess?" Breken asked again. His hand rested on her upper arm and the pad of his thumb caressed her shoulder. His eyes seemed to beckon to hers until they locked in place.

"You look exquisite this evening," Breken cooed. He took a step closer to her, and her mouth dried instantly. "You're too kind, my lord," she half whispered.

Breken leaned in. She felt what was coming, but a sinking feeling in the pits of her stomach told her to pull away, and so she did.

"I'd better return to the party," she said, taking another step back. The displeasure on Breken's face was obvious, and Kat was even more glad she had pulled away. "Thank you so much for your help."

Without waiting for a response, Kat reentered the grand hall and put as much distance between herself and Breken as she could. As she looked around the room, she realized something had changed. What was warm and inviting at first, now seemed disillusioned and inhospitable. The veil had lifted, and she realized she had been right about the whole thing from the beginning; It was nothing more than a competition.

She had hoped to salvage the night, but the moment she had shared with Rollin Breken and everything Daniel had said kept replaying in her mind. Jerren might not have understood what Daniel meant about her making the same mistake, but she was beginning to.

Had it all been a mistake? In the throes of anger, she certainly thought so, but the more she thought about it, the more she realized it hadn't been a mistake to choose Daniel for any of it. Besides Jerren and a handful of others in attendance, he was also the only one she knew had her best interest at heart.

Try as she might to focus on her guests, or anything else, all she could think about was Daniel. She flexed the hand he had gripped and remembered the horrified look on his face when he realized what he had done. She sighed. Maybe she was being ridiculous. She was sure Daniel felt something between them the way she had, but maybe it really was all in her head.

Each time she tried to justify everything that happened, she pictured the girl sitting on his lap and could only see red. She felt like a ball being tossed back and forth in a circle she couldn't escape.

When the night finally ended, and the last guest had gone, Kat fled to her room. The first thing she did as she entered was retrieve her pendant from the vanity where she left it. It offered little comfort on its own, so she recited her poem. With each word she spoke, though, her heart grew a little more heavy. She made it about halfway through when the tears streaming from her eyes allowed her to go no further.

It had all been too much; the feast, the dance, Daniel, Breken. She couldn't make sense of her own emotions. It felt as though the entire world had come crashing down on her. The day had begun wonderfully. How could *she* have been so stupid? How could *he* have been so careless? *Why did it hurt so much?*

Kat fell onto her bed, wrapped her arms around her pillow, and fell into a restless sleep full of bitter dreams.

Reap What You Sow

Kat watched from above as she slid into the river. She bobbed up and down, struggling to keep her head afloat. Suddenly, Daniel was there. He swam hard and fast to get to her, but he couldn't. The harder they swam towards each other, the more the river seemed to shove them apart. She disappeared beneath the murky surface, then everything went black.

❖   ❖   ❖

When she opened her eyes again, she was in the grand hall. She and Daniel stood in the middle of the room, surrounded by the whole of the kingdom. They began their dance, but stopped suddenly when everyone in the room burst into laughter and called out cruel things to them. Daniel stepped in front of her, shielding her, until he disappeared, and she was facing the mob all on her own.

The surrounding mob backed her into a corner. A menacing laugh exploded over the crowd, and the floor opened up beneath her. She was in free fall. Falling further and further down into a never ending pit of blackness. The only source of light being the hole in the floor she had fallen through. Daniel appeared over the hole and reached out to her, but she just kept falling.

❖   ❖   ❖

Kat was on the balcony. It was cold. Daniel suddenly appeared, and wrapped his arms around her. He held her close, and whispered sweet nothings in her ear. He leaned down and was about to kiss her, but she pushed him back. A wicked grin emerged on her face and she began to shout and yell at him, but it wasn't her at all. Daniel hung his head and retreated, devastated and alone.

Kat tried to shout for him, but no sound left her throat. Slowly, Daniel faded away, and still she was fighting to reach him. She tried to yell out once more, but the deafening silence lingered. Something grabbed her arm hard and whipped her around. It was her, but it wasn't. Her smile was menacing and her eyes had a glint of evil in them.

Kat struggled to break free of her twin's hold, but the more she struggled, the tighter and more painful the grip on her arm became. She turned her head and called once more to Daniel for help.

"Daniel Please!" she yelled, but he couldn't hear her. His faded image finally disappeared, and fear gripped Kat's

soul. *Her nightmare twin laughed maniacally, then lunged at her. Kat screamed and everything went black once more.*

❖   ❖   ❖

The princess woke with a start, as a light sweat beaded across her forehead. Her eyes darted back and forth as she tried to take in her surroundings. She was in her room, but she was still wearing the gorgeous gown her father had given her. *The same gown she'd worn in her nightmare.* Immediately, she rose from her bed, walked to her balcony, and flung the doors open, letting the frigid morning air consume her. The nightmare was over... She was home... *She was safe.*

A deep sigh of relief escaped her throat, and she immediately relaxed against the door frame. Slowly she lifted her gaze, following the line of the frame opposite her. The image of Daniel standing there, holding her hand and singing to her, just a few short months ago, gripped her heart. She pressed both her hands against her face, rubbing the image away in frustration.

The nightmares she had endured, mixed with the events of the previous evening, weighed heavily on her causing a soft sob to escape her. A light knock at the door made her jump, and she turned to watch as her brother appeared in its frame. "Not now, Jer, please," she begged.

He hesitated, but ultimately ignored her plea, and entered anyway. She readied herself for another send off, but stopped when she saw a small parcel in his hands. The strange expression on his face heightened her curiosity, but she was too stubborn to make an inquiry.

"I'm not here to lecture you, just to make a delivery."

Kat scoffed internally. *Why would she need a lecture?* "You can keep whatever you're delivering. I don't want it."

Jerren's mouth formed a hard line. "It's from Daniel. It was one of the few things left in his room, and it has your name on it."

"What do you mean *left*?"

"I went to talk to him this morning, hoping to sort out whatever happened between you two last night, and most of his belongings were gone. This was on the bed," he said, holding up the parcel.

The image of Daniel fading from her dream invaded her mind. Her heart stopped, but then she became frustrated. "Well, that's a bit dramatic, don't you think?"

"After what you said last night, are you surprised?" Jerren shot back.

Kat's defenses rose in an instant. "What I said?! And I couldn't possibly have any reason for being angry with him, could I?!"

"Angry or not... what you said was out of line and you know it!" Jerren replied, reprimanding her. Kat folded her arms and turned her back to him. *How could her own brother not be on her side?*

"Look, I don't know what happened-"

"NO! You don't!" Kat blurted, turning back to him. "You don't know! So why are you coming after me?"

Jerren took a deep breath, attempting to check his temper. "My sister is hurting, though I'm not sure why, and my best friend is gone."

Kat rolled her eyes. "Oh stop. He's not gone. You know full well he's at the inn," she said, hoping to convince herself as well as her brother.

"I hope you're right," Jerren sighed.

Kat turned away once more and looked out at the tree line and the village beyond that. Her nightmare flashed through her mind, and a shudder ran up her spine. *He'll come back. He has to.* She twisted her pendant between her fingers, trying her hardest to harvest whatever power it held.

"Look, I know you have this preconceived notion already in your head, but there's something you should know."

Kat let out a huff, then turned to face her brother once more, knowing he wouldn't leave her alone until she at least heard what he had to say.

"I had nothing to do with yesterday morning... All I did was wake you up."

Kat gave her brother a perplexed and rather annoyed look. "What'd you mean? What does that have to do with anything?"

Jerren took a step forward. "Maybe if you knew the truth, it could help you see things a little... *differently.*"

"The truth about what?!"

"Daniel planned *everything*," Jerren explained. "From where we went, to what we would do, all of it. The whole thing was his idea..."

He paused, waiting for some kind of response, but Kat was too busy trying to process his words.

"He knew how important that little tradition with Uncle Will had been to you... He wrote to me for weeks, trying to plan something special. Something he hoped that might make you smile and maybe forget, for just a moment, about what you were missing."

"But, I thought-"

"I know, and I told him he should've said something, but he told me it didn't matter who got the credit, as long as you were happy."

Kat shrunk inwardly. It was just like *Daniel* to do something so completely selfless like that, and it was just like *her* to run her mouth and ruin it all. She sat back sadly on her sofa, trying to wrap her head around what it all meant. Jerren could see the conflict in her eyes, and it softened his heart. He sighed heavily, then took his place on the sofa beside her.

"Kat... I don't know what happened last night... and I am *so sorry* that it hurt you," he paused. "And I don't want to make excuses for him... but there was *a lot* of drinking involved, and despite how *we* see him, he is only human and very capable of making mistakes."

Kat scoffed a little, and Jerren's look grew stern.

"All of that aside, I know *for a fact* he would *never* hurt you... unless... Unless he thought he was protecting you somehow."

Daniel had always protected her... Perhaps last night was just another example. Jerren placed the parcel on Kat's lap, squeezed her shoulder, and stood.

"I hope this helped a little."

Jerren paused, and looked as though there was more he wanted to say.

"Just say it..." Kat urged, readying herself for a much deserved reprimand.

Jerren rubbed the back of his neck, carefully contemplating how to say what needed to be said. "Kat... Daniel cares about you. *More than you realize...* he always has... Just, *please,* try to remember that." Jerren left his message at that, then made his way towards the door.

"Jer..."

He paused.

"Are you going to go find him?"

Jerren smiled to himself, then looked back over his shoulder. "I'll look, but I don't think I can be the one to bring him back," he said, giving his sister a telling look. "I'll let you know if I figure anything out."

She knew her brother was right... *about everything.* The insults she had hurled at Daniel sprung to the forefront of her mind, and even though a small part of her still felt at least some of them had been justified, it didn't compare to how horrible it made her feel now. "I didn't mean it..."

"I know."

Jerren left, and Kat stared down at the parcel in her lap. The small box was nothing special, but she knew whatever it held had been picked out with the greatest of care. Strands of twine wrapped like a ribbon around the box and tucked into the twine was an envelope, and *a thistle*. Kat sighed. Carefully, she pulled the thistle from the twine and brushed her fingertips along the head of the bloom before setting it aside. Then, she reached for the envelope, broke the seal and began to scan the letter held within.

Princess Katiana,

There are no words to justify my behavior tonight. You can't imagine how embarrassed and sorry I am. Of all the shameful things I have done in my life, hurting you will always be my biggest regret.

I wish there was some way to repair the damage I have caused, but that seems impossible. You were right; I don't belong here, not anymore. I always knew this day would come, though if I'm being honest, I had hoped it wouldn't have come so soon. You and your family took me in when you didn't have to, and I will be forever grateful.

I'm sorry I spoiled your special day. Please believe it was the last thing I ever wanted to do. I hope one day soon, you'll find someone worthy of your special moment, and I hope they do not waste it as I would have. You are truly a wonderful and beautiful woman and whoever you choose is sure to be the luckiest person in the world.

I meant to deliver this gift to you in person, but I fear I'm too much of a coward to face you again. You will always be more than just my princess, and should the day ever come that you need me for anything at all, I promise to be there. You deserve the world, Kitty Kat, and I hope one day you get it.

D.

P.S. I tried my best to fix it, but I'm sure you'll find someone to do a better job than I could.

"*Why did you have to be so stupid!*" Kat said, partially to the letter, partially to herself as tears welled in her eyes. "*And why are you always crying?!*"

She read the letter once more, and guilt coursed through her. The thought that she had pushed Daniel so far that he had truly left broke her. *He'll come back. He has to.*

She turned her attention back to the parcel. She untied the twine, and slowly opened the box. To her amazement, she found the choker she had ripped from her neck hours before laying on top of a drawing tacked to a thin board. Tears welled in her eyes as she lifted the necklace from the box. The clasp was bent, and sloppily soldered back together, but other than that, it seemed just as perfect as it had been when her father had given it to her. She wiped her eyes, then carefully placed it in the jewelry box that sat on her vanity.

She reached for the drawing, and when she took the time to truly examine the gift, her heart stopped beating. It was a nearly perfect likeness of her mother, and her uncle, sitting side by side, laughing. Her mother's head leaned against her uncles, and his arm draped around her shoulder. They looked so happy and carefree, and Kat imagined it was a perfect depiction of how they must look at that very moment.

Her heart swelled seeing a picture of the two of them together. She sighed and hugged the board to her chest. A bittersweet feeling came sneaking in, and she felt worse now than she had before. A small stream of tears trickled down her cheeks as she propped the picture up on the table beside her bed. *It truly was the perfect gift.* She brushed her fingertips along the image until they fell once more on the thistle that had accompanied it.

There was no doubt in her mind she had made a terrible mistake, and she was determined to make it right. Her own feelings and heartache aside, Daniel *had* earned his place here. *He belonged here*, and she knew she was the only person who could bring him home.

Emerlyn Mae Scott

Kat entered the village on her horse, surprised by how quiet it seemed to be. It was mid-morning, shops were open and there were a few merchants in the street, but everything seemed so calm, so slow.

When she arrived in front of the inn, she saw that there was a sign hanging informing patrons they had closed for the day. The place looked dark, but she could hear noises inside.

The front door swung open, and Lady Leanna appeared. Kat swallowed nervously. *What she must think of her.* She grew even more anxious when Daniel's mother seemed to be disappointed to see her.

"Oh, Princess... I was hoping you were the healer."

Kat's eyes grew large, and she dismounted. "A healer for what? What happened?"

Leanna sighed as she looked up and down the street. "Ada has gone into labor, and I'm not sure I can help her all on my own."

"I can help," Kat replied instantly, speaking before thinking. She wasn't sure what had possessed her to say *those specific words,* but there was no turning back now. The only birth Kat had ever witnessed was the stillborn birth of what would have been her little brother, which had ultimately led to her mother's passing; and the only other experience she had in the matter was from a few lessons with the healers. At that moment, she wished she had paid a bit more attention to them.

"I mean, I could run and fetch water or linens, or even just hold her hand. Or if you tell me what to do…" she trailed off.

Could she do this? Was she ready for something like this? Aunt Ada had always been so kind towards her, loving even. When she was upset, Ada was always willing to help cheer her up; and every time Kat entered the inn, Ada had only treated her like family. *Ada was family*. She shook the uncertainty from her mind, determined to do whatever she could to help.

"I can help!" She said with more confidence.

Leanna took one last look up and down the street, sighed, and nodded in agreement. She called for Declan to take Kat's horse to the stables around the back of the building. He obeyed, and Kat followed closely behind Leanna.

Kat had never seen the inn so dark and empty. It was a little unsettling. She discarded her outer layers at an empty table, then followed Leanna into the kitchen. She could hear

Ada calling out in pain from the room above them, and her heart constricted.

Leanna gave Kat a rather large apron with full sleeves to put over her dress, then loaded her arms full of linens and a pitcher of warm water. The pair raced up the back staircase towards the private quarters, and Kat almost lost her armload of supplies when Leanna stopped abruptly.

"Are you sure about this?"

The hesitancy in Leanna's voice shook Kat's confidence, but she knew it was a question of preparedness, rather than ability. She thought about how hard labor had been for her mother, but this one would be different. *It had to be.* Kat took a deep breath, then gave Leanna a confident nod. "Positive!"

Leanna led the way into the room where Tom was sitting beside Ada, holding her hand and doing his very best to comfort her. They both looked up, obviously surprised to see Kat enter behind Leanna. Kat tried to ignore their shock, then closed the door and quickly followed the instructions Leanna gave her.

Aunt Ada seemed weak and worn, and seeing her in such a state made Kat anxious. She realized the labor had been going on for some time, and it hadn't been easy, but she hoped it would end sooner rather than later. When it was time for Ada to push, Leanna instructed Kat to take Ada's left foot and carefully push it so that her knee was nearly at her shoulders. Then instructed Tom to do the same on the right.

"She's going to push back, but you'll need to hold her in place. Can you do that?"

Kat nodded in agreement and did her best to secure the position, while Tom did the same on the opposite side. Seeing all of this, and being a part of it, was not as simple as Kat had assumed it would be, and more than once, she had to wipe the mixture of sweat and tears from her face.

After an hour of screaming, and pushing, and mess, they brought the most perfect baby girl into the world. She was beautiful, and delicate, and the smallest creature Kat had ever seen. Even her cry, though loud as it was, seemed melodic, and any unease Kat had previously felt about the situation dissipated in an instant.

Leanna cleaned the infant as well as she could, and wrapped her in a small blanket. Ada reached out for her daughter, and Kat could see the immediate love in her eyes. Tom sat beside Ada, completely in awe of them both. It was such a tender moment that Kat felt suddenly out of place, until Leanna informed her there was still work to be done. Tom wrapped his daughter snugly into his arms, while Leanna doled out more instructions to Ada and Kat.

The after birth seemed just as draining for Ada as the original had been, and by the time it was over Kat could tell she was spent. Tom curled into the bed beside Ada with babe in hand so that they could 'ooh and awe' at the tiny creature.

"What will you name her?" Kat asked, as she helped Leanna gather the soiled undersheets. Ada and Tom exchanged a small smile, then looked over at Leanna. "Her name is Emerlyn Mae."

Leanna froze, and slowly lifted her head to them. What started as a small grin, erupted into a face splitting, all consuming smile; tears welled in her eyes, and a joyous giggle bubbled from her throat. Kat watched curiously as the bittersweet tears slid down Leanna's cheek.

Emerlyn? The name seemed so familiar, but it took Kat a moment to realize why. *Daniel's sister.* She smiled and stood to the side of Leanna, putting her arm around her waist. "That's a beautiful name," she smiled. Leanna reciprocated the tender embrace, and put a loving arm around Kat's shoulder, then wiped a few more tears from her eyes. A joy purer than anything Kat had ever witnessed seemed to fill the room. Then, she suddenly remembered the reason she had come to the inn and felt as though she had no right to be a part of such a special and meaningful moment.

She discreetly pulled herself away from Leanna's embrace, with a lingering squeeze. She had intruded enough, and today was too important to be ruined by her presence. *Today was for Daniel and his family.* She would have to make her amends tomorrow. Kat took one last glance around the room, taking in the perfect moment, then reached for the door.

"Would you like to hold her for a while, Kat?" Aunt Ada asked, startling her. She must have sensed Kat's unease, because the warmth in her smile grew with each passing second. Kat chewed her lip slightly, obviously waging an internal war against herself. "You helped bring her into this world after all," Ada cooed sleepily, giving her the encouragement she needed to step forward. Slowly, she made her way towards Ada and sat just to the side of her while Tom gently placed the infant in her arms. Less than a minute had passed, and yet Kat was utterly in awe of the sleeping babe; she truly was beautiful, and her name seemed to suit her perfectly.

Tom excused himself, and it wasn't long until Ada drifted off to sleep, too exhausted to fight the fatigue any longer. Leanna asked Kat to take Emerlyn into the room across the hall so that Ada could rest while she finished cleaning up, and she hastily agreed, unable to fathom leaving the infant's side.

It surprised Kat how easily caring for a baby had come to her. Even if it was only for a few minutes while the babe slept. In the minimal time she had spent with Emerlyn, she had already grown very much attached. Her heart ached a little at the thought of not seeing her again. Kat looked behind her to see if anyone was around and whispered to the sleeping babe as she paced the room, just in case this was her only chance.

"Hi Emerlyn, I'm Kat... I may not be around much after this, so I thought you should know just how lucky you are to have so much love in your life."

Kat swore she saw Emerlyn smile, and the thought warmed her heart. "You have the greatest parents in the world, and they love you more than you'll ever know. Your Aunty Lena loves you. Your cousin's Archer and Declan will love you... and if you want to know a secret, *I love you too.*"

A tear ran down Kat's cheek, and she wiped it away. "But, you know who is going to love you even more than *anyone else*?" she paused as if waiting for the baby to respond. "Your big cousin Daniel..."

His name seemed to catch in her throat, and she quietly cleared it. "He's going to love you so much."

She knew the moment Daniel saw her, he would be head over heels for the little girl. She imagined the elated look on his face when he held her for the first time, and the thought that the words she had spoken to him would sully the moment in any way killed her.

"He is going to love you, and cherish you, and let *nothing* bad ever happen to you. Not so much as a scraped knee," she sniffled. "And may the Gods help the boys who might someday break your heart."

As much as Daniel protected her, Emerlyn was sure to have all of that and then some. "I don't know if you know this but, your cousin is a knight... The most honorable, brave, and all together extraordinary knight in the entire kingdom... with the biggest heart you could ever imagine."

Kat silently wished she would have remembered that the night before.

"I just know he will do anything in his power to make sure you are happy and know just how much we all love you.

He'll draw you beautiful pictures and sing you songs, and he'll always dance with you, even though he says he hates it. When you're sad, he'll take you to the most magical places, just to see you smile; and best of all…"

Kat had to pause her speech to compose herself as a small cry escaped her throat. She took a deep breath, wiped her eyes once more, then continued on.

"Your cousin, Sir Daniel Trystane Enid, will make you feel the best about yourself, even when you don't feel it. He'll make you feel beautiful, even if you can't see it; and he'll make sure you never feel alone, no matter how far away he is… Trust me, I know."

The hairs on the back of Kat's neck stood alert, telling her someone was behind her. She glanced at a nearby mirror and saw Daniel in the doorway. Her heart spluttered, and she wasn't sure how much of what she said he had heard. There was more she wanted to say, but wasn't sure if she could utter the words with him standing there. She closed her eyes and prayed to the Gods for strength. When she opened her eyes again, she knew she had nothing to lose.

"And just between us girls… He has a tendency to be a little down on himself… and sometimes *selfish, horrible, hateful* people say nasty, hurtful things to him and make him feel bad… *even if they don't mean them.*"

Kat glanced in the mirror and saw Daniel suck in a small breath. "So… it's going to be up to you to remind him just how wonderful and special and brave he is... Do you think you can do that for me? I'd very much appreciate it."

Kat gently shook Emerlyn's hand, then kissed her forehead. "Now, I know I've built him up quite a lot, but I promise you he's going to exceed every expectation you have. And I don't want you to be shy when you meet him, okay? He may seem real tough, but in reality, he's just a big marshmallow."

Kat took another deep, cleansing breath, preparing herself to face him. "Ready?" she whispered, though she wasn't sure if she was asking Emerlyn, or herself. Prepared or not, it was time to face the music. Kat turned and walked toward Daniel as nonchalantly as possible. He blushed a little, realizing she caught him eavesdropping, but Kat made no move to reprimand him. She could see that he had gotten little to no sleep; he was pale and there was a slight shadow of facial hair on his cheeks. He looked at the ground, she assumed to avoid eye contact.

She had caused him all this suffering, and for what? Because he didn't feel the same way she did? He looked up for just a moment, and Kat could see the emptiness in his eyes, like the light inside had extinguished. She sighed, disappointed in herself, and tried her hardest to keep her own emotions at bay. *Now was not the time.*

Kat placed the sleeping babe into Daniel's trembling arms. "Sir Daniel Enid, I am pleased to introduce the newest member of your family, Miss *Emerlyn* Mae Scott."

Kat looked up to see the reaction on his face and saw a small, joyful smile inch across his lips. She looked back at Emerlyn and brushed the knuckle of her finger against the child's hand.

"Now, Emmy… I want you to take excellent care of your cousin, okay? He's the best man I know, and *he* deserves the world."

Kat glanced up into Daniel's eyes. She thought maybe she had seen just the slightest glimmer of hope in them, and she felt a small sense of relief. She pulled her gaze from Daniel, and back to Emerlyn, kissed her forehead once more, then whispered, "And so do you."

The expression on Daniel's face was a mixture of gratitude, guilt, and something else. Carefully, Kat leaned up on her tiptoes and left the softest of kisses on Daniel's cheek. "Thank you for always being there for me… I'm so sorry for everything I said, and I hope one day you can forgive me."

Kat didn't stop to see his expression or to hear a response. She just left the room as quickly as possible, raced down the stairs, gathered her belongings, and hurried out the back door. She had just made it to the small stable when he called out to her.

"Princess, wait!"

Kat could no longer contain the tears she had fought so hard to hold back. She turned to face Daniel, though she kept her eyes low. When he was mere feet in front of her, she lunged at him, wrapping her arms around his torso.

"Daniel, I am *so, so*, sorry. I didn't mean a single word I said last night. I was horrible and rude... and maybe a little jealous," she admitted. "I had no reason to act the way I did, and I didn't mean any of it! You are so much better than I am in so many ways, and you have more than earned your place here, and you prove it time and time again. You are the kindest, most wonderful... amazing person I have ever known, and the castle wouldn't be home if you're not there."

Daniel hadn't accepted her embrace, or made any sort of response, and Kat felt increasingly awkward. She released him, took a step back, then wiped her face. "I just wanted you to know that before you made any permanent decisions."

Daniel remained silent, and Kat was unwilling to look him in the eye for fear that it had all been for nothing. "Thank you for the wonderful present... and for making Jerren get me out of bed yesterday morning. He told me what you did."

Daniel opened his mouth to speak, but Kat, who still had her eyes on the ground, interrupted him... *again*.

"And thank you for being my first dance. I don't care what anyone else says or thinks, I'm glad it was with you. I know you were just trying to protect me from maybe feeling a certain way, but you should know I don't think it was a mistake and I don't think *the other thing* would've been a mistake either... I may have overheard what you said to Jerren in the garden."

Daniel waited once more to see if she had finally finished, then sucked in an amused smile as her nervous ramble continued.

"And I'm sorry I slapped you! And I'm sorry if I made you feel you'd done something wrong, because you didn't! I was acting selfish and foolish and a lot of other things and I'm just so sorry."

She paused, but then, again, continued, causing Daniel to stifle a small chuckle.

"And I'm sorry I said you couldn't call me Kat. Having you call me anything other than 'Kat', even 'Kitty Kat' just seems wrong and I wouldn't want you to. Not that it matters much what I want right now…"

Kat couldn't think of anything else to say and because Daniel still had yet to reply, she knew the damage was done, and nothing she could do or say could change it. She turned back towards the stables, feeling desperately heartbroken. Until she felt a gentle tug on her hand.

"Kat?"

When she glanced over her shoulder back at him, warm blue eyes and a kind smile greeted her disheartened gaze.

"Don't I get to say anything?"

Kat sighed, and relief flooded her system as she turned to face him. "Daniel, I'm so-" is all she got out before Daniel placed his free hand on the side of her neck and pulled her into a tender, affectionate kiss.

Kat was momentarily stunned, but it took only a half a second before she melted into it; *into him.* He pulled her closer to him, deepening the kiss. It was everything Kat had hoped for her first kiss to be; a soul melting, heart stopping, unearthly kiss, and it could've only been with Daniel.

"I hope it was still okay for me to do that," Daniel said in a low voice, still holding her close. Kat couldn't do anything but nod. "Does it feel wasted?"

She shook her head, still rendered speechless, and Daniel's answering grin made her heart flutter. "Good."

He lifted Kat's chin until her eyes met his, then turned the hand he had been holding until their fingers intertwined. "You *never* need to apologize to me for anything, *ever* again."

Kat opened her mouth to say something, but Daniel stopped her.

"I mean it," he said almost firmly. "And.. I'm sorry I hurt your... I don't know what got into me... I was being so stupid... I would *never, in a million years...* even *think* about hurting-"

"I know..." Kat said, reaching up to rest her free hand on his chest. Daniel smiled at her response, and tucked a loose strand of hair behind her ear, then let his hand rest against her cheek. Kat's gaze dropped slightly, her mind racing with questions.

"What is it, princess?" Daniel asked, noting her curious expression.

"Does this mean you're going to come home?"

The corner of Daniel's eyes crinkled as his grin broadened. "Do you want me to, Kitty Kat?"

"More than anything!"

"I guess that's settled, then." Daniel chuckled with a puckish glint in his eyes. "After all... I couldn't leave the Princess without the most honorable, brave, and all together extraordinary knight in the entire kingdom," he said, mimicking what she had said to Emerlyn.

"Daniel Enid!"

Kat blushed and playfully slapped his chest, making him chuckle once more. Suddenly, everything was right in the world, and the night before, erased without question. Kat wrapped her arms around Daniel's neck, pulling him into a warm embrace, one that he gladly accepted and returned.

"Congratulations on the newest addition to the family," she whispered.

"Thank you, Kitty Kat."

Kat loosened her embrace but left her hands in place, resting on the back of his neck.

"Can I ask you something?"

"Anything."

"Your drawing was so... *perfect.* How'd you do it? If I didn't know any better, I would've thought they had posed for you."

Daniel shrugged, but the color in his cheeks told Kat her praise meant more. "I - uh, well, I had some sketches of

Wil- Sir William, and then there's that portrait of the queen hanging in the library..."

"But she's not smiling in that one..."

Daniel cleared his throat, obviously embarrassed, though Kat couldn't understand why. "The smile..." he began shakily. "I got that from watching *you*..."

Kat's heart fluttered once more, and it was her turn to blush. A bold thought crossed her mind, and she took a flirtatious step forward. "Can I ask *one* more thing?"

Daniel swallowed hard, clearly anxious about how close she was, then nodded.

"Would it be okay if you were my second kiss, too?"

Kat looked up at him through her long eyelashes and watched as a shy smile crept across his lips, and it was all the answer she needed. Kat stood on her tiptoes and used her already perfectly positioned hands to pull him to her.

"Your brother is going to be so jealous," Daniel chuckled, as their lips finally parted. "He's been trying to get me to kiss him for years!"

Kat laughed and shook her head at his joke. "I keep trying to tell him I'm your favorite, but he refuses to believe me!"

Daniel chuckled once more, then stroked her cheek with the pad of his thumb. Kat didn't want the moment to end. Their second kiss had been just as perfect as their first, and she craved more. And even though she knew none of it meant anything, it would be a moment she would never forget.

She could have easily spent the remainder of the day with Daniel's arms wrapped around her, but she knew it was time for her to leave. She stepped shyly from his embrace, and turned back to the stables, but Daniel caught her hand before she got too far.

"Thanks, Kitty Kat…"

"For the kiss?" Kat asked, thoroughly confused.

Daniel laughed and shook his head, "No… Well *yes*, but *no*… Thank you for what you said before… upstairs."

Kat looked at the ground and shuffled her feet. "Well… I meant every word… Emerlyn is lucky to have someone like you in her life… *So am I…* I'll try to remember that next time my temper gets the best of me."

Kat met Daniel's warm gaze and her heart raced. They walked the rest of the way to the stables in silence. Not because they didn't know what to say, but because nothing more needed to be said. Daniel helped her onto her horse, but kept a gentle grip on her hand.

"I know there are exciting things going on here… but promise you'll be home soon?" Kat asked. Daniel chuckled, but gave a firm nod. "I promise," he said, leaving a kiss on her hand before finally releasing it, and watching as Kat rode up the path back towards the castle.

For the rest of the day, the only thing Kat could think of was Daniel. The way he smiled at her, and held her in his arms. The way he looked at her, and *truly saw her* – but mostly, she thought about the way he kissed her, and the feeling it had left in its wake. Just the memory of their kiss filled her stomach with butterflies and made her heart soar; and as splendid as the memory was, she *prayed* it wouldn't be the last time she felt his lips on hers.

Only time would tell, but as Princess Katiana Scarborough drifted to sleep that night, she was *certain* of one thing; the Gods themselves couldn't have crafted a more perfect moment, *or person* for her.

It had always been, and it would always be... *Daniel*.

375

Printed in Great Britain
by Amazon

3ec8a65c-ea60-4290-b0ed-b38d6d2e0e95R01